"THIS ONLY HAPPENS ONCE IN A BLUE MOON."

Cleo wasn't just referring to the stalled Ferris wheel that had left them stranded at the top. She was talking about this moment when there were no confines to her enjoyment. She was free to touch the sky—to touch Clark.

"Actually, it's an orchid moon," Clark mused, intent on the big luminous ball above.

Smiling, Cleo rested her head on his shoulder. "Call it any color you like. When I'm with you I'm color blind. All I know is that I could stay here forever."

Clark pulled her toward him and kissed her. There was something different in his kiss, and in his manner when he gazed at her and said very solemnly, very gently, "Sooner or later we have to get off...."

ABOUT THE AUTHOR

California dreaming was the inspiration for
Orchid Moon, Gail Anderson's first novel. This
imaginative author observed all the sights and
sounds of her San Francisco area home and
wondered "what if?" What if a woman met a
fabulous man on her way home from work? What
if he swept her away on a mad, impetuous junket?
The result was a delightful Superromance—and
lots of fun!

Gail Anderson

ORCHID MOON

Harlequin Books

TORONTO • NEW YORK • LONDON
AMSTERDAM • PARIS • SYDNEY • HAMBURG
STOCKHOLM • ATHENS • TOKYO • MILAN

Published August 1987

First printing June 1987

ISBN 0-373-70272-8

CHAPTER ONE

SHE SHOT OUT of the elevator like a race car driver in the lead, with nothing left to do but burn up the road to the finish. She stepped quickly down the corridor, leaned into the turn to central Xeroxing and headed down the straightaway to where the black and white distribution bins made a checkerboard of the wall. Control was comfortably in her grip until she arrived at the bin marked with her name. It was empty.

"I don't see my reports," she said, raising her voice to the clerk at the reception counter. She didn't turn away from the huge distribution grid. Instead, she began to check each and every bin. If the reports were simply missorted, she would find them.

Her words intruded on the duty clerk, hunched over the morning newspaper. His face soured, but when he looked up, his ready sarcasm was blown away on the breath of a slow, silent whistle.

A slim woman stood with her back toward him. She was on tiptoe, teetering a bit, as she peered into the top row of bins. There was a sweet innocence about her, like Dorothy in the Land of Oz. But she didn't belong in Oz or in this distribution room. In a soft, white suit and high-heeled, lilac sandals she was a doll on top of a decorated cake, all sugar and icing. He recognized her as one of the associate directors in financial planning—the starchy one . . . yeah, Cleo Holmes. But she sure looked different today.

"When did you submit it?" he asked.

Cleo Holmes spun around quickly, enchanting him even more with a lilac blouse. "Yesterday afternoon. I need it for Porter Franklin by ten o'clock," she answered crisply.

"I'll check," he drawled, glancing at the bold face of the wall clock, which marked the time at nine-thirty, but easing off his stool too slowly to have been tinged with any motivation. He strolled into the interior operations room, turning to Cleo once more before disappearing. She was as tight as ever, he decided, but gee, she was pretty.

Cleo paced in front of the counter, her cool exterior masking the inner fire, until the clerk reappeared.

"We managed to run all the copies," he said, draping himself over the lower half of the Dutch door, "but the collator was jammed." He shrugged. "I guess someone should have called you."

He watched the pretty doll purse her lips, his eyes dropping to the lilac shoes as she stepped around the counter and marched toward him. He barely had time to jump aside as she pushed open the gate and forged past him.

Cleo went directly to her copies, stacked crosswise on an idle machine as work in progress. She picked up an empty cardboard box from the floor and immediately began to load the copies into it. "Where are the binders?" she snapped above the hum of the other copying machines.

Someone limply pointed, and Cleo flew to the supply shelves. There she counted out fifteen report covers and rushed back, her lips still moving from the count. The covers hit the box with a snap as she spotted a hole punch on a nearby workbench. Quickly she retrieved it and with both hands lowered it into the box. Then she lifted the load, leaning back with its weight, and stormed out. The clerk clucked his amusement. To Cleo, he did not exist.

Next door in a vacant conference room, Cleo sorted pages and collated the reports at a furious, self-righteous pace. She could have recruited help or simply phoned Porter's secretary to announce a delay, but she measured performance only in terms of her own capability. She knew she could make the deadline, and at precisely ten o'clock she was in Porter Franklin's office. At two minutes past ten she returned to her office and slammed the door.

Porter had been on the phone when she had walked in with the finished reports cradled in her arms. He had glanced up as she bent over and deposited the culmination of three months' work on the edge of his massive desk. "Good girl," he said, covering the mouthpiece of the receiver momentarily.

She was twenty-nine years old. She had been making Porter Franklin look good for eight years, and he had said, "Good girl."

The padded carpet absorbed her angry footsteps as she stomped to her desk and took command of her coffee mug. She threw the cold, bitter liquid down her throat in measured gulps. *You're overreacting, Holmes,* she told herself repeatedly.

An accurate assessment, it was still no solution. After eight years of unfaltering commitment to the corporation, Cleo could no longer pretend that the paper pushing was of any world significance. Yet she couldn't tolerate even a sixty-second tardiness in delivery of a report that Porter would probably not even review.

Frustrated, Cleo set the mug down, folded her arms and surveyed her office objectively. It was a landscape of

tasteful corporate gray, poised on the edge of an unsur-
passed view. This was her universe, this corner office on
the fifty-first floor of the California Investment Tower,
where breathtaking floor-to-ceiling windows wrapped blue
sky around her and placed San Francisco at her feet. But
it was a glass encasement. She couldn't touch the sky, the
city or anyone. *A prison of your own making, Holmes,*
she told herself in a lucid moment, and an all too familiar chill ran down her spine.

She reacted instantly, busying her hands in the layers of
paperwork strewn across her desk. Her mind followed.
There was still refuge in discipline.

At eleven-thirty someone opened the door hesitantly.

"Knock, knock." It was Mira Sands, the second and
newest member of Cleo's staff. "Oh, oh, you look
gloomy. Something wrong?"

"Nope," Cleo said, smiling quickly. "We're right on
schedule. The study is in Porter's hands. We wait."

"Great. I can't believe we have this breather. I've never
worked so hard in my life. I see you're cleaning up. Josh
and I are digging out, too." Josh McCall was the other
half of Cleo's staff. "Here's your deli order." Mira placed
a small paper bag on Cleo's desk, and reached into her
pocket to make change. "By the way, your outfit is terrific. I've never seen you in such a dressy suit before."

"Oh, this." Cleo shrugged, flipping one of the lapels.
"I haven't been able to get to the dry cleaner. I'm down
to the suit I wore to my sister Cassy's wedding shower."

"Your sister should get married more often. So what
happens with Porter now?"

Cleo regarded her thoughtfully. Mira had only been at
California Investment for three months, the life of the
current project. Cleo spoke cheerfully, choosing her words
with care. "Well, Porter presents our study to the execu-

tive committee at the noon luncheon meeting. I won't know anything more until the phone rings. It's the custom. Porter calls and I run up with an explanation or additional numbers. Since this is a major study, I expect him to call at least three times today."

"How stupid. Why can't Porter prepare himself decently, or better yet, why doesn't he include his associates at the meeting?"

"You tell 'em, kid." Cleo winked.

"I just may. It's Friday, and I'm in no mood to work the weekend just because someone upstairs didn't understand what he was looking at."

"You and Josh have the weekend off, I promise," Cleo said routinely, removing the sandwich from the lunch bag. "I can handle any revision alone. I planned on working this weekend anyway so—"

"Cleo, please don't work this weekend." Mira spoke rapidly with a sort of maternal desperation. "It doesn't matter whether the revision is submitted on Monday, or Tuesday or next year. It's all the same."

Cleo was stunned, her mouth already agape from her unfinished sentence.

"Uh, do you still want the door closed?" Mira asked quickly, acutely aware that she had overstepped a boundary, but not sure how.

Cleo nodded blankly, and Mira was gone. But Cleo could not make as clean an exit on the subject. How could someone as young and unseasoned as Mira see things so clearly? She had been so careful to shelter Mira, to keep her out of corporate politics, to make sure her illusions were not destroyed too early. But Mira had no illusions. *Where have you been, Cleo Holmes?* she asked herself, biting into her sandwich and tasting nothing.

BY TWO O'CLOCK there was still no phone call from Porter.
Cleo had filed every stray paper, replaced every file and
even dusted the top of her desk with a tissue. Any further
work hinged on the forthcoming decision of the executive committee. She had nothing left to do but wait. And
in the void, the chill in her spine came home to stay.

There was nowhere to hide. She had tried to outrun the
truth long enough. So, with a firm resolve, Cleo reopened the credenza and confronted the long row of feasibility studies that had comprised her life for the past
eight years. It was nothing more than a parade of illusions she'd kept intact for almost a decade. The tabs on
the file folders now reminded her of tombstones in a
graveyard. She gazed at the open file for a long while before walking to the north window.

The Goodyear blimp was gliding over the Golden Gate
Bridge in a flight pattern typical of summer afternoons.
Cleo always waved to the blimp in fun, but today she
waved in sadness to adventure that was passing her by.

"Hey, are you dating the blimp captain again?" Josh
was leaning into her office, one hand on the doorknob,
the other anchored to the frame. "Forget it, Cleo. That
man has no shame. Look!" He pointed at the window.
"He advertises right on that balloon—an offer of one
good year, and then it's gone with the wind."

"But Josh, honesty is his most endearing quality."

It was a game they played. Josh was always accusing her
of preposterous affairs. He knew, as did everyone else,
that Cleo was married to the company.

"Cleo, are you okay? You don't usually have your door
closed."

"I'm just waiting . . . thinking—that's a new one, isn't
it?"

"No word from Porter?"

"No."

Josh mumbled something about five-martini lunches, then pulled the door shut. Alone again, Cleo stared at the closed door. Josh was a sweet kid, she thought. At twenty-four, married and a recent father of a baby girl, he couldn't possibly know what she was feeling.

Returning to her desk, Cleo sighed. Both Mira and Josh thought she was worried about the executive committee. And why not? This was her life.

She dropped into her chair and glared at the company pen set, an award for service that sat on her desk like the horns of a bull. She was a fixture at California Investment like everything else in the room. But somewhere in this office there had to be evidence of a separate identity, some token of another life.

She leaned back in the chair and looked critically at a small painting that hung unobtrusively in a niche beside the door. It was the only thing in the office that belonged to Cleo. It had been with her from the beginning. On scrutiny, the picture was quite beautiful. And once it had been real.

Cleo focused on the small spot of color, recreating a memory of another summer afternoon, deliberately pulling herself out of the hermetically sealed, temperature-controlled office and into the painting where it was hot, sun-drenched, where the sun streamed over miniature marigolds at the windowsills. And the smell of baking orange bread spreading delightfully into the air made it possible to taste the sunshine. Yes, it had been real once, and now Cleo concentrated on making the image real again....

SHE HAD BEEN SITTING among the lumps of a tattered sofa, her legs tucked beneath the gathers of a skirt faded by summer sun, her lips in the crescent of an irrepressible smile. Her smile had deepened, electrifying the happiness in her face when the artist had winked at her.

Partially screened by the tall easel, Perry Paul Spencer III stood in the middle of the room, barefoot on a hardwood floor that creaked affectionately beneath his toes. His slender body was clothed only in denim cutoffs, a fringe of unraveling threads dusting the top of his taut and tanned thighs.

The sunlight claimed his golden head of curls as its own, and sparkled in the blond furring of his chest, arms, legs. He was an eternal host not only to sunshine but to all the best things in nature that rushed to project within a soul so gentle, pure and unassuming.

The chime of the cooking timer touched off the usual performance. Perry pantomimed surprise, and playing to Cleo's audience, scurried in a Charlie Chaplin gait to the kitchen alcove, where he delivered his orange bread from the old stove like a caring but hurried stork.

With several taps to the pan, he flipped the loaf onto a wooden cutting board, sliced a hefty chunk and ambushed it with a cloth napkin before the steam could escape. Then he rushed it, piping hot, to Cleo's outstretched hands, pivoted on his heel for a quick return to the easel and resumed painting within a record click of the stopwatch.

Holding the bread to her lips, Cleo nibbled, relishing the chewy pieces of orange rind. She met Perry's eyes as he peeked at her rhythmically from behind the canvas, his eyes sometimes distant in concentration, sometimes playful. What he saw when he squinted, Cleo could not guess. It could be the sands of the Kalahari or the flames of Kilauea, for he could create anything with a turn of his mental kaleidoscope.

Finally, he stepped back.

"There, I've painted you," he said with the enthusiasm of a bright child.

Cleo had left the sofa, coming forward to stand before the easel as Perry moved aside and draped himself on a wooden stool. He watched her with a contented grin, absently helping himself to crumbs from the cutting board.

Cleo was at once caught up in the visual delight of the variegated watercolor. Knowing Perry too well to have expected a portrait in likeness, she studied, then savored the message he had painted from the heart.

It was an abstract of a woman sitting in a bevy of bunched bananas, no doubt the immediate inspiration of the yellow sofa, but more likely symbolic of all the crazy times they had shared. The woman was done in shades of violet, her mane of black hair swirling through an array of intricately detailed candy and confections—peppermints, truffles, bonbons, ice-cream cones and parfaits. The whole image was held in check by thin, silver lines of concentric rectangles. Lost in a Perry original, Cleo marveled until his voice broke her reverie.

"Give it a few more minutes to dry, then you paint *me* into it."

Cleo's mouth flew open. "I can't paint," she exclaimed, surprised and excited by the novelty of his suggestion.

"Come on. This is special," he coaxed, rising from the stool to stand behind her at the easel, his arms encircling her waist. "I want it to be us."

"I can't paint," Cleo repeated, settling back into the comfort of his young body. "And I certainly can't paint *you*," she added to further the impossibility.

"Why not?" he asked, nibbling her earlobe.

"You've said it yourself," she answered with a laugh, her finger tracing in the air the geometrical lines in the painting. "I'm too arrested, conventional...."

"So damned structured." He crooned the familiar quote into her ear while his hands burrowed under her flimsy blouse. "There's a whalebone corset under here somewhere," he accused, as she twisted in his arms in an affectionate struggle, giggling at the tickle of his search. "You girls are wearing the corset higher this year," he said with scholarly authority as his roving fingers found her brassiere.

"Per-ry," Cleo protested lightly as he unfastened the hook. His hands moved to cup her breasts while he nuzzled the nape of her neck. Then he tugged gently on the front of her bra, and Cleo, surrendering to his will, slipped the strap off one shoulder, then the other, and threaded her arms through the loops so that Perry could pull the bra from beneath her blouse.

He dangled the limp halter before her, delivering a eulogy in his inimitable style. "Behold, the padded bra. Exhausted property of a wanton hussy." He flung it into a corner.

"Wanton hussy?" Cleo sputtered, the words spilling out in laughter as she retaliated in kind, grabbing the nearest paintbrush and dabbing his nose a healthy green.

"What a start! I can feel this talent," he shouted, as he captured her hand. Tightening one arm around her waist, he positioned her hand at brush length before the canvas, coaxing, "Come on. I'll help you. Paint me."

He rested his chin on her shoulder, presenting the tip of his green nose in her line of vision. *What a darling nose,* she thought. *Lead and I follow as I have a hundred times before.* So, tucked tightly against his body, she nodded her readiness to take up the challenge.

"You're a child of the sun...." she mused, and instantly her hand, held firmly by his, daubed the brush into yellow paint and went to work on a quick orb in the upper corner of the canvas.

"You've got some green in the sun," Cleo warned.

"My nose, sweetheart," he answered casually.

She nudged his ribs and continued, intrigued with the process. "And you're a child of the moon...."

"You flatter me," Perry whispered, nuzzling her temple. He kissed the top of her head, and then he bleached the brush with enough white paint to throw a crescent moon onto the canvas opposite the sun.

Cleo watched carefully, admiring the ease with which the moon appeared. Her eyes riveted on the canvas in definite purpose, she stated with certainty, "Now I need gold."

Perry let go of her hand and unscrewed the cap from a new tube of paint using his thumb and forefinger. It was oil paint this time, metallic gold, shiny. He squeezed it generously onto the palette, dipped a fresh brush and handed it to her.

For a short while, Cleo held the brush upright like a long-stemmed rose, contemplating. Then, frowning, she sought Perry's face. "I needed this for your very essence. But I don't know how to show it. How you breeze through everything."

He looked at her kindly, amused by her distress. "Like this," he said, smiling an elfin grin and taking charge of her hand, snapping it to spray gold flecks across the painting.

"Gold dust," Cleo whispered in awe, reverently placing the brush on the ledge of the easel. "You've captured your essence."

"No," he said, kissing the palm of her hand and raising it above her head. He twirled her like a music-box dancer to face him. "*You* have captured my essence." Still holding her hand above her head, he kissed her lips tenderly, then set his music-box dancer in a reverse twirl so that she rested against him once more to view their painting.

With Perry's arms wrapped securely about her waist, Cleo studied the canvas, lulled by his breathing, the rise and fall of his chest. "It's us," she announced at last.

"So titled!" he proclaimed. "*Us*. No fuss. No muss. Just *Us*." He gave her a squeeze as she groaned at his strained poetry.

"You know," she said, inclining her head to see him, "now that it's a joint portrait, it's only fair that we each keep it for alternating time periods...trading it on the same day each year."

Perry shook his head, chuckling, "Too precise, my earthbound angel. You'll never learn to fly." He breathed into her ear, his voice sinking an octave. "You keep the painting, and I'll keep you." He lifted her energetically into his arms to spin her around and around. She clung to his neck, and their infectious laughter became one sound as they rotated.

Abruptly, he stopped, pressing her tightly against his chest. "Shh. Listen. Did you hear it? That marigold—it just said, 'I love you.'"

He carried her to the nearest window, where sharing his spontaneous fantasy, she pointed with urgent interest. "Was it this one?" she asked.

"No." He shook his head.

She pointed to another, her eyebrows raised. Again he shook his head. "Ah, it's this one," she said, smiling knowingly. "I see it winking at you."

She plucked the tiny orange bloom and rooted it in the curl of Perry's hair, just above his ear. She drew back to judge the effect, but could not be objective. His face tugged at her heart. He was too cute, too lovable. She folded her arms about his neck, claiming a kiss that lasted while he lowered her to the mattress on the floor.

He hovered above her, his smile and adoring gaze the mirror of her own. Cleo licked her fingers and touched them to his nose to wipe away the green of her first artistic foray. Lovingly, her hand lingered on his face, brushing slowly over his lips as he kissed each finger individually in passing. Fondly she plucked the marigold from his hair and brought it to her lips, looking deeply into his twinkling blue eyes.

"I have a confession," she said, dropping her eyes, toying with the flower. "This marigold didn't really say 'I love you.'" Her eyes returning to his face, she savored his sensitive features, now alert with curiosity, then whispered, "I did."

His expression was awash with emotion, and he showered her with kisses. "Then come to Athens with me," he urged breathlessly, his mouth pressed into the hollow of her neck.

"I can't, silly," she answered with practiced ease, her supreme confidence unshaken until her eyes met the painting looming in the easel above. Suddenly chilled, she pressed into the golden warmth of Perry, closed her eyes and let the watercolors dissolve....

CHAPTER TWO

CLEO OPENED her eyes to the cool gray of her office. She shivered. The temperature was unquestionably a perfect seventy degrees, but the room seemed as cold as an Arctic wasteland.

She fidgeted in her chair, chiding herself for having slipped into some melancholy dream. It was after four o'clock. What was happening with Porter? Cleo thought irritably, forcing herself to forget that she had once carelessly thrown away a chance to be happy. She prayed for the phone to ring, and when it did, she pounced, her professional sail unfurled.

Porter's voice bubbled. "Cleo, the study is superb! All recommendations have been accepted."

"Great. I thought the ratios looked pretty safe." Cleo instinctively picked up a pencil.

"Needless to say, the new division vice-president is impressed. Get ready, Cleo. You and your staff have just become the lead team."

Her pause was slight. "Josh and Mira will be glad to hear that."

"I'm sending down a bottle of champagne. I'd come down myself for a little celebration, but my wife is throwing a party tonight, and I am under strict orders to come home on time."

All the appropriate responses flowed from Cleo's lips, and after she put down the phone, she sat quietly, listening to the echoes of the conversation in her mind. She had sounded happy and Porter, of course, had sounded happy, *was* happy. He would never know nor care that on the phone Cleo had merely gone through the motions—just as she had done with the carefully constructed feasibility study that was now upstairs swelling chests with corporate pride.

The study was hardly a masterpiece of analysis. It was a formula piece—laborious, comprehensive and, above all, well packaged. Cleo had summarized three months of data by writing to the level of the limited abilities it had been her duty to observe in the past committee meetings. She had used words of embarrassing simplicity and had belabored the obvious, often being redundant so that no one would miss the point. And it had been a success. Small, hollow, but a success nonetheless.

Stop it, Holmes, she scolded. She lurched out of her chair and strode through the door to relay the official word to Mira and Josh.

"They bought it, hook, line and sinker," she announced. "Porter's sending down champagne."

Before the whoops of self-satisfaction had subsided, Porter's secretary arrived with the promised libation, purchased from the lobby spirit shop.

"Stay and have a drink with us, Sally?" Cleo invited, as she accepted the bottle.

"No thanks," Sally declined with a hasty wave as she left. "Got a hot date tonight."

"Speaking of dates," said Mira, pulling on her blazer in a rush, "I wonder if I still have a husband? He won't believe I have the weekend off. We were only tentatively planning to drive down to Monterey." She became animated. "Cleo, I know this is short notice, but can I have Monday off?"

Cleo nodded.

"Great!" Mira waved goodbye as she bounded energetically to the door.

"Have a good time," Cleo called out quickly before Mira was gone. Turning to Josh, who had just put down the phone, she tilted the bottle of champagne toward him.

"Why don't you take it home," he suggested, pointing his finger at her. "You deserve it all. I just called Glenda and told her to start the barbecue. Have a good weekend, Cleo." Standing in the doorway, he saluted her and was gone.

A good weekend, Cleo thought. Her weekend plans to work had been canceled. Now what? She retreated to her office and never felt more alone. The place was immaculate. Not a paper out of place. Not a trace of personality.

Cleo swiftly packed a briefcase—out of habit rather than necessity. She looked at her name, Cleopatra S. Holmes, lettered prominently in gold beneath the handle of the case, another pompous gift from the corporation, another meaningless trapping. Cleo ran her fingers across the lettering and was once again the first daughter of Leo and Patty Holmes. *Cleo has a business mind,* she heard them say. Would they be proud of her now? She snapped the case shut and headed out the door, returning a second later to grab the champagne bottle by the neck, toting it with her in resignation.

The corridors were deserted; the weekend was a powerful magnet. Cleo entered an empty elevator, and when the doors closed, the isolation was complete.

She watched the indicator lights flash the floors in descent like the diminishing numbers of her options. She did not want to be alone tonight. *You're a smart woman,* she told herself, *do something.* Frantically, she remembered

Owen in general accounting on the fortieth floor. She had always taken his interest in her for granted. Sure he was dull, but she was hardly in a position to be critical. Desperately, she stabbed the button for the fortieth floor, quite sure that her reaction was too late. To her surprise the doors flew open, serving up Owen's pleasant countenance, radiant with what could only be the mutual pleasure of seeing her.

"Hello, Cleo."

"Owen, I was just thinking of you," she gasped joyously.

Owen put his hand against the elevator door and looked expectantly down the hall toward the sound of jingling keys. Cleo's lips parted. She was about to explain the champagne and suggest dinner, when the only lawyer in the corporation with the physical assets to permanently tip the scales of justice her way tackled Owen from behind, and tickled him into the elevator.

"Oh, hello, Cynthia." Cleo spoke first to cover her shock.

"Hiya, Cleo," Cynthia answered, finding her niche under Owen's arm. "Oooh, champagne," she cooed to Owen. "Cleo's got the right idea. We need to pick some up, baby. Maybe some French bread...some oysters, too."

Behind a clenched smile, Cleo prayed her face would not reveal her feelings. She couldn't believe that Owen was with Cynthia, the sexiest woman in the company. They looked so happy, and Cleo felt so left out.

At ground level, Owen and Cynthia sailed out of the elevator like a champion ice skating pair. Cleo hung back, feeling she had been dropped more than forty floors.

She walked through the deserted lobby, listening to the echo of her heels on the polished floor. She felt flawed and worthless. She passed through the revolving door into a beautiful summer evening that seemed to exclude her. Slowly, she walked down the steps of the plaza to the street level below. She was totally alone until she heard someone scold her.

"No, no, Cleo. You carry champagne, you look-a so sad, is-a not right." It was Emilio, a compassionate saint of many years, and proprietor of the flower stand at the cable car stop. Long ago he had adopted Cleo, whom he had come to know as the young woman who ate sandwiches on the plaza steps so that she could return to work before an entire lunch hour was wasted. Cleo greeted him meekly, embarrassed at having been caught in obvious depression.

"Whatsa matter? You have-a so much work, you have-a no weekend?"

Cleo shook her head.

"Come here," Emilio instructed. "Take down your hair," he insisted, pointing to the clip that secured her hair in a loose twist above the neck. Cleo obeyed. His concern made her feel better.

Her dark hair dropped over her shoulders and Emilio nested two giant orchids, the same shade as her silk blouse, into her hair like an off-center crown. Satisfied with his creation, a princess in white and orchid, he produced a piece of what had once been a much larger mirror.

"I make-a you a picture," he promised. "Maybe tonight you fall in love."

Cleo peered into the mirror and lit up with pleasure under the spell of the orchids. Invited into paradise, her deep blue eyes went violet beneath the balmy tropical headdress. Emilio had indeed made her a picture.

"Emilio, what would I do without you?"

"What's to worry? You have-a me." He spread his arms wide.

It took a while for Cleo to persuade Emilio to keep the champagne. After much gesturing, he accepted the bottle and sent his princess on her way with his blessing for whatever adventure might befall her on such a lovely evening.

Cleo walked confidently down California Street to the Bay Area Rapid Transit station. Emilio had forced her out of her stupor, and his gift had restored her self-esteem. Today she had scored a substantial career success, and on top of that, she had a friend who cared enough about her to create a floral crown fit for a queen. What more did anyone need?

The bounce in her step was strengthened by the even pendulum swing of her briefcase. She was charged with energy and receptive to the party atmosphere in the streets. Commuter crowds were always relaxed and mellow on Friday evenings. She couldn't help but smile. The weight of the orchids on her head made her feel pretty, and the sweet scent circling her face made her happy.

Cleo knew she was attracting attention. In particular, a man in a tweed sport coat standing on the running board of a slow-traveling cable car was watching her. A crop of red hair topped his friendly face. Boldly, Cleo smiled at him. After all, she was Cleopatra, Queen of the Nile. How many kings of the Nile were there? When the stoplight turned green at the intersection, the cable car carried him out of her life.

The entrance to BART at Embarcadero Station was a hub of activity adjacent to the Hyatt Regency Hotel and the cable car turntable. There was a constant stream of people, tourists along with commuters, often clustered around street musicians and entertainers.

Cleo walked by a hot pretzel stand doing a rapid business and then stepped onto the escalator to the BART station, located below street level. It was then that she realized she had forgotten to buy a newspaper from the corner vendor. She made a mental note to pick one up before leaving the station.

While she fumbled in her purse for her BART pass at the turnstile, there was a tap on her shoulder. Turning, she found herself face-to-face with the redhead from the cable car. Cleo blushed.

"May I have a moment?" The charming inquiry came on the wings of a British accent. He stepped to the railing and beckoned Cleo to follow, directing her attention to the giant macramé sculpture that hung from the top of the tunnel to the train platform below.

"Would you mind taking this pretzel to that starving chap with the sunglasses?" He pointed to a tall man at the base of the sculpture.

Cleo leaned over the railing, then faced the redhead squarely, trying to decide why he should ask this. His face exuded a wholesome goodness that denied suspicion or the possibility of a joke.

"Please?" he added politely over a winning smile. That was the deciding morsel. It was an odd request, but harmless . . . and sweet. Why not? Cleo thought. It would be her bit for British tourism.

"Sure," she agreed warmly. "This must be a British custom."

"You could be knighted for this."

"Wonderful," Cleo said, extending her hand. The Britisher placed a large pretzel heaped with mustard into her palm. This was an antic that had a Perry-flavor. Maybe it was possible to recapture the past, Cleo thought.

Then he motioned her ahead of him through the electronic turnstile, and before she could tell him about her BART pass, the gate was activated, allowing her passage, and his behind her. How she was able to enter without a ticket or a pass Cleo did not know. Puzzled, she turned to him, but her question was lost in his instruction. "Tell him this exactly. 'Dinner is catered by Alex,' and 'this is the very best I can do.'"

Cleo nodded, repeating the message under her breath. "Would you believe I've never done this before?" she quipped.

Feigning shock, the man said, "Incredible...truly."

He ensured that she stepped safely onto the escalator that made the final descent to the depths of the BART tube. Carrying the pretzel and briefcase left Cleo no free hand for balance. Then he hung over the railing to bid her a bon voyage. This was fun, Cleo thought, although illogical. The man was so close to making the delivery himself. Oh, well. It was Friday.

Once on the subway level, Cleo made a path to the rope sculpture, deciding at once that the very tall, dark-haired man at its base was infinitely more interesting than the dusty piece of macramé. He was impeccably dressed in a navy business suit, the line of fit the credit to no tailor, but to an athletic build. His carriage was distinct. He paced expectantly. The aviator sunglasses completed the look of stylish intrigue.

"Take me to your leader," Cleo addressed the pretzel.

As she neared, Cleo felt as if he were tracking her progress, but it was impossible to tell because of the sunglasses. Then he seemed to recognize the pretzel as a letter of introduction and, with a flicker of a smile, he appeared to scan the upper levels for his British companion.

Cleo's heart rate accelerated in anticipation. Finally, the moment of contact. She stood before him. "This is for you, from Alex," she announced buoyantly.

Bowing his head, he lowered the mysterious sunglasses to study Cleo before focusing on the twisted dough in her outstretched hand. The intensity of his steel-gray eyes penetrated her poise, rendering her speechless. This was definitely King of the Nile. Totally flustered, Cleo, too, dropped her eyes to the pretzel.

"I have a few lines I'm supposed to recite here," she said with a nervous laugh. "They seem to be slipping my mind." Her voice was lively as she tried to articulate the reason for this exchange. Her mind raced. She wanted desperately to be charming and captivating and witty. What could he be thinking of her? She forced herself from the paralysis of shyness to look up at him, only to find that he was gazing beyond her, not listening.

"Excuse me," he uttered blandly, moving past her.

Instantly, she yanked herself back from the depth of a schoolgirl crush, feeling inordinately foolish. She glanced around self-consciously, sure that a million eyes had witnessed her abandonment by this handsome man, while she melted at his feet. Then irritation overcame humiliation. She realized that she had been left with custody of a pretzel heaped with mustard. It lay smugly in her palm, defying her to dispose of it. She hated mustard. But the pretzel wasn't hers. How could she just toss out a gesture of someone else's goodwill? She would insist that the tall stranger take this responsibility off her hands, literally.

She turned and located him immediately. His height was an easy mark as he moved beyond the throng of people gathering for the incoming train. Eyes fixed on the head above the crowd, Cleo proceeded in his direction.

"Paper, ma'am?" asked a small boy in a baseball cap.

"Oh, not right now," Cleo mumbled, barely taking her eyes from the stranger, who had stopped two benches down the platform in the company of a thin, heavily mustached man, small enough to be a jockey. He, too, wore sunglasses.

"But I'm giving 'em away. Last two," the boy stated with tenacity.

Cleo returned to earth. Surely her need should have priority over this ridiculous errand. Indicating acceptance, she turned to the boy, who then demanded urgently, "Please hurry, Missus. I'm gonna miss my train."

A quick transaction appeared tricky as the briefcase hung from her left hand, the pretzel sat in the palm of her right, and Cleo had no intention of carrying a newspaper tucked under her arm against a white suit. She lifted her briefcase high, catching the base against her hip to form a landing onto which the newsboy slid the paper and was gone. Smiling at her ingenuity, Cleo plopped the pretzel on top of the paper, as a finishing touch, using her briefcase as a tray that she carried in front of her like a sacred offering.

She walked against the crowd toward the tall stranger and the jockey, seated together on a stone slab bench. They enjoyed more and more privacy as the crowd receded from them to channel onto the train. The tall stranger appeared to be doing the talking. He had removed his sunglasses. The jockey was still a tightly shrouded form in sunglasses. Absorbed in their own proceedings, they did not notice Cleo until she stepped directly in front of them, presenting the exultant pretzel, her briefcase about eye level to the seated men.

"You forgot this." Her voice held only a hint of the annoyance she felt.

Her reception was immediate and unexpected. The startled jockey leaped to his feet, pushing Cleo to the floor as he bolted for the outbound train. Cleo tumbled backward. Luckily, she dislodged her hands in time to brace her fall. She landed knees bent, hands behind her hips, with the pretzel bonded by mustard glue to her chest. More concerned with her awkward position than the reason for the assault on her, she straightened her legs and tugged at her skirt, conscious of the dark-haired man above her, who was focused on the flight of the jockey. Then, as the train rocketed out of the station, he dropped upon her, placing his hands firmly on her shoulders like the talons of an eagle in a grip she interpreted as assistance but could have compared to restraint.

"That's what I call an adverse reaction. Do you suppose he doesn't like mustard?" Cleo said to her presumed rescuer.

His answer came in the form of hands traveling rapidly down her body, along the sides of her breasts, around her waist and hips, then down her thighs. Her mouth opened, but she did not protest, not certain of the nature of the encroachment. Was he checking for injury? Broken bones? His hands moved deliberately, with remarkable efficiency, or erotic skill, or both. Before she could comprehend the action, it was over. He held on to her wrist, reaching across the floor to her briefcase.

"Is this yours?" he asked abruptly.

"Yeah. Who else's would it be?" Cleo fired back while peeling off the pretzel with her free hand and giving it a slam dunk into the trash container, which was now her neighbor at ear level.

The British tourist appeared at a run.

"Who the hell is she?" the tall stranger demanded.

"I just picked her out of the crowd," came the answer in alarm. There was not a trace of British accent.

"I frisked her. She's clean."

"Frisked!" Cleo howled, trying to jerk her hand away from him.

He tightened, then relaxed his grip on her wrist, but otherwise ignored her. "Take a look at her briefcase," he said.

The Britisher's eyes darted to the briefcase, and he then swore under his breath. He looked worried—and guilty.

"What's going on?" Cleo demanded, more impatient than angry, more curious than alarmed.

The attention of the dark-haired stranger was once again on Cleo. He discreetly flashed identification from his wallet. "We work for United States Intelnet," he said in a guarded voice. "I'm Clark Cannell." He indicated the redhead. "He's Alexander Matlow."

There was a loaded pause. Expectation hung in the air, hung on the faces of the two handsome men hovering over her. Cleo regarded each of them in succession in blank comprehension, then exploded into laughter.

Her outburst slapped surprise into their solemn faces. As they watched her, bewildered, the one named Clark released her wrist.

"This is so funny," Cleo sputtered at last. "What can I say?" she continued, throwing her hands in the air. "Welcome to San Francisco."

Still, the mood did not lighten, and Cleo began to focus her awareness. Clark observed a serious silence, while the redhead, Alexander, seemed to be withdrawing into a private horror. What was wrong with them? Here she was sitting on the cold concrete platform with mustard all over her blouse. If she could laugh, why couldn't they?

"You're...not laughing," Cleo said haltingly to the man crouched in front of her.

"No, I'm Clark Cannell," he replied patiently. "And you are?"

"Cleo Holmes," she answered, reaching up, accepting his handshake.

"Are you hurt?" he asked, retaining her hand.

"No. I'm alive, well, and sane—more than I can say for you."

"Point taken," he said calmly as he gripped her hand firmly and pulled her from the floor. It was a natural movement that brought her to her feet and gracefully maneuvered her to the bench. Her body followed his flow, and she sat down without much thought. "Here." Clark handed Cleo his handkerchief, which she applied as offered to the mustard on her blouse. He pivoted, shooting Alexander a question. "Odds on a setup?"

"My angle, zero," Alex reported, drawing in a breath. "I was doing you a favor, Clark. Strict dinner break. How about your end?"

"Pidgeon was terrified."

"Did you get an origin?"

"Negative. We got to stage one. Protocol only."

Cleo listened as she dabbed at the mustard, an amused grin taking over her lips. What a show, what a show! And here she was, front row center. The station was rather quiet now. The last two trains had cleared the commuter herd, leaving only the stragglers. So Cleo was getting a private showing of *Spies at Work*—and act one had certainly been a comedy. Oh, oh, Clark was turning toward her. Act two.

Clark studied Cleo for a moment and slowly sat down beside her. She had been folding his handkerchief so that the mustard stains would not show. "Thanks," she said, handing it back to him, somewhat hesitantly.

He took it from her in a relaxed, easy motion. He moved slowly and spoke even more slowly. "I don't suppose," he began contemplating his folded handkerchief, "you'd consider coming with us." He looked at Cleo casually. "Somewhere where we could talk."

"No...I don't suppose," Cleo responded with a friendly smile, mimicking his easy "aw, shucks" manner and questioning her sanity in refusing to follow these gorgeous men to the ends of the earth if necessary.

"Ah, yes." He managed a knowing chuckle and folded his handkerchief another time. "I didn't think so." He nodded his head. "You realize, of course, you don't have to be afraid of us." He glanced at the ceiling and shook his head slightly. "Would muggers and thieves be carting pretzels through a BART station?" he asked, throwing Alex a resigned look. Alex didn't notice. He was maintaining a keen vigil in all directions.

Cleo smiled at Clark. She liked him. "So you're not muggers and thieves. What's going on?"

"I was hoping you'd tell me." He took a controlled breath and an easy grin came to him. He was so calm. Cleo liked calm, controlled people. She, herself, was prone to excited fits.

"Tell you what," he offered, reaching for his wallet. "Here's my ID." He removed the laminated card. "Take a look at it. I'll even let you hold it in your hand."

Cleo succumbed to his folksy coaxing. "So this is where my tax dollars go." She accepted his ID between thumb and forefinger.

"Looks official, doesn't it," he jested.

"Good picture," Cleo chimed. She examined the ID closely, just to be polite. She was more interested in the man beside her. Out of the corner of her eye she could see he was smiling. He had a friendly smile. But why was he doing this? And why was she going along?

"Can I see your driver's license?" he asked respectfully, cautiously, like a child addressing another for the first time on a playground.

Cleo broke into a laugh. So that's what this was all about. "Good grief, why didn't you just ask?"

He shrugged shyly. He was acting like a kid, and Cleo thought he was adorable.

In a burst of energy, she thrust her hand into her purse. Immediately, Clark braced himself. Alex stepped back. "My God—why so jumpy? Here," she said, producing her wallet and flipping it open to her license.

"Ah, would you mind..."

Cleo laughed lightly as she anticipated him. "I will even take it out. I will even let you hold it."

He took the card from her and read aloud, "Cleopatra Simpson Holmes." He showed it to Alex and repeated, "Cleopatra Simpson Holmes." They looked dejected, depressed. Disappointed Boy Scouts.

Cleo spoke cheerfully to Clark. "Let me guess. Now we hand back the IDs?"

"Right," he answered. "You've done this before, I see."

"Just yesterday." She took one last look at his identification. The large serial number ZEB 786786A imprinted on her mind, and she consciously chose to freeze it in memory.

"Is anyone expecting you this evening?" Clark asked.

"No..." Cleo answered idly, noticing how oddly Clark took his ID from her, handling only the edges. "I mean yes. Yes...I'm meeting someone."

"Excellent hedge, Ms Holmes." Clark's smile was gentle as he raised his finger in mock reprimand. "But you're not supposed to be afraid of telling us you're on your way home to Oakland. Where do you get off?"

"MacArthur Station."

"May I ride with you?" Clark's smile rested nicely on his face, causing crinkles at his temples, which warmed his eyes and suited his easygoing manner.

"I can't stop you," Cleo said brightly.

Clark and Alex exchanged glances, and Alex stooped to pick up Cleo's newspaper and move her briefcase within her reach. He handed her the newspaper. "Goodbye, Ms Holmes. Thank you for being such a good sport."

"My regards to the queen," Cleo joked, but he did not hear her. He left as swiftly as he had come, bounding up the staircase and then out of sight.

"He had a British accent when I met him," Cleo explained. Clark digested the information silently. Cleo was very glad that he, too, had not walked away. She liked him. She felt comfortable with him.

"Well," she said to fill the silence as she picked up her briefcase and placed it on her lap. She opened the case wide, tossed in the newspaper and clicked her case shut again. Clark smiled at her. She smiled back.

"How long have you worked at California Investment?" he asked.

Cleo's mouth dropped open. "How did you know?"

He indicated the briefcase.

"Oh, no." Cleo was shaking her head. "No, you couldn't possibly have read the fine print on those folders. I didn't have it open that long." Clark continued to grin. "Wow, you *are* a spy!"

"Occupational hazard. I read anything flashed in my face."

"Okay," Cleo said playfully. "What's the date on my *Wall Street Journal*?"

"Wednesday, the fifteenth." The answer was unpretentious.

Cleo reopened the case to verify. "Uncanny," she stated emphatically. "I'm impressed."

"I'm flattered." He adopted a humble stance. "So what do you do at California Investment?"

"You tell me." Cleo threw down the challenge.

"Hmmm," he answered, unconcerned. "You're an analyst of some sort."

"Egad!"

"Egad?" He pursed his lips softly to hide a laugh.

"Egad," Cleo repeated firmly. "What else do you know?"

"That this is your train." He lifted her briefcase off her lap and began to escort her by the elbow. Cleo moved along easily with him. He had such grace. But it was more than how he handled his body. He was at home with himself. Comfortable in his own skin and able to transfer that feeling of comfort to others.

Like the station, the train was not crowded. More than half the seats were empty. Clark guided Cleo away from the regular seats, choosing instead the two seats along the side of the car facing the aisle and adjacent to the door. "Better view," he explained as he situated himself.

Cleo laughed. "What view?" she asked as the train sounded its futuristic whistle and moved forward. "This is the last San Francisco station. We're going into the tunnel under the bay." The train accelerated and then there was only pitch-blackness outside the windows.

The train sped into its descent, causing pressure on the eardrums. "Exciting," Clark said, swallowing hard.

"Exciting? I do this every day." She thought a moment. "You're right. This is exciting. Doing eighty miles per hour on the ocean floor with ninety feet of water above. I'm sitting next to a spy—oh, excuse me—that was crass. I mean intelligence agent...secret agent...operative...?" She turned to Clark, but he was not listening.

"We're slowing down," he said, not to her, not to anyone in particular. He was monitoring the situation, reporting to himself aloud.

"It's common. Characteristic of our beloved BART. Delay."

"We're stopping." His eyes scanned the windows. He was intense. The interior lights blinked out for an instant.

"You guys are really jumpy, aren't you? Just sit tight and hope there's no earthquake."

"Dead stop in midtunnel," Clark announced. He moved to the edge of the seat and peered down the aisle toward the connecting car. He clasped his wristwatch.

"Take it easy," Cleo said concerned. "I didn't mean to scare you with the earthquake business."

The public address system came alive. "There is a tie-up at MacArthur station. Trains are stopped on the track. There will be a slight delay. Service will resume as soon as possible."

The tension visibly drained from Clark. He sat back in the seat.

"Are you claustrophobic?" Cleo asked, touching his arm.

"No. I'm not." He was firm, conscious of her once more. "I just don't like to be a sitting duck," he added, again as if he were thinking aloud rather than speaking to Cleo.

"Sorry I even mentioned earthquakes," she apologized.

Clark turned to her. She could see him thinking, the gears turning in his head, as he brought himself back from a distant stare. His eyes struggled for the subject of conversation. "Earthquakes? No, you don't have to worry about that. This tunnel is not anchored to the ocean floor. Reinforced steel and concrete. I doubt it will crack. Fire could be a problem." He ran his hand over the seat. "The upholstery is fire resistant," he reported. "There'd probably be a lot of smoke. Just keep calm, pull the handle on the door, exit onto the walkway, head for the inner passageway between the tracks."

"You sound like you have it all planned."

"I do." He was staring ahead. "I'd take you and the woman over there in the brown jacket with me."

"Why?" Cleo asked, intrigued, looking over at the woman in brown.

"She'd probably have difficulty in the rush. She has a cane."

Oh, yes, Clark Cannell, Cleo told him silently. *I do like you.* "Then why would you take me?" she ventured. "See? No cane."

"Because you haven't told me what happened back at the platform." He grinned.

Cleo threw back her head in laughter. "What happened? Come earthquake or fire, you still want to know?"

"Yes," he said easily.

"Then I wish I could tell you. I really do." She paused. "My guess would be as I said before, the man had an adverse reaction to mustard—just the sight of it drove him crazy."

"Actually, the smell of it on your blouse is driving me crazy. I am so hungry. Whoa, we're moving again."

Oh, the dear man, Cleo thought, as the train accelerated in the darkness. He hadn't had dinner. And neither had she. Perhaps... Suddenly the train emerged from the tunnel, breaking into the daylight and squelching Cleo's bold thinking.

"Oakland West Station. Oakland West," came the announcement over the intercom.

"That's the Port of Oakland," Cleo said, playing tour guide. "Largest container port in the world." She pointed to the huge structural elevators towering along the berths for the loading and unloading of container ships. "They look like those walking war machines from *The Empire Strikes Back*."

"Yes. They do, don't they."

"I don't remember what they were called in the movie. Nobody seems to."

"They were called at-ats."

Cleo sat back. "Did anyone ever tell you you have a terrific memory?"

"Occupational hazard." He smiled. "Things just seem to stick. But I do ward off trivia."

"I'm glad you don't consider at-ats trivia. I saw *Star Wars* three times, *The Empire Strikes Back* twice."

The train entered an underground track. "12th Street Lake Merrit Station... 12th Street."

"This is City Center," Cleo explained. "Downtown Oakland. Like our graffiti? The convention center is above."

Clark nodded politely during the stop, and then the train was a burst of speed again, traveling just seven city blocks. "19th Street Station... 19th Street."

"This is still downtown," Cleo said when the train stopped. "We're practically in the basement of Emporium Capwell's, the largest store here—" Clark nodded, but Cleo stopped abruptly, then asked, "Am I filling your head with useless information that you'll never get rid of?"

Clark laughed freely for the first time. A hearty, good-natured laugh. "Occupational hazard," he insisted, coughing to clear his throat.

"Flypaper memory," Cleo commiserated jovially, "Chalk it up to the downside of—" Cleo faltered, thinking it a mistake to label him a spy "—of what you do."

"There are no downsides to what I do," he said confidently.

The train emerged from the underground network and moved onto aerial tracks paralleling the freeways. "MacArthur Station . . . MacArthur. Last transfer point for Fremont and Richmond. This is a Concord bound train."

"Our stop," Clark said.

"No . . ." Cleo hesitated. "Actually, my stop is Rockridge." She gritted her teeth. *Oh, I've been such a fool,* Cleo moaned inwardly.

Caught off guard, Clark quickly consulted the transit map mounted on the wall of the train. Rockridge was the stop after MacArthur. "Very clever, Ms Holmes."

Cleo tried to read his sober remark. She couldn't tell if he was offended or impressed. His expression turned reflective. His head nodded slightly. "If there is a downside to—" he paused as she had "—to what I do, it would be that I can't stay on with you to Rockridge. I can't ask you to dinner."

Cleo was touched by his sentiment. This was indeed a memorable encounter. She spoke from the heart. "Well, thanks for the excitement. I'd been having a bad day—feeling sorry for myself, worrying about my boring, little life. I feel redeemed.''

Clark stood as the train slowed. ''Thanks for putting up with me.''

''Goodbye, Clark Cannell, ZEB 786786A,'' Cleo said brightly.

The use of his ID number startled him. He stopped and looked back at her. ''*Real* sorry about dinner,'' he said. He turned and stood alone in the door well as the train came to a smooth halt. The doors were slow to open, and Cleo saw him impatiently place his wristwatch against the molding. It seemed to give the doors a boost. They opened and he stepped onto the station platform.

So that was how Alexander had tripped the electronic turnstile, Cleo decided. She prepared to wave, waiting for Clark to turn around. He didn't.

CLARK CANNELL WALKED quickly down the platform to a rendezvous with Alex. He was anxious to hear the latest report. He was in big trouble, and it had nothing to do with the woman he had just talked to. She was innocent, just as Alex had assumed. God, she even had orchids in her hair that shook when she laughed.

Damn Alex and his kindhearted sentimentalism. It was a good thing Alex was getting out; he was definitely losing his edge. Clark would have to make sure Alex got out alive. But after what happened on the platform at the Embarcadero Station, he wondered if any of them would get out alive.

CLEO HOLMES FELT renewed, rewarded. She was tingling, giddy from a rush of feelings she did not sort out until the train pulled away from MacArthur Station. And as the train accelerated, two truths, two opposing truths, organized her consciousness. She had just met a most interesting man, and she had just let him walk away. Stupid, stupid, she told herself. Why didn't she get off the train with him? Oh, well, she would learn from it. For next time.

But a next time would be a miracle. There weren't many men who could interest Cleo in a short flash of time. Even Perry, the dearest man in her life, whose loss she had come to regret, had not been an instant attraction. Perry had had to work his way into her heart, wearing her down with his antics and constant attention. In the beginning, she had resisted.

Her sister, Cassy, had pointed out her unrealistic standards. "That's why you're not married," she had said. "You expect to be swept off your feet by a man."

But Cleo had always contended that she knew what she liked. Could tell immediately. And this evening, triumphantly, she had proved herself right. She would call Cassy tonight, she crowed to herself. Too bad she had let him walk away.

"Rockridge Station...Rockridge." There was hope, Cleo thought. He had inspected her driver's license. He knew her address. Surely he would remember it. Maybe he'd call, send a postcard. Maybe.

Cleo stepped off the train onto the open-air platform. She looked toward the bay, graced by the San Francisco skyline against a setting sun. And in the foreground, she could see the outline of MacArthur Station on the track. *Go back. He may be there. Do one foolish, impulsive thing in your life.*

Reason was to prevail. Contented with a lovely memory, Cleo caught the escalator down to the street level. And then the public address system crackled with an unusual announcement. "Cleo Holmes. Phone call at security booth. Cleo Holmes."

Her face lit up with joy. "It's him! It's him!" she whispered. "It's got to be him!"

She flew to the glass-enclosed booth near the entrance to the station, her heels clicking on the concrete floor. The BART security attendants anticipated her, handing her the phone, as she responded to a quick check of her name.

Cleo took a deep breath. "Hello," she said happily.

"Cleo Holmes, this is Clark Cannell." *Oh, it's him! It's him!* Cleo shouted inwardly.

"Please wait where you are. I have to talk to you." His voice was crisp, firm.

"Sure. I'll be here," Cleo said, enchanted.

The receiver clicked in her ear. *I'm in love,* she thought, *I'm in love.* Then she turned away from the curiosity of the BART attendants, self-conscious of blushing, glowing.

The station was largely deserted now that it was past rush hour. Cleo stayed at the security booth, her eyes fixed on the escalator, awaiting the arrival of the train from MacArthur Station, which would bring Clark Cannell to her. Then, all of a sudden, Clark Cannell was running to her. He had come not by train, but from street level, through the main entrance. He was wearing sunglasses again, but Cleo would have known him anywhere. Waving, she began to walk toward him. He was still running. How romantic. She breathed inwardly. Just like in the movies.

"Hi," she said shyly, but he did not listen as he reached out and clasped her shoulders firmly.

"Ms Holmes. The man who ran away from me at Embarcadero Station was killed on the tracks at MacArthur."

"Oh, how awful!" Cleo gasped, instantly aware that she had misread his haste and too overwhelmed to be embarrassed.

Clark spoke rapidly and with authority. "We have to get this straightened out. Come with me to headquarters. I promise you an answer."

Cleo had barely nodded her consent when Clark took her briefcase and wrapped his arm around her, sweeping her into a pace that alternated between a quickstep and a run. They retraced Clark's course to the main entrance.

Outside in the empty parking lot, a Bell helicopter, painted white with a blue stripe and U.S. government insignia, waited. The rotor blades began to turn at their approach, and the whine of the engine became pronounced. Cleo's hand automatically shot up to restrain her hair and secure the orchids against the wind from the rotor.

Alexander Matlow gave a silent greeting at the door, pulling Cleo into the body of the helicopter as Clark propelled her forward and climbed in himself. They were barely inside when the helicopter lifted off the lot.

It was Alex who oriented Cleo, wide-eyed and agape, into a cabin seat. Clark crawled in next to the pilot and immediately plugged into a set of headphones.

"Ever been in a chopper before?" Alex shouted above the noise of the engine. Cleo's expression was his answer. He took her hand for reassurance. "Sit back and enjoy yourself."

Cleo nodded, smiling tentatively into his trustworthy face. She appreciated his effort to settle her. She would have no doubts about taking another pretzel from him, she decided.

When Alex let go of her hand in order to write in a notebook, Cleo edged to the window. The view was spectacular as the helicopter gained altitude, made a sweeping turn away from the bay and headed over the Oakland foothills. Cleo was totally engrossed, reveling in the landscape, thrilled by the sight of her own town house and thirty others like it nestled in a row on the side of a hill. She was sitting in the sky, mentally and physically.

CHAPTER THREE

CLEO RECOGNIZED the landing point as the research laboratory for defense weaponry in the valley. For reasons of national security, not much was publicly known about projects conducted at the lab. Cleo had never given the place much thought. It was just there. Still she was surprised to discover that Intelnet was part of the facility.

The helicopter touched down on an asphalt landing pad. Away from the bay breezes, Cleo stepped into an evening that was oppressively hot. It was a silent Alex who helped her out of the craft and escorted her to a single-story cement building, which Cleo guessed was a penthouse for an underground installation. Her first thought as she walked into the building with Alex was of the efficiency of the air conditioners. The climate inside was a total mastery of the natural heat.

Clark, who had been conferring with the pilot, caught up to them in the corridor, silently taking a position on the other side of Cleo. He was still wearing sunglasses, which made his face even more of a somber mask.

Taking her cue from her silent hosts, Cleo did not attempt conversation as she walked between them through the maze of cool, sterile corridors made ultrawhite by rows of fluorescent lights. The dull whir of computers and Teletypes from the interior ran through the air.

When they came to a door marked Visitors' Lounge, the purposeful pace came to a halt. Clark turned to Cleo mechanically. "Just relax. Give us a while to work it out," he said. It was Alex who responded to Cleo's agreeable nod and held the door open for her.

Cleo stepped into the lounge. The cozy environment was in stark contrast to the antiseptic hallways. Much like a special airport waiting room, it had all the comforts of home. Sectional sofas in gold brocade were set at right angles on a burnt-orange rug. The opposite wall was surfaced in amber mirror tiles. There was a television console in one corner, a wet bar in the other. Vibrant blue porcelain vases filled with dried fronds accented the decor nicely.

Cleo was charmed by the room's ambience. Still she wanted to see more of the installation. She turned and opened the lounge door gently. A baby Marine, whose youth reminded Cleo that she was really getting old, had taken up guard. The message was blunt, and Cleo respected the restriction on this hospitality. It was, after all, a secret government facility.

Not expecting to remain long, Cleo sat down on the couch. What a story she could tell at the office Monday. She picked up a *Newsweek* and started to flip the pages until her reflection in the tiles caught her eye. The orchids in her hair were much too flamboyant now. The mood had passed, and she felt silly. Carefully, she removed them, remembering how Emilio's floral creation had restored her spirits, but having little recollection of how miserable she had felt beforehand. She set the orchids on the coffee table and stroked the petals a bit, as if the gesture would somehow prove her gratitude to Emilio.

Then she resumed flipping the pages of the *Newsweek*. She did the same with a *Time* and then another *Newsweek*. An article caught her eye. She read it. Afterward, she became aware that a serious amount of time had passed. Maybe they had forgotten her.

She stood and headed for the door just in time to receive a dinner on a silver service cart, pushed into the lounge by yet another baby Marine. Cleo was struck by the courtesy offered in the Visitors' Lounge. The least she could do was be patient. She smiled. Clark Cannell had, in a sense, taken her to dinner.

"How long must I be here?" she asked the Marine, playing a long shot that she might be able to get some information low on the totem pole.

"Don't know, ma'am," he replied with military politeness while removing the cover from the dinner plate and exposing wild rice and chicken. Cleo guessed it was Chicken Kiev by the plump golden shape. The aroma rose invitingly. "If you need anything else, you can call on the intercom, ma'am. Press the red button, then ask for the kitchen," he said before putting his shoulder to the door.

Need anything? Cleo thought as she looked at the glass of wine, green salad, spinach soufflé, croissants and chocolate mousse topped with a green cherry. Recalling the cottage cheese in her refrigerator, just this side of the expiration date, and the box of graham crackers in her cupboard, she raised the glass of wine and toasted her reflection in the amber tiles. Then she took a big gulp and sat down to dinner, indulging heartily in the novelty.

She spread the heavy napkin on her lap and played to the mirror tiles, pretending to be a restaurant critic. She tasted a bit of everything first before settling down to eat in normal progression. She would definitely tell an amazing story at work Monday.

Close to nine o'clock, when Cleo was yawning at regular intervals, Alex appeared. "Will you come with me?" he said gently. He looked drained. He tried to give her an encouraging smile. Cleo could see he was making a great effort.

He led her just next door to a narrow room where a burly man with sandy hair sat at the head of a long conference table, lighting a cigarette. Clark was in the far corner of the room, pouring coffee into a Styrofoam cup. His white shirt was open at the neck, the sleeves rolled almost to the elbows. There was a computer terminal on the table, emitting pleasant-sounding beeps, but it was the wall the room shared with the Visitors' Lounge that had Cleo's attention.

On this side, the amber tiles she had been looking into all evening were part and parcel of a two-way mirror. She had been observed for the duration. Cleo went cold at the realization she was under surveillance, under suspicion. For what?

"I don't believe this," she gasped. "I pick up a pretzel and I end up here?" She shouted at Clark, a fearful quiver entering her voice. "How dare you! You asked me to come here for a...for a mutual solution. I came with you in good faith."

The burly man rose from the table. "That you did, Ms Holmes." He was a steady, unshakable kind of man. "I'm Phil Edmondsen. It's Cleo, isn't it?" He extended his hand, motioned her to a chair, then sat down again.

Alex took a chair across from Cleo. Clark moved to the far end of the table and stood with a foot on the chair, his arm resting over his knee. His face was devoid of expression, but he did look tired.

Styrofoam cups littered the table, remnants of a rough evening. Certainly, no Chicken Kiev had been served here.

Cleo got her bearings. "This has gone far enough. Why am I here? Look, I'm sorry that a man has died. But it doesn't concern me."

Edmondsen was absorbed in his cigarette. He took a puff, savored it and then cleared his throat. Shuffling papers, he began a monologue, his voice a dull monotone. "You have no criminal record, no questionable affiliation. Legitimate employment. Fingerprints check clear."

Fingerprints! Of course, Cleo thought. Taken from Clark Cannell's identification card. What a sly trick he had pulled while she was lapping up his "aw, shucks" charm.

Edmondsen was now reading from a computer printout. "Graduated from U.C. Berkeley, employed by California Investment for eight years, voted in last election, only living relative, sister Cassandra in San Luis Obispo..."

"What is going on?" Cleo insisted, almost at a shout. Alex shifted uncomfortably in his seat, but her outburst had no effect on Edmondsen. A fire in his shoes wouldn't faze him.

"Your profile as an average citizen," Edmondsen said.

"Oh, wonderful," Cleo tossed in sarcastically.

"I ask you, Ms Holmes, have you ever seen either of these two men before today?" The tip of his cigarette subtly pointed out his colleagues at the table.

"No," Cleo stated flatly, raising her hand in frustration. "Trust me, men who look that good don't grow on trees," she added flippantly. Still she was unable to ruffle his composure.

"So you swear that you had no knowledge of Mr. Alexander Matlow before he drafted you as a..." He paused. "A pretzel courier?" He shot Alex a derisive look and noted Cleo's nod. "And Mr. Matlow claims he singled you out of all the women in downtown San Francisco—" another derisive look at Alex "—at random, and that you did nothing to solicit his attention."

Solicit? Cleo flinched. She had flirted with him a little. Was she on thin ice? *My God,* she thought. *I conduct a life that would not be at odds with sequestered nuns. I smile at one man in years, and it's an inquisition.* A blush spread over her face. "I did smile at him, but I—I didn't expect to see him again," she stammered.

Sensitive to her difficulty, Alex spoke on her behalf. "Again for the record, she had nothing to do with it. I considered her Clark's type. That was my only motivation."

Edmondsen nodded and lit another cigarette. Cleo relaxed. Her innocence had been upheld, and in the process, her respect for Alex entrenched. She no longer felt victimized or accused. The feeling of control seemed to return all at once, perhaps on the knowledge that she was Clark's type. It was a sort of personal triumph. Her appeal, and not random chance, had brought her here. Yes, she decided, she did have some control, though she didn't have the foggiest idea of what.

Her ears pricked up when Edmondsen began again. "Ms Holmes, you have been unwittingly involved in an unfortunate situation. The United States government is in serious need of your help. And though we regret any inconvenience, we trust you will be able to arrange for a two-week absence from work."

"A vacation is possible," Cleo said matter-of-factly. A vacation was at least three years overdue.

"Then you agree to spending that time with us in interest of national security? You will be paid a stipend, of course, to be negotiated later." He paused for her answer.

"For reasons of national security? That hardly leaves room for refusal, does it?"

"Good," he continued in stodgy exposition. "Mr. Cannell, behind you—" his eyes indicated Clark who had just sunk into a seat in a preoccupied haze "—is the internal force behind CLEOPATRA, code name for a project that until now we had every reason to believe was top secret. We can't explain the reaction you got from our contact agent today. We don't know who he was and, obviously, we can't ask him now. But we suspect the name Cleopatra on your briefcase triggered his reaction, which points to a serious leak in our organization.

"CLEOPATRA is in motion and cannot be stopped. That leaves us to deal with neutralizing the association of Mr. Cannell with CLEOPATRA while we patch up our security. Clark has proposed that we draw the spotlight on you, thereby denying existence of the code name and the project. The arrangement is that you accompany Mr. Cannell for two weeks, after which time CLEOPATRA will be in place. The best cover is as his wife, from a verifiable marriage."

A verifiable marriage? Cleo's lips parted in disbelief.

"Fortunately, for all who know Clark," Edmondsen continued, looking once more at Alex, "you fit his taste. It would raise no question. It's certainly plausible on the surface."

Cleo began to fidget.

"Think about it, Ms Holmes. This is a serious two-week agreement on your part. If you feel you cannot handle it, please say so now."

Oh, what a twisted day, Cleo thought. First, a home run with the bases loaded at the office, an encounter with a spy, and now... She glanced at Clark. And now a two-week vacation with a man who earlier today had captured her interest as no man had ever...

"I urge you to say yes, Ms Holmes," said Edmondsen. "Ms Holmes?"

"Okay," she blurted, surprised by the sound of her voice, but mostly afraid she might be blushing. Alex instantly breathed relief, and Cleo subconsciously used his reaction to solidify and validate her spark decision.

"Only the three of us in this room are to know of the arrangement," Edmondsen concluded.

"Four," Alex interjected, indicating Cleo.

"Four," Edmondsen amended in begrudging agreement.

A page from the intercom broke into the silence. "Mr. Edmondsen . . . Mr. Phil Edmondsen to Level Four."

Edmondsen's bulky form was slow to rise. "Good luck to you, Ms Holmes. I will be in touch when this is all over." He glanced briefly at Alex, then Clark, and left the room.

Cleo inhaled deeply, trying to understand what had happened, wondering if she'd had too much wine. She was exhilarated. She was confused. It was Alex's supportive look that helped her grasp the situation. She lifted her shoulders, then let them drop. "This is not my typical Friday night," she told him. His smile was full of empathy.

Then she summoned her courage and shifted her eyes down the length of the table to find Clark Cannell. He was certainly attractive, even as he sat there, silent, within himself, his eyes expressionless in a face drawn with gloom. A man of many faces, all appealing, all . . . Was Alex observing the way she looked at Clark? Yes, he was. Cleo blushed. She lowered her eyes to the table but raised them when Clark spoke.

"We'll be flying to Oakland Airport in twenty minutes," he said blandly, staring at a point on the wall behind Cleo. "I'll drive you to your house. Pack one case only. We'll drive to Lake Tahoe for the weekend. From there, we'll play it as it comes."

"What do you mean?" Cleo asked and felt color rise in her cheeks as Clark fixed his eyes on her and skewered her with his irritation.

"Exactly what I said." He spoke with almost hostile precision.

This was a confrontation, Cleo thought incredulously. She didn't know how to handle it, so she lashed out, "I know exactly what you said at the BART station, and you lied to me. You didn't tell me I was going into a fishbowl to be watched and researched and—"

"And if I had told you, would you have come with me?"

Cleo was trapped. She admitted he had a point. She was not used to being wrong, not used to losing an argument. She didn't know how to get out of this gracefully. "Well, I think you're wrong to manipulate people for your own purposes," she finally retorted.

Clark rose painfully from the table and took a slow stride to the door. As his hand reached the doorknob, he turned to Cleo. "Ms Holmes, you don't have to like me. In fact, *dis*like me. I'll even let you stick pins in me."

Infuriated by his tone, Cleo gripped the table and opened her mouth for combat. But Alex immediately stretched across the table and covered her hands with his own. Startled, Cleo faced him, and in that instant, she heard the door close as Clark left the room.

"You should be yelling at me, not him," Alex said gently. His voice, his face, his body stretched awkwardly across the table disarmed Cleo. He was reaching out to her with his entire being. "It's not his fault," Alex explained. "I'm sorry for what happened. I can't change it." He looked down at the table before meeting Cleo's eyes again. "All I can say is that being with Clark will not be so bad. I've known him for a long time." There was a pause. "I owe him my life on at least two occasions that I can recall. He is under a strain now that no one should be under. Give him a chance. Please? He's the finest man I know."

Cleo was taken by Alex's sincerity and his genuine effort to mend the situation. "Gee, Alex, if someone was harboring a bad opinion of me, I would certainly want you coming to my defense."

He smiled appreciatively. "Let me show you to a rest room. A guard will take you to the copter when you're ready."

Dear Alex, Cleo thought. A kind, considerate man.

CLEO STOOD under the awning on the helicopter deck next to a young Marine, watching Clark flight-check a small, two-seater helicopter. He was apparently the pilot on this flight. Cleo tingled with the excitement, the adventure.

Mechanically, Clark ushered her to the helicopter and dismissed the Marine. Without a word, without a wasted motion, he led her by the elbow, seated her in the copilot's seat, handed her the helmet and buckled her in. Then he sprinted over to Alex, who had just come onto the landing pad toting a small canvas suitcase with many zippered compartments. Clark took the suitcase, slapping Alex's arm in a show of comradeship.

Returning, Clark stowed the suitcase behind the pilot seat and swung into place with the grace of a leopard. Cleo smiled politely. "Alex is very nice. He thinks a lot of you," she remarked, wanting to establish some basis for communication. Clark merely tapped a gauge on the instrument panel. He started to put the key in the ignition.

"Clark," Cleo said quickly, causing him to look at her. "I just want you to know I'm not going to stick pins in you."

"Your choice." He shrugged and turned the key.

The helicopter rocked with vibration, the engine whining, the rotor turning. Clark waited for the necessary rpm, and then lifted the craft off the ground. One hand on the control stick, one hand on the collective lever beside the pilot seat, and both feet on the rudder pedals, his entire body melded with the motion of the aircraft.

Once again Cleo reveled in leaving the ground, only this time her thrill was magnified by her front-seat view in a flying bubble. High in a night sky and surrounded by stars, she was sitting next to Clark Cannell, a member of an elite band of intelligence agents. Secret agents? Professional spies? Whatever. Who was he, really? He did have a good friend. That indicated worth in Cleo's book. He looked good. He moved well. And he had certainly stolen her senses on the BART train. Yes, she decided. She could stand being married to this unusual find for two weeks. How would Josh ever top this one?

Clark skillfully brought the helicopter to rest at a military hangar at the Oakland Airport. Cleo was sad the flight had come to an end. How she envied Clark's ability to fly. She removed her helmet and said cheerfully for a new beginning, "If we taxpayers taught you to fly, it was well worth the expense."

There was no response.

An Air Force sergeant informed Clark that a maroon Thunderbird, an Avis rental, was ready for him in the parking lot. Once again Clark seated Cleo in the car without a word. Determined to break his mood, she waited until he took his place behind the wheel. "You know, I was wrong. I thought you were quite amiable this afternoon."

He put the car in gear and uttered dryly, "In your boring, little life, anything must seem good." He must have felt her recoil. "Look, I'm sorry." His eyes never left the road.

"Forget it," Cleo said curtly, trying to put the cruelty of his remark in perspective. She had used the words "boring, little life" herself on the BART train, but she never expected to have them thrown back at her by someone who had validated them through investigation. She refused to let him know how much it hurt. "I'll give you directions to my house," she offered.

"I've read the map," he informed her. "It's a little skill I picked up at no cost to you taxpayers."

Cleo was seething with fury. She wanted to be out of the car, out of her agreement and rid of Clark Cannell. What gave him the authority to be so rude? She closed her eyes and controlled herself. She had made a commitment. She was no quitter. The issue was not Clark Cannell. The issue was national security. Clark cracked the window for air. It helped to cool her distaste for him.

True to form, Clark was having no trouble navigating to her house. At each critical junction, Cleo waited for him to fail, prayed for him to fail. But he hesitated at no turns, asked for no assistance and now was driving up the final winding road.

Suddenly, headlights flooded the windshield. An oncoming car had taken too wide a turn. "Look out!" Cleo screamed, preparing for a crash. But Clark swerved, hung on the edge of the road, recovered and it was over. Reaction and nerve. He never blinked. Was this the man with the cute fear of earthquakes? Cleo watched him study the rearview mirror.

"That was close," she said shakily.

He remained serene, silent. She hated him.

Clark rolled to a stop in front of Cleo's home. "Do not get out of the car," he ordered. "I'll come around and get you. Have your key ready."

In deference to his authority, which she presumed she should respect, Cleo waited, her hostility setting new highs. He collected her and led her firmly by the elbow to her front door. She resented his proximity but felt obligated not to shake him away. She could feel his muscles tightening, taut and alert for action. He watched shadows as if expecting an ambush. Obviously, he was playing some game, and Cleo found his behavior ridiculous.

She opened the door, and Clark slid past her. She closed the door behind her while feeling for the light switch. When the light came on, she saw that Clark stood ready, his revolver drawn and pointed to the ceiling.

"Oh, *really*," Cleo snorted. "This is my home. You are quite safe here. No guard dogs. No attack goldfish."

"Draw the drapes," he commanded.

She muttered in disgust and did so. Then she turned, folding her arms in front of her while Clark cautiously inspected her living room. "You case the joint. I'll make coffee," she said, shaking her head.

When Clark joined her in the kitchen, she thrust a cup of coffee into his hand, a move to assert herself in her own home rather than a gesture of hospitality.

"I'm going to check around, open drawers, look at photographs," he announced with a slight note of inquiry in his voice, as if to ask permission.

"Be my guest," Cleo replied sarcastically. "How bravely you risk the boredom."

Cleo heard him inspecting the kitchen cabinets as she climbed the stairs to the bedroom to pack. She heard the refrigerator door open. She winced. She should have wiped up the orange juice spill from this morning.

Cleo turned on the light in her bedroom. The comforter on her bed had never looked more inviting. Going to sleep would be nice. Waking up in the morning to find that none of this had happened would be nicer. Cleo dismissed her wishful thinking and forged ahead. She was a trooper. Hadn't Perry always said that?

So, from the depths of her closet, Cleo retrieved a small Samsonite Pullman and opened it on her bed, not bothering to brush off the dust. Then she moved through the bathroom, gathering her toothbrush, hair dryer and other essentials, which when deposited on her bed made quite a pile. Cleo shook her head over how much hardware was necessary even when following the directive to travel lightly.

She went to the closet again, not at all dismayed that the bulk of her working wardrobe was either at the cleaners or in the laundry hamper. Somehow her nine-to-five attire didn't fit the occasion, and without hesitation she selected her favorite clothes and laid them across her suitcase. She refused to admit that she was bent on impressing the fanatic whom she could hear rummaging downstairs.

She guessed that he was correlating his findings with his impression of her, somewhere between ordinary and drab. Certainly her home was cozy and comfortable, warmed perhaps by the feminine touch, but it had a rather bland personality. Conventional and conservative, it evidenced no artistic flair, no interesting hobbies, no exciting travels.

She entertained the instant wish that her home could reflect a life so scintillating as to singe this Clark Cannell's eyebrows, and bring him to his knees in apology for his erroneous assessment of her. It would be so gratifying to explain matter-of-factly to his gaping regard that, yes, she trained jaguars and had a private line to the chairman of the Federal Reserve Bank. But it was not to be and Cleo wondered why his opinion of her should even matter. It disturbed her, but she continued to pack her best clothes, remembering to include accessories for dramatic combinations, as if she were dressing for a two-week date.

She heard Clark directly below her. She heard him raise the piano keyboard. *Yes, Mr. Cannell, I do play the piano,* she projected herself saying haughtily. Clark hit a few arpeggios, followed by a chromatic chord. Oh, no, that wasn't the prelude to "Chopsticks," Cleo moaned to herself. And, of course, he would see her beginner music sheets.

Motivated anew, Cleo moved purposefully to her bureau and gathered up her laciest, most feminine lingerie. Hesitating only for a second, she located, at the bottom of the drawer, an expensive nightgown, which she had never worn. She intended to torture Clark as the ravishing embodiment of his "type," even if she didn't measure up in substance. Devilishly, she laid the seductive items in her suitcase. Then her practicality ran headlong into her desire to conduct life in the fast lane. With a resigned sigh, she threw in her worn flannel nightgown over the whole naughty display.

When she was satisfied that everything had been assembled on the bed, Cleo removed her suit jacket and slipped out of her lilac blouse. Noticing mustard stains on her camisole as well, she removed that, too. As she folded the soiled clothes on top of the dresser, Clark walked in, either oblivious, or totally unconcerned, that she was undressed. Cleo saw through the mirror that he was absorbed in her address book as he took a seat on her bed and leaned against the headboard. She was indignant. He was trespassing on every facet of her life.

Pretending experience with strange men sauntering into her bedroom while she was undressed, Cleo attempted to pull a clean white camisole over her head. Her calculated coolness was unfortunately betrayed as she struggled with placement of the shoulder straps and got stuck. For a frantic moment she feared she might spend the rest of her life trapped in a nylon hood. Finally, she extricated herself with much flailing of arms, and peeked over the edge of the camisole, hoping that the world had shared her blindness. No such luck. Clark was eyeing her curiously, a witness to the whole performance.

With a resigned tug and all thoughts of grace out the window, Cleo straightened the camisole without taking her eyes from him. He held her gaze for a long time, then said, "Cleo" with a clarity that cleansed the air. He paused, then spoke again.

"Edmondsen didn't tell you the whole story. Everything he said was true, but he didn't mention the danger—maybe to make you feel at ease, or maybe he doesn't fully trust you. Anyway, there was no reference to risk, and I feel you have a right to know."

Cleo swallowed hard as he continued. "First, let me say, I never thought you were part of a setup. I never meant to lie to you. I called you as soon as I found out the cause of the tie-up at MacArthur was the dead body of our Mr. X on the track, because...because, quite frankly, someone may want you dead."

"Me?" Cleo said, astonished.

"Not you, personally. But you, for whoever someone might think you are or might think you know."

"I don't understand," Cleo whined.

"Neither do I. What do you remember about the man, Mr. X?"

"He was small—like a jockey," Cleo recalled, walking to the bed and sitting on the end.

"That's about all I know, too. He was someone who contacted us with an interest in informant status. By his own cunning design, he chose to conceal his identity. He is unknown and untraceable. He is also dead. Either he threw himself or was thrown in front of a BART train. In any case, his reaction to you cost him his life. I'm speculating that you are a target by association, Cleo. I don't know. But if you are, I give you my word that I can keep you alive. Humility serves no purpose here. Your best chance for survival is with me."

Arms folded against her chest, Cleo felt herself getting numb. "Cleo. Talk to me," she heard Clark say.

"I'm okay," she said, jarring herself out of a trance. She popped up from the bed like a jack-in-the-box and began to tuck the remaining items into her suitcase, hoping that physical activity would give her the illusion of composure. She did not want Clark to know she was shaken, although she realized the chance was slim of being anything less than transparent before him. His words continued to frame her incredible predicament.

"As Edmondsen said, you and I will be buying time for project CLEOPATRA. If you are targeted, you will draw out what we need to know. If you are not, you will diffuse my association with CLEOPATRA, while Alex and Edmondsen work internally to retrace connections for leaks. Your house will be under surveillance, as will your friends. Your phone lines will be tapped, as will those of your friends. Alex is at your office right now, combing through your files for any clue, any contact you might have that would link you to the subway incident."

Cleo closed the suitcase and swallowed hard. She was overly aware of her own breathing.

"This is my rule," Clark continued. "Never leave me. In public, always stay within my grasp. In private, never lock a door between us."

Cleo nodded as she walked stiffly to the closet. She took her favorite white blouse from a hanger. It was trimmed with white satin ribbon, embroidered at the neck, and had long, billowy sleeves cuffed at the wrist. Combat uniform would be more appropriate, Cleo thought. Here she was packed for an all-expense-paid vacation, when U.S. Intelnet was hoping, at best possible expedience, that she would be bait for the unknown. Turning at the sound of Clark's voice, she slipped into the blouse.

"I'm going to break an agency rule," he said. "I don't think it's fair to make you sit defenseless." He produced a miniature gun no longer than a credit card, easily mistaken for a toy. He motioned for Cleo to sit beside him, which she did, in a state of hypnosis. "It must be fired at close range. There are only two bullets. This is the safety. This is the trigger. Try it." Clark placed it firmly in her hand and made sure she knew how to use it by explaining simply and repeatedly. "Carry it with you at all times," he concluded at last.

Cleo inhaled deeply. She would have settled for an electromagnetic wristwatch. Grateful that Clark had told her the score, she was more afraid of admitting fright than feeling fright.

She walked over to her purse on the dresser. Entranced and repulsed by the gem of lethal technology in her hand, she rooted in her purse with no particular purpose, totally unconcerned that Clark was buttoning the back of her blouse.

When she finally found the resolve to drop the gun into her purse, Clark put his hands on her shoulders and swung her around to face him. Strongly reassuring, his voice resonant, he said, "You won't need it, Cleo Simpson Holmes. You have me."

In his protective hold, Cleo looked up into his dark gray eyes. He was commanding, firm, towering over her. She shivered, and his strong hands deliberately rubbed a burning warmth into her shoulders. Everything was so unreal, except for the man who now held her. A current ran through her body. She did believe this man could save her from anything.

Clark carried her suitcase downstairs while Cleo rushed to the kitchen to pour the remaining coffee into a thermos and grab the box of graham crackers. She noticed her hands were shaking slightly. She was still confused, but she met Clark at the door, as ready as she would ever be.

"One more thing," Clark began.

Cleo held her breath in order to hear him more clearly. She attached vital importance to anything he had to say.

"I'm sorry," he said, simultaneously turning out the lights.

After locking the door, Cleo followed Clark to the car parked beneath the street lamp. *I'm sorry, too, Clark Cannell,* she uttered silently. *I'm sorry for thinking petty thoughts, throwing nasty little barbs at you when your only crime was having too much character, too much integrity. I like you, Clark Cannell, I really do.*

CHAPTER FOUR

CLARK AT THE WHEEL, the rented Thunderbird pierced the night easily. The hour was late and hardly a car competed for the road.

"It's about a three-and-a-half-hour drive to Tahoe. I can spell you anytime you like," Cleo offered.

"Thank you. It won't be necessary," Clark answered freely. The barrier between them was gone. Cleo sipped from the cup of coffee she had poured for Clark, which he didn't want.

"Are we being followed?" Cleo asked.

"No...not yet, at least."

"Will you tell me when we are?"

"Yes."

That satisfied Cleo for a moment. But she needed more. Much more. It was hard to be logical when she didn't know where to begin. "What is CLEOPATRA?" she ventured.

"I'm sorry. I can't tell you." Clark seemed to reconsider. "It's basically a plan that restores leverage against terrorist reign in the Middle East. If it's exposed prematurely, many years of work will be lost and an untold number of lives will be in jeopardy."

"What are you going to do now?"

"Distance myself from CLEOPATRA operationally. Let Edmondsen and Alex do the work. My function is to look married. Someone out there may be interested. So let's get to know each other fast. What do you do, exactly, at California Investment?''

It was the first of many direct questions Clark fired at Cleo. She answered quickly, precisely, acutely conscious of sharing any detail that would help Clark build a credible relationship. She was cooperating not only because her life hung in the balance, but also because she now embraced the crisis personally, if not through the facts, then through tangible respect for Clark Cannell.

No matter how varied the questions, Cleo's answers always centered on her work. Finally Clark asked, ''Where do you go regularly other than work?''

Cleo could hear the seconds ticking by as she searched feverishly for an answer. The void dismayed her. How could she have let herself become so deficient?

''The BART station,'' she answered meekly.

''Good,'' he returned, to her surprise. ''We met there. I've been in San Francisco for a week. I arrived on July eighteenth, stayed at the Hyatt Regency through the weekend, did all the tourist things. I am on business from Washington, D.C., which I call home. On Monday we shared a seat on a BART train. What time were you there?''

''Seven forty-five.''

''Seven forty-five,'' he repeated. ''What reason did I have for heading to Oakland at that time? Any outstanding attraction?''

''There's Sun Moon Garden, a Szechuan restaurant in Oakland Chinatown. Oh, wait. It's closed on Monday.''

''Good. You told me that on the train, invited me to your home. We spent every night this week together, except last night, when I picked up Alex at the San Francisco Airport, seven-fifteen, TWA from Boston. As you might expect, he is my best friend. We entered Intelnet together. That brings us to now.''

Cleo conscientiously slotted the manufactured history into her memory.

''You don't need much detail about me,'' Clark said. ''My work is secret. If you are ever quizzed on my past, claim that I'm elusive and cryptic.''

Cleo concentrated on the meager personal biography he gave her. Dedicated to memorizing every detail out of duty and a keen interest in the man himself, she hung on his words. It was just as well that his background remained sketchy, she decided. It was believable that any woman would be infatuated with his superficial acquaintance. Just looking at him would be quite enough.

He was born in September in Vermont, thirty-eight years ago. He attended MIT, joined the Air Force, spent four years with the CIA, then the past eight years with Intelnet, six of which had been on European assignment. Consequently, he spoke German fluently, Russian passably, some Turkish, some Arabic, and in his words, enough French to order from a menu. His older brother, Daniel, was a research chemist in Vermont, married, with three children.

''My younger sister, Claudia, is a prima ballerina with the Eastern Art Ballet Company.''

''Claudia Cannell!'' Cleo exclaimed. ''She's lovely. I've seen her on public television every—''

''Tell me about your family.''

Cleo realized Clark wasn't breaking cadence. Business first. There was no time for small talk. She obviously knew enough about his sister.

So Cleo threw herself into a description of her family, about the Holmes sisters, Cleo and Cassy, two girls from

Bakersfield. The spotlight never fell on Clark again. Cleo was the subject of study, she, herself, supplying data with exhausting detail as Clark grilled her relentlessly.

After the landmark facts had been established, he probed her personality with carefully worded inquiry. He set a conversational rhythm, allowing her full rein to ramble, and she responded as openly as if lying on an analyst's couch. Her willingness to participate was attributable as much to her penchant for honesty and her inexperience with guile, as to Clark's expert method of interrogation. He asked about her likes and dislikes, her friends—and her lovers.

"He was an art major," Cleo began, "and I was a conventional accounting student. I would never have known him if we hadn't lived in the same Victorian house on the north side of campus. He rented the attic. I had a room below. Knowing him was a nonstop trip into craziness. Like the night I was cramming for a midterm—he crawled through my window claiming to be Robin Hood and insisting I go with him to Sherwood Forest, which of course, turned out to be the Baskin-Robbins on the corner and an ice-cream cone I needed badly. We went our separate ways after graduation. I got a postcard from Athens and that was it. If we had both been older, it probably wouldn't have ended like that. But I was young and didn't recognize happiness as a commodity. I thought it was the by-product of a well-ordered life, a life made meaningful if you worked very hard at your job."

"How do you define happiness?" Clark asked, and so it went, on and on. Around the break of dawn, he said, "Have a graham cracker," concluding the study like a schoolmaster rewarding a good pupil.

Cleo obeyed him reflexively, putting a cracker into her mouth, although her throat was dry from talking. Clark lapsed into solemn silence, and Cleo chewed quietly, careful not to intrude upon his thoughts.

Dawn introduced a disturbing reality. Greatly fatigued, Cleo recollected how much of herself she had given on demand to the handsome stranger beside her. Under cover of night, she had poured forth her soul freely, openly sharing very private thoughts. She found this terribly personal, terribly unsettling, as daylight melted over the mountain peaks. This man called Clark Cannell knew everything about her. And what did she know about him? He was not the easygoing man she had known on BART. There, he had been wearing an expression calculated to make her feel comfortable, for he was an expert, skilled at extracting information. Who was Clark Cannell really, and what was she doing here? Oh, what the hell, she thought. In two weeks, she'd never see him again.

They drove the perimeter of Lake Tahoe, a giant bowl of blue encircled by mountains and evergreens. The sun was just creeping over the mountains; the road was still shadowy. Fresh morning mist clung to the forest, and the air was pure and clear.

Tahoe's playland, the south shore, was still asleep, judging from the quiet street that received the slowing Thunderbird. As they crossed over the state line into Nevada, the flashing lights of the large casinos, once streaking excitement across the night sky, looked drained against the rising sun. Without people, the street seemed lonely and depressing.

Clark pulled off the main road and parked in the driveway of one of the many wedding chapels that advertised every convenience, except a drive-in window. Cleo cringed. Fortunately, what she was about to do here was meaningless. How could real lovers find it within themselves to wed in these sleazy traps that prospered along the gambling strip? Marriage wasn't meant to be mixed with lucky nights at the roulette table.

They walked across the gravel driveway of the Tahoe in Love Wedding Chapel with the neon Open 24 Hours sign blinking in their faces. The bell on the door chimed their arrival as they entered a waiting room that bombarded the senses. Cleo was much too tired to deal with red wallpaper flocked with hearts, a plaster statue of Cupid, a simulated fountain of love, vases of plastic red roses in need of dusting and, of course, an exhibition wall of hundreds of blissfully wedded couples.

A round, elderly man in wire-rim glasses made an appearance at the counter from behind a beaded curtain. He was accompanied by three excited dachshunds, wagging their tails into a blur. Resembling a wholesome farmer from the heartland, he was an incongruous addition to the gaudy setting.

"Hello, hello. Bright and early are we. Going to be a beautiful day," he bubbled.

In abrupt metamorphosis, Clark said a cheerful good-morning with all the zest of a man about to be married. Cleo heard herself echo his greeting, but fall short of his award-winning delivery.

"Name is Bill Smith," the proprietor told them. "I'll be doing the ceremony this morning. Here's a little paperwork for you," he added, pulling a form from beneath the counter.

Clark's pen flew over the information blocks. Cleo followed his data responses closely, believing it necessary for her to supply information. But Clark did not hesitate. He came to the block requiring her driver's license number. Cleo had a hunch. She was right. Clark filled it in. All he needed from her was her signature.

The proprietor's wife burst through the beaded curtain with two more dachshunds underfoot. Gretchen Smith wore a pinafore apron over her plump body and looked as if she, too, belonged on a farm. Slapping her husband's back, she spoke like a popcorn popper. "I told Bill we'd have a wedding early this morning. 'No, no,' he says to me, but I feel these things in my bones." She buzzed on and on like a crazed bee. "Did Bill offer you coffee, some tea? I should leave a table by the door so you folks will know we have it." Her practice was to talk continuously, stopping not even for answers to her own questions. "Our powder room is over here. Have you freshened up, dear?" This time she did pause long enough to look at Cleo. Cleo, in turn, sought Clark.

"Go ahead," he advised. "I can handle the arrangements."

Released from responsibility by a definite understatement, Cleo escaped from the ornate parlor to the relative peace of the rest room. The sink was clam-shaped. The faucet was in the form of a fish. The windows were dressed in a print of primping mermaids. But everything was powder-blue, and Cleo found the room cool and soothing.

She approached the mirror apprehensively, dreading the sight of a pale face bearing every trace of the night before. To her surprise, her appearance was fine. She supposed her body had not yet comprehended its fate, and therefore held together in abeyance.

Cleo brushed her hair, then lightly touched the mascara wand to her already dark lashes. She used crimson lipstick to electrify her satin face against the soft white blouse. The use of vibrant color would make her ordinary face very striking. Color technique was the legacy of a certain young artist in her past. She thought of Perry for an instant, but let him go. There were more pressing matters ahead.

Cleo was smoothing her skirt when Gretchen Smith joined her in a twitter. "Do you need any help, dear?" Again not waiting for any response, Gretchen rambled, "Your husband-to-be is such a handsome man. He chose the snow ceremony in our winter chapel. My favorite, too. I've never seen anyone run through the choices so fast."

It's his job, Mrs. Smith, Cleo wanted to say.

"You know we have studio chapels in all four seasons. Most folks choose the current season or the one they met in. Did you meet in winter, dear?"

"No, but it was rather chilly, Mrs. Smith."

Gretchen was willing to accept anything from a dizzy bride and rattled on. "You must like snow," she said, satisfied with her own answer. Cleo considered it an appropriate deduction. They were, after all, engaged in a snow job.

"Goodness, look at me," Gretchen exclaimed, calling attention to her plump hands. "This is the bouquet your husband chose for you. Why am I hanging on to it? Goodness!" As Cleo took hold of the small arrangement of baby roses, the same color as her lipstick, Mrs. Smith drew a breath. "Oh, you are so lovely, my dear. That blouse!" She lightly touched the embroidery at the neck. "Those long sleeves. Come, come, let's not keep your fine gentleman waiting."

And so Cleo was forced to leave the blue-walled sanctuary behind, realizing that the curtain was rising on another episode of this crazy production. With hesitancy akin to stage fright, she moved toward her costar in drama, anxious for the company of someone equally as nervous. But she could find no evidence of kindred difficulty.

Clark, with a crimson baby rose tucked into his lapel, was leaning against the counter, smiling. Mr. Smith was laughing, undoubtedly entertained by Clark's wit. Clark had certainly turned on the charm requisite for the occasion. Both proprietors were eating out of his hand. Apparently, he could be whoever he wanted. A real professional, Cleo thought, feeling even more disconcerted. Driving all night had not dampened his manufactured style in the least.

Mrs. Smith stole away first in preparation for the ceremony. Mr. Smith was next, leaving Clark and Cleo alone. Cleo avoided Clark's eyes. She didn't have a coherent thought in her head. She dwelled on trivia. Where had all the dogs gone?

"Are you ready, Cleo?" Clark asked, with a broad smile.

"Yes," she replied faintly. She walked toward him, struggling with every fiber of her being to match his total cool. She tried to paint a picture of familiarity around him, to make him real by fusing the facts she had learned about him last night. Instead, she drew a blank. *My God, what was his name?*

Clark led her down a dim hallway, retracing the departure of the Smiths. His hand was at the back of her waist, patting her now and then for reassurance. Her heart was pounding. Suddenly it occurred to her how much she treasured a wedding ceremony as a beautiful symbol of commitment. And now here she was, on the brink of an ugly ceremony in ugly circumstances with a man she did not know. She braced herself for the onslaught of the winter chapel. It was sure to look like the rummage sale of a defunct repertory theater. It was sure to smell of mildew.

Cleo heard the music first, a sweet mixture of piano and violins. Then she saw the winter chapel, a small studio as sweet as the music itself. The walls were curtained in white. The fabric was textured in a pattern of raised snowflakes. In the soft pink lighting, the studio was an artistic impression of winter, as quiet and classic as a white dove of peace embossed on a snow-white Christmas card.

And when Cleo found herself standing with Clark at an altar within a gazebo of glass panels, etched and frosted at the edges with snowflakes, she felt as if she stood in a crystal castle that existed at the very heart of Christmas. Mr. Smith, his silver spectacles twinkling, was the perfect image of Santa Claus. His wife and a snowy-haired witness were perfect stand-ins for Mrs. Claus and a good-hearted elf.

Cleo clutched Clark's arm tightly. Only his presence would prevent her from drifting too deeply into a beautiful storybook. He, alone, his flesh hard and vital, would remind her in her weariness that they were partners in a pretense, that this was not real.

The ceremony was a lyrical love poem, which Cleo felt rather than heard. She was floating on its beauty, not sure whether to enjoy it, or to deny it.

Two silver wedding bands were presented on a silver-rimmed, glass tray. "...as a ring of life goes around and around, may you exchange rings..." Clark disengaged his arm, and Cleo instinctively knew that letting go of his arm would shake her stability immeasurably.

She watched as a ring was slipped on her finger, then reenacted what she had just seen, placing the remaining ring on Clark's finger, thinking from afar, mind out of body, suspended in time.

"I pronounce you husband and wife. You may kiss the bride."

The kiss. The final moment. Cleo felt the palm of Clark's hand lightly on her cheek, turning her toward him, lifting her face upward. She looked at him for the first time since entering the studio and was not prepared for what she saw. Her eyes must have been swimming in the emotion of the imagery. She did not see just another face imposed for the occasion. She saw instead a face of integrity, a special face, rich with compassion and inner strength. Cleo tried to deny what was before her, but it was useless. In the short time she had known Clark, he had given her reason to believe that his face was the mirror of his character.

She felt his hand drop to her neck as the perfect man, out of a perfect ceremony, drew near. She had barely placed her hands to his chest when the kiss came delicately on her lips. In that instant, she felt helpless, lost, inadequate.

"Congratulations!" Gretchen Smith shrieked, showering them with white confetti.

Saved by Mrs. Claus, thought Cleo. More confetti followed from the elf.

Clark was radiant in his enjoyment. He shook hands with Mr. Smith, thanking him for the ceremony. Following Clark's lead, Cleo heard herself praise the chapel.

"My wife's niece decorated this," Mr. Smith confided in a whisper.

"Stay right there!" Mrs. Smith shooed Cleo and Clark back into the gazebo. She held a huge box camera. "A picture on the house. You two are too beautiful." Smile. Flash. Deeper smile. Flash. "I must have your picture on the wall."

Cleo gave a start. To be on the wall for eternity. *It's not possible, it's not real,* she screamed inwardly.

"We would be honored," Clark said, as gallantly as if he had bowed from the waist.

Mrs. Smith drowned in the depths of his charm. "I'll have a print for you in twelve hours."

"Thank you. We're staying at the Hanna Hotel," he informed her.

Mrs. Smith grabbed the confetti from the elf and showered them out the door.

As they drove away, Cleo wilted in the seat of the car, letting her eyes rest on the bouquet of roses on her lap, a foreign reminder of a hazy experience. It had been done. They were married.

CHAPTER FIVE

CLEO SAT DOWN to breakfast with Clark in a restaurant in the hotel. Their bags had been sent ahead to their room by the desk clerk, and Cleo would have preferred to follow them. She was tired and uncomfortable. She felt out of place. They were seated at a window table beside a view of the timeless evergreen forest. Naturally, they were in the line of sight of everyone attracted to the view.

Cleo picked at her scrambled eggs and slices of buttered toast, while Clark ate heartily. The wedding band on her finger shocked her anew each time her left hand crossed her line of vision. *What am I doing here?* she thought, becoming more and more uneasy. She wanted to talk to Clark, but she was growing more uncomfortable with him. He knew everything about her. She had no privacy from him. That he was so at home here only escalated her shyness. It became exceedingly difficult for her to meet his eyes.

"What happened to the spitfire I knew last night?" Clark inquired, setting down his glass of orange juice.

"I guess I'm just no fun after I'm married," Cleo replied weakly, feeling the color rise in her cheeks, feeling as stupid as the blushing bride cliché.

"You're giving me a pitiful reputation. I've always held myself out as a fun guy to be married to."

"Oh, I'm sorry." Cleo was jolted into the reality of her role. She felt a strong twinge of guilt for her poor form.

She was obviously failing. "I'm sorry," she said again, not knowing what to do.

"You're allowed to be tired. Put your hand on the table," he requested, indicating her left. He reached out and covered it with his own. He winked. "Eat your eggs. Or at least try."

Their hands on the table passed as a convincing display of marital bliss, making conversation, or any other contrivance, unnecessary. Clark was, indeed a professional. Thoroughly impressed, Cleo resolved to do as he said. With childlike regard, she ate her scrambled eggs.

Their room was on the eighteenth floor, overlooking the lake. After drawing back the curtains to let the sun in, Cleo sat cross-legged on the bed to write postcards to her sister and two close friends, as instructed, with the buoyant message, "Married in Tahoe today. See you in two weeks." Finishing the three cards, she lay across the bed and closed her eyes for a moment. For just a moment, she thought.

Her eyes opened at a much later hour, as told by an evening sky. The situation was only faintly familiar. She lay still, as her drowsy mind attempted explanation. The bedspread had been thrown over her. Her feet were without shoes. The television screen showed a newscast, but there was no sound. A man was seated in a chair reading a newspaper, his feet propped near hers on the bed. This was really happening, she told herself. She closed her eyes to escape, to awake on another dream channel. *No,* she declared silently. *You are here, and you're a trooper, remember?*

Purposefully, she raised up on her elbow. "Are you Clark Cannell?"

The newspaper lowered with a snorting laugh. "Can't swear to the odds, but in this town, it's a good bet."

Cleo sat up. "It's clear I hogged the bed. Were you able to rest?"

"Quite comfortably, except for your snoring."

"Oh." Her eyes darted to the bedspread. Had she snored? Oh, in heaven's name, why must she be trapped here? She wanted to shrink into the mattress.

"What *did* happen to the spunky sport with the tricks up her sleeve? I thought it was just lack of sleep that wore down your batteries this morning."

Cleo spread her arms. "Well, here I am—fully charged." Reaching for a pillow, she hugged it against her stomach. "I guess I'm just a product of my boring, little life. I'm completely lost out of my element."

"I made a dinner reservation for seven-thirty. How does that sound?"

Cleo consulted Clark's travel clock on the nightstand. It was slightly after six. He had evidently moved in while she slept, surrounding himself with his personal articles. The art of a perpetual traveler, Cleo thought.

"Seven-thirty is fine. I even have time for a shower," she said, getting off the bed. She walked toward her suitcase, and stopped short.

"I hung up your clothes while I was at it," came the explanation. How could he be so relaxed?

"Wear the red dress tonight," she heard him say as she closed the bathroom door. She remembered not to lock it. She felt odd.

She ran the water for a shower and stepped into the smooth, shiny tub. It was mint-green, as were the towels and some of the tiles in the mosaic pattern set along the walls. Even the soap was green. A little, tiny bar of green soap, just unwrapped in her hand, brand-new... *Holmes, what's wrong with you?* Cleo scolded. *You are in Tahoe,*

*standing naked in a shower with a strange man outside the
door, and all you can think about is little green soap?*

She pushed her face into the shower spray. *Sober up.
Sober up. Somebody might want to kill you, remember?*
Ridiculous! Recalling the tone of the television spy shows
of her youth, she conjured up the official form of Edmondsen. *Your mission, Ms Holmes, is to spend two
weeks with Clark Cannell.* It sounded crazy, but apparently she hadn't thought so when she agreed. And she had
agreed. *If you have to do it,* she told herself, *do it well.*

With the steam from the shower still masking the bathroom mirror, Cleo began to package herself for the evening. Dutifully, she slipped into the red dress, a
fashionable silk chemise, dormant since its debut at the
last company Christmas party. As the smoothness of the
elegant cranberry silk flowed over her body, an enthusiasm began to brew within her. It was Saturday night and
she had a date. Already enlivened by the color of the
dress, her face emerged in beauty as she lightly applied
some makeup. Then she fastened a string of pearls around
her neck and brushed her dark hair over her shoulders.
With a finishing touch of cologne, she sallied forth from
the bathroom, ready to conquer the world. But her self-
created invincibility was short-lived.

Clark stood at the foot of the bed, naked to the waist,
in the process of changing shirts. His broad shoulders
were massive and appealing. His chest was hard with
smoothly crowned muscle, his stomach flat and tight.
Dark fur covered his chest and tapered to his belt line,
giving a savage quality to his powerful form.

Cleo was mouselike, staring meekly, helpless before the
megadose of perfection she was forced to ingest. She had
considered it her trump card that she was supposedly the
image of his taste in women. She knew that card to be

worthless now. It took more than a mere image to claim such a man.

He smiled at her as he buttoned his white shirt from the bottom up, ignoring the top button for comfort. He was completely unaware that his tantalizing chest exceeded the legal limit on the power of attraction.

"You look gorgeous," he told Cleo warmly.

"Thank you," she murmured softly, knowing the compliment to be seriously misplaced, misdirected. She had spent an hour on her looks in the privacy of the bathroom. He had stolen the show without the slightest contrivance.

Cleo stocked her purse with tissue and tried to blend into the wall, while Clark fastened his shoulder holster and settled his revolver. A light wool sport jacket concealed the weapon, and Cleo erased it from her consciousness.

His grooming complete, Clark's eyes traveled over Cleo, head to toe. She felt the assessment ponderous.

"You are definitely too stiff," he concluded. He was beside her before she could offer some excuse, any excuse. "Kiss me," he said clinically, embracing her firmly. "Come on. Put your arms around my neck."

Cleo was like a schoolgirl, hesitant but obedient. It had always been in her nature to follow instruction, to conform to requirement. She raised up on tiptoe and gave him a virgin kiss, conscious that she was already on record for the amateur technique she had displayed at the altar that morning.

"Again," came the quiet command.

Had she failed the assignment? *Get it right, Holmes,* she agonized. Again, she complied. This time her kiss was more certain. Surely this would suffice. Still he was not impressed. He was such a strict schoolmaster.

He kneaded his hands into her back. "Get comfortable," he instructed, swaying with her from side to side. "Get used to me. I'm your husband."

Reminded of the purpose for their association, Cleo was once again a big girl. She had a responsibility, and she never failed a job. She tightened her arms around his neck and planted a firm kiss on his lips with a respectful resolve. He met her lips with equal pressure, parting them slightly as the kiss deepened. She felt a momentary thrill, but ignored it. She drew back, still locked in his embrace, satisfied that this response equated to a passing grade, yet suddenly unsure of her performance. She waited for judgment.

Clark frowned. He struck a contemplative pose. "I've seen powerful witchcraft like this before. Don't you dare stick pins in me."

Caught completely off guard, Cleo choked on a laugh, and instinctively swatted his shoulder. The ensuing peals of laughter broke the ice formed in the crystal castle of the winter chapel.

THE FLICKERING CANDLE LANTERNS on each table at the Starlight Pavilion, high atop the Hotel Hanna, kindled a romantic glow. A string orchestra played for a few couples silhouetted on the dance floor.

Everything excited Cleo—from the plush carpet beneath her feet to the intricate chandeliers high above her head. She was conscious of the maître d's regard as he seated her formally. She was in proper costume, in the company of a stunningly handsome man and seemingly born to this divine setting.

Her eyes danced around the room. What a perfect way to spend a Saturday night, whatever the reason. The reason, in fact, she had momentarily lost, thrilled by the classic ambience of the Starlight Pavilion.

"Do you expect trouble here?" she asked abruptly, having great difficulty imagining to what kind of trouble she could be referring.

"Just enjoy yourself. I'm certain nothing will happen tonight," Clark answered, smiling.

"You will tell me at the first sign of, ah, trouble," she said, again unsure of what she meant by trouble.

"You will be the first to know," Clark murmured with sexy charm.

"I beg to differ," Cleo rebutted saucily. "I believe in present company I could only hope to be the second to know."

"Flirting becomes you, Cleo." He gave her a provocative glance, before dropping his eyes to the menu.

Dinner with Clark was an animated pleasure. He was interesting, he was debonair, and he was witty, when just his smiling face across the table would have been enough. He was like the man she had met on BART, Cleo decided, only now he was suave, sophisticated. This man spoke to the waiter in French. This man would order a béchamel or béarnaise sauce. This man would never ask for mustard. *Who are you, Clark Cannell,* Cleo mused. *You're probably none of the men I've seen you as. Just an actor with many faces. Oh, I don't care. Entertain me.*

Conversation flowed easily in what could have passed for mutual attraction. They had ordered bouillabaisse, and it was served with tongs and other gourmet utensils for eating shellfish. They made a joint effort out of cracking the clams, and with each successful foray into culinary dissection, they toasted each other with large drafts of white wine.

Even as he participated in the festivities of dinner, Clark remained alert to surrounding activities, never losing sight of the slightest changes around them. His discipline was a reminder to Cleo that this man ran much deeper than the popular notion of a Saturday night date. His company, however, made that easy to forget.

It was over the most decadent chocolate torte ever created by a pastry chef that Clark announced matter-of-factly, "There is a woman engaged in a predatory stare to your left, behind you. I want you to turn and look at her."

Cleo froze for an instant, and then regained herself taking her cue from Clark's face. He maintained the air of a happy diner, but his eyes were in control, and silently urging Cleo to maintain the same control. She turned as instructed, and was rewarded by a moment of harmless recognition. She raised her hand in a polite wave.

"That's Francine McMillan, another associate director at California Investment," Cleo explained, turning back to Clark. "I can't stand her," she added flatly.

"She's coming over," Clark informed her.

"She's an unabashed opportunist," Cleo grumbled. "Got her job by marrying the vice president."

Clark stood when Francine reached their table. She flashed him a seductive smile and focused her attention on Cleo, as if she was about to pounce on a poor, unsuspecting creature. "Cleo, how interesting to see you. I thought your side of the hall never saw weekends." She pivoted her tall, voguish frame slightly. "And what are you doing with this sexy animal?"

Cleo glanced up at Francine and wondered what kind of answer she wanted, what terrible secret, what juicy tidbit she expected. There was only one answer, however, that Cleo was allowed to give her. "This is my husband," she said sweetly.

Francine's jaw looked dislocated. "No wonder no one at work ever got anywhere with you," she blurted out before regaining the haughty composure she wore so well. "I could have sworn your tastes were provincial. I am shocked at you, Cleo. How could you have kept him hidden for so long? Although I can't say I blame you."

"We were married this morning on impulse," Cleo explained, barely breaking the trance Clark's body had thrown Francine into.

"Impulse? Is there any other way?" Francine purred, unable to resist flirting with Clark.

After Francine returned to her table and the stuffy Joel McMillan, Cleo congratulated herself royally. It had been her first lie for the team, and she could not have imagined enjoying it so much.

Missing none of the cattiness of office politics, Clark cautioned, "Careful, Mrs. Cannell, you're gloating."

"I can't help it. I've upstaged her," Cleo expounded with enthusiasm. "I work long hours at California Investment. She knows that I earn my money, and she does not. I do a good job, and she does not. And it takes the fact that I'm sitting here with you for her to give me some credit."

"Too bad you didn't mention that I'm a terrific dancer," Clark said coyly.

"Pity."

"Want to show her?"

A blind man could have seen the delight in Cleo's face as Clark led her to the dance floor. Holding Cleo closely, Clark caught her smiling gaze. He lowered his head so she could whisper in his ear. "Make it easy and just tell me what you can't do."

"Nothing." He paused. "Thanks to you beleaguered taxpayers and your infinite generosity with lessons, of course."

"And I used to think that government was fiscally irresponsible."

Having jumped at the once-in-a-lifetime chance to flaunt her magnificent escort—and husband—before Francine McMillan, Cleo had forgotten she could not dance. But melting into Clark's lead, she was nothing short of a dancer. There was no need to look for reaction from Francine. The moments were too divine to seek aggrandizement.

At the height of the dance floor's popularity, Cleo and Clark left to stroll the gambling strip and tour the four major casinos. Cleo recognized this as Clark's bid for visibility, but she was too enthralled to ponder the consequences. Tahoe was exciting, and she had no quarrel with the world.

The night was alive with pulsating neon signs that ran like rainbows along the streets filled with swarming crowds of gamblers eager to seek the pot of gold at the end of every rainbow. The casinos buzzed and sizzled with action. With Clark's arm firmly around Cleo's waist, sometimes around her shoulders, they strolled in the appropriate aura of two people in love. More than once, they attracted attention; the world seemed to revel in the infectious happiness of lovers. Her lips fixed in a perpetual smile, Cleo walked as if led into a fantasyland.

A little after midnight, they returned to the casino at the Hotel Hanna. Cleo inserted a quarter casually in a slot machine, which rattled as it digested her coin. With a shrug, she accepted another from Clark. Again, she inserted the coin, pulled the handle and waited for the tumblers to come to rest. This time she was rewarded by the sound of clattering quarters.

Jubilantly, Cleo counted out twenty-five quarters into her hand and made a presentation to Clark. "Take the money and run before the house discovers your method."

Declining her offer, he said, "Do you ever really gamble?"

"I just won you an astronomical return on investment and you want more?" she teased.

He led her to the roulette table, whispering into her ear, "I once spent an entire summer undercover in Monte Carlo. Mission made a profit."

Cleo laughed as she imagined her hero, clad in tuxedo, breaking the bank at a European casino. Indulging him, she converted five dollars to chips. She observed the croupier spin the roulette wheel, throw the ball and announce the winning number. After a few more cycles, Cleo turned to Clark, as the croupier called for bets. "I'm going to bet on the line."

Clark's eyes were fixed on the spin of the wheel. "No. Do a straight play, number twelve."

Agreeably, Cleo leaned across the table and placed all her markers on number twelve.

"Number twelve" came the announcement. Methodically, the croupier augmented her stack with payoff. Cleo flew into orbit, jabbing her elbow into Clark's ribs. He grunted, then clasped her tightly. "Let it ride," he whispered, and though Cleo floundered on his reasoning, she obeyed.

The ball clattered in the wheel, around and around, then slowed. "Number twelve again," called the croupier, and Cleo was on the moon. At Clark's prompting, she scooped up her chips to "oohs" and "aahs" from the crowd. At a thirty-five to one payoff, she knew she had more than six thousand dollars. Clark guided her away from the table.

"Calm down or you'll hyperventilate," he warned.

"I've never won like this in my life!"

"Take the money and run before the house discovers your method," he teased.

He took her to the cashier's cage where she converted her winnings to cash. Deliriously, she clung to Clark's arm as they walked across the lobby. "What are you going to do with your fortune?" she asked.

"Your fortune," he corrected. "Consider it a payoff for debts owed on taxpayer lessons."

Cleo was still light-headed at the registration desk, where Clark asked for messages. There was a photo envelope from the Tahoe in Love Wedding Chapel that Clark handed to Cleo while he read a brief message. "It's from Alex," he said, offering no explanation. Then together they walked to the elevator.

Back in the room, Clark checked for any sign of disturbance. Then he headed for the shower, chuckling to himself as he left Cleo sitting at the table, avidly reading the courtesy literature on How to Play Craps. This was too easy, she kept saying to herself. Why work?

When the hum of Clark's shower told her she was alone, Cleo opened her wallet to visit the six thousand-dollar bills. She couldn't believe her luck, which was changing as rapidly as her life.

Slightly giddy, she opened the envelope from Mrs. Smith like a Christmas present, and peeked inside. The photo was good, so Cleo removed the picture and studied it. She had smiled at the right moment, Clark was a natural, and together they looked very happy. It would be a nice souvenir of her Intelnet service. She could even buy

it a six-thousand-dollar frame. Cleo sat back in the chair.
What a day!

Clark came out of the bathroom clad in pajama bot-
toms, toweling his hair.

"I have a hair dryer," Cleo offered, trying to be non-
chalant as the sleek shoulders paraded by her.

"Thanks. This will do." He sat on the side of the bed,
still toweling his hair. "Alex didn't turn up anything at
your office."

"You mean *my* files didn't turn up anything useful,"
Cleo joked, thinking again of the six thousand she had
made so effortlessly compared to working at California
Investment.

"Actually, your safety is highly indicated. I'm sure that
in all of Tahoe, only Francine McMillan is aroused by
your presence," Clark stated.

Cleo wanted to say that she'd never felt unsafe with
him. Instead she continued to listen.

"You did a great job tonight. Your acting could even
have fooled me," he praised, resting his head on the pillow.

Cleo sat back in the chair. Had she been acting? She
wasn't sure.

"I was worried this morning that you wouldn't be able
to pull it off," Clark continued, his voice getting slower.
"But you have the mettle of a double agent." He let the
towel cover his face.

Cleo was at once struck by the honesty of his statement. He had actually been worried about her ability this
morning, and now he was complimenting her. She had not
made any special effort since the morning. She had simply enjoyed herself. She felt obligated to make this
confession.

"Clark?"

"Hmm."

"I had a good time tonight. All acting aside, I want you to know that. I almost feel guilty. I know what we are doing is serious, yet I can't remember when I've had so much fun." She paused. "Clark?"

As she suspected, he had fallen asleep. *So even he runs down,* she noted with amusement. It was her turn to take care of him.

She moved silently to the bed and gingerly removed the damp towel from his face. He was peacefully asleep, and Cleo took the opportunity to study his face. He did not look like a person who would carry a gun. Why would anyone want to work for Intelnet? Then again, why did she work for California Investment? Intuitively, she wondered if their reasons were the same. Basically, they were both very good at their jobs.

Cleo sighed. She wondered what kind of an everyday person he was, how he did his laundry, how he bought his socks. Asleep, he looked rather vulnerable. Unable to resist, Cleo lightly brushed his hair back from his forehead. She wanted to touch the temples, which crinkled when he smiled. Instead, she simply turned out the lamp on his nightstand.

Bending over him, she took hold of the turned-down sheet and blanket. "Clark," she whispered softly against his ear, as she gently touched his shoulder. Without waking, Clark followed her suggestion and rolled toward her so that she could free the covers to place over him. He remained fast asleep, though hanging somewhat precariously at the edge of the bed. If anyone could sleep in that position, Cleo supposed he could. Amazing.

They hadn't discussed sleeping arrangements, and the room had just this one king-size bed. It would be all right to sleep there, Cleo decided as she undressed. They were adults, and she was no prude. Besides, they would never find each other in it. It was all so pure, so platonic.

She slipped into her special pink nightgown, feeling too festive to wear her regular flannel. Getting married and winning at roulette were not bad ways to spend the day. She laughed at herself for thinking this morning that the two events made an unsavory combination. Such thinking came only from people who led dull, ordinary lives. On with the new, she thought. Just one day had expired on her two-week lease on adventure.

With her eyes glued to Clark, Cleo crawled carefully into bed, making every effort not to wake him. With a tiny, inaudible sigh, she admitted to her despair that she would have to give him up. He could become a habit. Then she turned out the lamp on her nightstand.

CHAPTER SIX

THE CALL OF GULLS woke Cleo early Sunday morning. She was immediately conscious of the fact that this was day two of her adventure. She smiled at Clark, asleep in the same position, his back to her, then crept from the bed to stand at the window, eager to see the miracle of a summer day unfold. Grander than she had imagined, the lake lay shimmering in the sun against the majesty of snow-capped mountains, and everywhere there were California pines.

After drinking in the view, she whirled away from the window, setting her nightgown in motion like a rose petal breeze. Gathering her hair from behind her neck, she flung her arms above her head, then stopped abruptly. Clark lay awake, his deep eyes fixed on her.

"Don't stop. It's only me," he said.

Cleo was speechless. All she could think about was her kimono lying on the bed. Against the sunlit window, her nightgown was nothing more than a pink film. She was virtually naked before him.

"I dreamed I was married to a beautiful princess. I woke up to see I was right."

Cleo stood without a breath. She hung on his words, wondering if they had been sincere or just polite tokens, whether she dared to respond or... And then came a forbidding knock at the door.

Clark was instantly on his feet, his revolver in hand. He motioned Cleo to the bed and took a position beside the door.

Cleo threw herself into her kimono, clutching it around her to muffle her wildly beating heart. Snatched from an idyllic scene, she was mentally unprepared for what lay beyond the door. Again, the awful pounding—like a deadly reckoning, forcing her to pay for her frivolous enjoyment of a serious situation. She had been wrong, so wrong.

"Who is it?" Clark demanded.

There was no sound.

Cautiously, he approached the peephole in the door, then swiftly drew back. Cleo realized he was about to make his move. She watched him silently free the locks. When the pounding came again, he ripped the door open in a burst of strength, using it like a shield against the intruder.

A man as thin and white as cooked spaghetti stood aghast in the doorway until Clark gripped his collar with one hand, and pinned him in the entrance. The intruder was no more than a teenager. He wore the uniform of a hotel employee, and there was a room service cart in the hall.

"Why did you block the viewer?" Clark demanded, keeping his revolver out of sight behind the door.

"I didn't mean any harm," the boy spoke in a high-pitched whine, and Clark let go of him. "I don't want any trouble. There's supposed to be these college chicks in this room. The guys bet that I couldn't make them open their door. That's all! Honest!"

Clark was examining the room service ticket as the boy spilled his story. "You want the room across the hall, not this one." He eyed the boy squarely. "Go over and knock on the door. Announce yourself. No games."

"Room service," the boy squeaked pitifully.

A shrill, flirtatious voice replied, "Just leave it."

Clark dismissed the boy with a flick of his finger and remained poised at the door. Moments later, three nightie-clad young women with hair in bright pink curlers claimed the cart while gawking at Clark. Having confirmed the circumstance, Clark closed the door.

"False alarm, Cleo."

Cleo had sunk to the bed, hand over her mouth. "I half expected you dead in the hall."

He sat beside her, his arm protectively over her shoulders. "Half expected? That's encouraging." He was using his folksy "aw, shucks, ma'am" approach on her again. He rubbed her shoulders vigorously, but saw immediately that she could not be comforted so easily.

"You have to be in some strange business, Clark Cannell," Cleo said, her voice breaking. "I'm petrified, and all I know is that it can't be happening. It's Sunday. It's beautiful. And you're ready to use your gun."

Clark looked at her sympathetically. He brushed her hair back over her ear. She was scared, baffled, struggling. "There's something I forgot to tell you about this 'strange business.' We never work on Sunday. Quick. Get dressed. There's a holiday out there waiting for us."

ALL THROUGH BREAKFAST, Clark was a wellspring of peppy anecdotes, formulated primarily to restore Cleo's peace of mind. But Cleo was no longer naive when it came to his manipulative skill. She was well aware of Clark's methods and untouched by them. She would come to her own decision on what the morning should mean to her.

She was not, as Clark seemed to think, afraid for her life. She was not part of this game where every knock on the door was a threat, and life was protected by a gun. She could not be afraid of what she considered absurd. Perhaps she was just ignorant. No matter. She liked this ignorance.

Clark, on the other hand, took this game seriously. He lived by its rules. And as she saw this morning, he could die by them, too. Obviously, with rules like that, it was more than a game to him. Why did he choose to live this way? Personally, Cleo felt the world would be better off without Intelnet, but she didn't control the world.

She studied him across the table. She did not know who he was. She could not define him. But she liked him. He was committed to something she didn't understand. And yes, she was not afraid for herself. She was afraid for him.

Right now he was working very hard to erase any fear from her mind. And Cleo could see his growing bewilderment that, for all his superior technique, he was failing. He probably wasn't used to being wrong, Cleo decided, not used to people he could not mold like butter. She didn't like the way he used his many guises to serve his purpose. It was devious, dishonest. Yet she found that she would very much like to crawl into this man's lap, enjoy his company and believe whatever he told her. But she could never believe that he could be safe in his game.

"Clark, you don't have to cater to me," Cleo said at last. "I appreciate what you're trying to do."

"Appreciate? I owe it to you." He took a strained breath. "Tell me what I can do for you. I don't want you to be afraid."

Cleo believed him. He seemed genuinely concerned. He was principled. He was decent. And she was fond of him.

She decided to give him what he wanted—her willingness to forget the morning. "I'm not afraid, Clark. Really. I tell you I am not afraid."

After a heavy breakfast, they struck out on foot in the direction of the lake. Cleo noticed that Clark chose well-populated routes. She chose to ignore his reasons. In no particular hurry and with no particular destination, they meandered toward the shore.

They arrived at a state beach dotted with sun umbrellas, colorful beach towels and groups of playful children splashing and racing at the water's edge. Cleo sat in the warm sand to unfasten her sandals.

"Walking on the beach is one of my favorite pastimes," she told Clark enthusiastically.

"I can tell by your tan," Clark said with a smile, pulling her to her feet and placing a floppy straw hat on her head. He had purchased the hat on the way to protect Cleo's indoor-office complexion from sunburn. Cleo had not resisted the purchase, partly because Clark was right, and partly because she would do anything he asked. And Cleo was well aware that the floppy hat added a touch of storybook romance to her off-the-shoulder cotton blouse with ruffles at the neckline to match the ruffle at the hem of the skirt.

Clark's nicely tanned complexion met the sun in health and vigor. He reminded Cleo of nature's master, dressed casually in a light-weight safari jacket with sleeves rolled up to the elbows. Like a fool in paradise, she suppressed the knowledge that the jacket concealed the ever-present shoulder holster.

They strolled along the water's edge, hand in hand, and Cleo's bare feet flirted with the rushing tide. Motorboats crisscrossed the lake, pulling water-skiers.

"Do you water-ski?" Cleo asked idly.

"Yes."

"I had to ask," she moaned. "And, of course, you swim well."

"What's your definition of well?"

"Olympic gold medal freestyle."

"Gold medal freestyle!" He whistled. "Do you think I'd have the audacity to stand here and tell you I could win the gold?" The pause was small. "Silver, yes." He glanced at her slyly.

"What an ego! You're insufferable."

"You mean honest, Cleo."

A dog pranced toward them and dropped a Frisbee expectantly before Clark. He tossed it long and hard. The anxious dog took off in frenzied chase and returned to Clark for two more throws before his owners called him back.

Alone once more, Cleo and Clark continued over the sandy stretch of beach and moved into shoreline terrain, infinitely more quiet and private. Intermittently in sun and shade, they walked beneath the low-hanging branches of trees. Cleo found it all so incredibly beautiful—the sun, the sky, the trees, the lake, the man beside her. It was like being in love. Was she in love? She peeked at Clark from beneath the brim of her hat and willed her lips into a silent "I love you." She was just testing, she told herself. The fantasy was sublime.

Perhaps when whatever it was was over, there would be another weekend on this beach and—suddenly Cleo stopped the projection. She chided herself for living out the fiction of her romantic dress. Her reality would be separate from Clark's in two short weeks. She wasn't even sure Clark *had* a reality. At any rate, she couldn't let herself start expecting postcards from this man. There could be no promises. She forced her mind to focus on the scenery.

They walked in silence for a long while, late afternoon breezes fanning over them, until Clark squeezed Cleo's hand. "What are you thinking?"

"Nothing new. Just how big the world is, and how little we are." She turned to him. "Sage, huh? But what do you expect for the price of a pretzel?" She smiled brightly. "Tell me, what's it like to be you, to eat dinner in a BART station, to sneak around in dark glasses, and discipline hotel employees?"

Clark chuckled. "I do exactly what you do—gather and evaluate data. The only difference is that I can actuate the final solution for a common good."

"For a common good," Cleo repeated dramatically, teasing him. "Sounds like a job for Superman."

"You said it. Not me."

"Okay, Superman, tell me how you know what the common good is?"

"The lady asks tough questions. It's a judgment call, isn't it?" He paused. "What can I tell the lady except that I care and that I never do anything unless I'm sure...and I try not to be wrong."

"Careful, you're sounding human, Superman," she quipped.

"The lady is cruel." A smile came to his lips. "Remember the westerns on TV?"

"Hmm, you're showing your age."

"I liked the westerns. The good guys. The bad guys. It was all so clear," he reflected.

"Oh, yes. The good guy rides off into the sunset...and he always gets the girl. Okay, tell me why you don't have a girl?" And instantly Cleo was afraid of the territory. Maybe he did have someone special. She felt herself blush, and she looked down to hide her face.

"Real good guys can't have a girl."

"What! You speak in riddles, Clark Cannell," she exclaimed, ignoring her feeling of relief.

"You seem to do all right in understanding," he said gently, taking a seat on the ground. From this angle he could see her face beneath the hat, see that she was blushing.

And she did understand. How could someone be married to Clark when his work required a one-hundred-percent commitment? "It's a paradox, isn't it?" She dropped down beside him. "You must not care in order to care."

"Oh, the lady is smart," he said appreciatively. "Once you care you lose your edge. All of a sudden your judgment is affected. You're a risk to others and a risk to yourself."

"But you can . . . quit?" Cleo advanced cautiously.

Clark nodded. "Alex is shifting to Class B status at the conclusion of CLEOPATRA. He's phasing out of active duty for the love of a Boston schoolteacher." Clark seemed pleased. "Megan is just what Alex needs. He's a hopelessly sensitive sentimentalist."

"Whereas you are a strong individualist, not given to sentimentality, quite happy leaping tall buildings in a single bound," Cleo lightly teased.

"I just hope nothing happens to Alex before we can get him out of CLEOPATRA," he said, becoming very sober. He stared out over the lake, and a slight frown came to his forehead.

Cleo sat very still. It was an honest moment soaked in the truth. She felt she was seeing the real Clark Cannell for the first time as he sat there, distant in private thought, worry in his face, and a weary slump weighing down his shoulders. And Cleo's heart went out to him. He lived a very dangerous life by choice and by conviction. His work was not just a meaningless commitment. She had to respect him for it. Cleo remembered that he had wanted to take her to dinner the evening they met, but could not. She wanted very much to help him, to help his friend, Alex.

"Why can't Alex pull out now?" she asked. The solution to her seemed obvious.

Clark looked at her immediately, his glance annoyed. Cleo hunted feverishly for the error of her words. Had she been too blunt? She had only wanted to help. But she had made him angry. Why? He had just given her credit for understanding him. She didn't want to lose that credit. She wanted to understand him.

The anger in Clark's face disappeared as fast as it had come. He was controlled when he spoke. "Because CLEOPATRA is too important. It is the most crucial defense project of the past twenty years. In my opinion it will make the largest single contribution to world peace in this century. No one would consider pulling out early. Especially Alex."

"Then don't worry about him." Cleo's voice was gentle and reassuring.

"Okay, kind lady," Clark said with a slow smile. He ran his fingers through his hair. "I'm sorry if I seemed ready to snap at you."

Cleo shook her head, throwing his apology aside as unneeded.

"CLEOPATRA means a lot to me," he explained. He paused, looking directly into her face. "And every day CLEOPATRA seems to mean more."

The code word fell softly on Cleo's ears. Clark was not speaking of her. But she heard only her name as she found herself swept into a moment as real as the kiss in the winter chapel. They drew closer, his eyes steady, hers framed in the dreaminess of the hat, closer until inevitably, their lips met and fused with desire.

Cleo kissed him hungrily, wanting him passionately. She did not need instruction. Her arms flew around his neck in desperate need to touch the man who had come so powerfully into her feeble existence. She felt his arms encircle her in a tightening embrace, pulling her against his hard chest, his fingers pressing greedily into her back.

Cleo clung to his neck as the breathless kiss deepened. She felt herself inwardly tumbling as Clark eased to the ground, bringing her with him, wrapped in the protection of his strong, muscular arms. Cleo burned to be nearer to him, her hands squeezing the flesh at his shoulders in her urgent desire to verify his existence. Her grip grew wild, fueled by the flames of the fiery kiss.

Too quickly Clark returned her to a sitting position. His arms still around her, he withdrew his lips. Her eyes opened wide.

"We have company," he said with a smile, and then gave her a quick, polite kiss to erase the surprise from her face.

Turning around at the crackle of leaves, Cleo saw a little boy whose need for a haircut exaggerated his forlorn expression. He stepped forward.

"Mister, can you get my plane out of that tree?" The child's small finger pointed to a red plastic airplane trapped in the branches of a tree at the edge of the clearing.

"Oh, that looks bad," Clark said, playing for tragic effect. "But we can get it," he added cheerfully. He ruffled the boy's hair bringing forth a smile from ear to ear. The little boy ran toward the villainous tree.

Gazing skyward, Clark asked Cleo, "How many planes would you say are flying around this lake?"

"Just one," she answered, tongue in cheek. Laughing, she leaned against his arm and gave him a push.

He stood and walked heroically toward the small boy. "This is rescue launch to rescue leader. I'll climb northeast. You let me know if they stop sending radio signals."

The child's eyes were wide with wonder. "Uh-huh." He nodded.

With one superb movement, Clark caught the lowest branch of the tree and levered himself upward. Finding a toehold in the bark, he reached to another limb and continued up the tree. When the plane was within his reach, he shouted, "The pilot doesn't want to come down till they've finished the in-flight meal. What should I do, little fellow?"

The boy had a giggle fit, and Clark threw Cleo a shrug. She blew him a kiss.

He then began to untangle the plane from the branches. "It's okay," he called down. "They're having pinecone pie for dessert. No one likes pinecone pie." He grimaced.

The child answered with a corroborating "Yuck" between giggles.

Cleo drew her knees as close to her chest as her skirt would permit. She rested her chin on them and watched Clark clown on the tree. *Go ahead. Show me how you employ that splendid body for the "common good." Then make me laugh. Show me that I won't be able to forget you...and tell me that I don't have to.* With that, she took off her hat. *Enough, Holmes.*

With a deep sigh, she rose and walked over to the base of the tree as Clark made his descent. He jumped the final distance and deposited the plane with its owner. Cleo claimed her hero with a possessive arm around his waist.

The little boy held the plane eagerly in his hands, as though it was a long slice of watermelon that was all his on a hot day. "Thank you," he said.

Smiling, Clark ruffled the child's hair again. "You're out pretty far, pretty late, son." He surveyed the late-afternoon sky as he spoke. "You'd better walk with us back down the beach," he instructed, pointing the way.

A tiny "okay" was barely audible as the little towhead obediently scurried in front of them and maintained his lead as they returned to the crowded beach area.

Cleo noticed that Clark enjoyed the sight of the child ahead of them. Two adults and one child. They looked like a family unit. Clark seemed charmed by the child.

"Does he remind you of yourself?" she asked.

"Are you kidding? I would never have lost my plane in a tree."

"I see. There were no trees where you grew up."

"Yes, there were trees," Clark said quickly, and Cleo bit her lip to keep from laughing.

"I was just kidding," she said with an amused twinkle in her eyes. "I believe you had a plane. And I believe there were trees. Lots of them."

"Okay, okay, you win. I have a big ego. As you say, I'm insufferable. But don't the good guys need something to keep them warm at night?"

Cleo flinched, and she realized that Clark had noticed. She had a million answers to his question, but couldn't share a one with him.

Mercifully, the subject was lost as their young companion motioned to a trailer camp, and with a small "bye," ran toward several families gathered around a barbecue. The smell of roasting hot dogs came up to meet them.

"I'm starving," Clark exclaimed. "Let's find a place to eat."

CHAPTER SEVEN

BACK ON THE MAIN STREET, they came across the Covered Wagon Grill, a down-home eatery jumping with the sound of country fiddling and raucous laughter. The aroma of baked beans and barbecued ribs, reminiscent of the camp fires near the beach, wafted over the western-style saloon doors.

Acknowledging Clark's lifted eyebrows, Cleo stepped through the swinging doors, leading him by the hand. Beyond a row of pinball and slot machines, the interior boasted the darkness of a cave. A bluegrass band played on a raised stage ringed in blue lights like an airport runway at night. A long bar with a brass railing was the dispatch center for the traffic of buxom waitresses in low-cut uniforms and net stockings, carrying trays loaded with mugs of beer. The size of the crowd immediately affirmed Cleo's decision to enter.

Pushing past the patrons standing at the bar, Cleo found a vacant table at the foot of the stage. She and Clark strained to be heard over the band and the audience appreciation as they placed an order with a waitress. Then they joined the knee-slapping, hand-clapping crowd.

A comedian was onstage when the food arrived—a feast of barbecued beef and french fries, along with Clark's beer, Cleo's coffee. Cleo ate with an appetite brought on by the day's activity. She was careful to divide her attention between her meal and the punch lines of the comedian, who succeeded not so much on talent, as on the boisterous enthusiasm of the beer-drinking crowd. The coffee struck Cleo as an error in mood. She sipped Clark's beer often, sipping him into an early second mug, then a third.

The bluegrass band returned on the heels of the comedian, and when they took five, a jukebox of incredible volume wailed the latest country hits. Cleo was thankful for the noise level. It emphasized the present and interrupted her thoughts on the future.

She kept wondering what it would be like twelve days from now when Clark was gone. Of course she would remember him. She'd send him a Christmas card, and he'd send her one. He might even send her a postcard. Maybe several. She might live for those postcards and then one day they would stop coming. And she would wonder if he just didn't want to send them anymore... or if he was dead. *Stop it, Holmes. Just get through this from moment to moment.*

THE NOISE LEVEL in the saloon remained with Cleo as a ringing in the ears during the walk back to the Hotel Hanna. Clark, too, experienced the ringing.

"Do I hear the moon humming?" he asked, drawing Cleo's attention to the large, full moon dominating the star-laced sky.

"It's the mice," she explained, resting her head against his shoulder. "The moon is made of good cream cheese."

"How do you know it's good?"

"The man asks tough questions." She smiled. "What can I say except that I just know," she stated adamantly. He drew her nearer to ward off the chill of the evening.

After their walk outside, the hotel seemed hot, stuffy and very bright. The main floor casino was abuzz with gamblers just warming up for a night of good fortune. No one noticed Cleo or Clark crossing the red and gold carpeting in front of the blackjack tables to the registration desk. There were no messages waiting, and they took the elevator upstairs.

Except for the simple strains of elevator music, they were undisturbed, the only two people in a small corner of the world. Abruptly, Cleo disengaged from Clark's arm. She wanted to be the first to turn away. Once in the room, there would be no need to continue this pretense. The day had ended, taking with it that moment of unrestrained, mindless passion on the shore. That kiss should never have been. Thank God for little red airplanes.

"It was a nice holiday," Cleo said to Clark nonchalantly. "I'll add this hat to my collection."

The elevator door opened into the rosily lit hallway. Cleo walked down the corridor, absorbed in her own thoughts until Clark gripped her arm urgently. Startled, she looked up at him, then followed his line of sight to the hazard on the path.

They were still too far away for a clear view of the recessed doorway to their room. But something was different. There was a foreign object at the door.

Taking hold of Cleo's hand, Clark walked in front of her. Cleo's heart raced. Once more she was forced into a reality that was not her own. The false alarm this morning had been only a reprieve from the night's dire consequence. How could Clark live this way, with vile threats beginning and ending his day?

Clark stopped at the door with a snicker, inviting Cleo to peer around his shoulder. The dreaded object was a bottle of champagne in an ice bucket wrapped as a present. Cautiously, Clark stooped to read the gift tag without touching the assembly. Then with a low chuckle, he scooped the bucket off the floor and motioned Cleo to the door as he inserted the key.

"Who is it from?" Cleo asked, once inside.

"It's for you," he said, locking the dead bolt.

Cleo held the tag to the light and read aloud, " 'Best wishes. Francine and Joel.' A wedding gift from Francine McMillan?"

Clark was thoroughly amused. "Shame on you for harboring a grudge against that woman."

"Dom Perignon," Cleo read the label, calculatingly. "I'm almost moved, but I know it's just a ploy. Francine is starting to scheme early."

Clark clucked his tongue to scold her.

"Oh, don't be so smug," Cleo retorted, thrusting the bottle at him. "Here, you open it."

Cleo rinsed out the glasses while Clark wrapped the bottle in a bath towel and popped the cork into the tub.

"It was thoughtful of Francine to include these glasses," Cleo said, holding them to the light. "But, of course, she'll pass them through her expense account, probably at twice the price. She is such a phony."

With a dour expression, Cleo sat cross-legged on the bed, holding the glasses while Clark poured.

"She's not so bad," Clark drawled. He took a glass from Cleo's hand and raised it in toast. "To Francine."

Cleo lifted her glass also. "To Francine and all her ulterior motives," she declared, then drank from the glass like a pouting little girl. Clark refilled her glass, then his own. "I suppose this means I need to send her a card of thanks," Cleo muttered sarcastically.

"Do what you would normally do, Cleo. Judging from that scowl, I wouldn't guess it to be much."

"It wouldn't be a problem if she had a genuine bone in her body. She wants something. I wonder what she has in mind.'' Cleo sipped the champagne steadily, her eyes narrowing.

Clark set his glass on the nightstand. He tuned the radio to an easy-listening station while casually unbuttoning his shirt.

Swirling the champagne in her glass, Cleo made a definitive statement. ''I know what Francine wants. She wants to get into bed with you fast.'' Cleo was at once shocked by the words she had let escape from her mouth.

Clark tilted his head back and roared with laughter. ''Why would she want to bed me?'' he asked, playing the sentence on his tongue roguishly, taking pleasure in baiting Cleo as he took off his shirt.

In the loaded silence, Cleo gulped the rest of her champagne. She knew she was on thin ice. ''You obviously don't know Francine,'' she said rapidly with her eyes downcast, trying to dismiss her indiscretion. Still Clark could not be deterred.

''No...I don't know Francine. Why would she want to sleep with me?'' he persisted, his voice deeper, his body moving closer. ''Why?'' he whispered into her ear.

Cleo felt his hot breath on her bare shoulder. She turned to him. There was no way she could craft an answer concerning Francine. Every fiber of her body was alive with her own feelings.

She looked into his dark gray eyes. Her senses reeling, she sat before him, helpless. He held her gaze, then drew nearer, taking the champagne glass, which she guarded with both hands, and setting it on the floor.

Cleo trembled. She felt the nearness of his breath against her cheek. She closed her eyes as their lips met slowly, her arms winding gracefully around his neck. He kissed her tenderly, softly, his arms moving slowly about her in a gentle embrace. His hands delicately caressed her back and floated over her shoulders, touching her as he would a treasured porcelain doll.

Her hands fell to brace against his chest as he relinquished her lips and drew back to gaze quietly into her face. His arms dropped to her waist. Cleo looked at his fine features and her heart melted, draining the strength from her body in a rush of admiration. "Oh, Clark..." she breathed before his mouth found hers again in another tender kiss.

His lips pressed softly, and he cradled her in his arms. She was a fragile flower in his hands. She could not have felt more loved. Slowly, the blouse fell away as his hands traveled over her shoulders, gliding along the smoothness of her skin, and finding the fullness of her breasts. Shivering, Cleo gasped with delight.

She wound her arms tightly around him, clinging, thrilling to the feel of his body, as he lowered her to the bed. He kissed the hollow between her breasts, and sensing the excitement pulsating through her, he returned to her mouth greedily, brushing her breasts to aroused peaks with his furred chest.

Cleo could feel his muscles tightening. She worshiped his animal perfection. Passion mounted. The kisses became more intense, each deeper and more fiery than the last.

His mouth moved hungrily down her neck while his hand inched up her thigh to dispense with her wispy underwear. He brought a startled moan to her lips as her body tingled with even greater excitement.

She ran her hands over the muscles of his chest, down his taut stomach, then she paused at his belt. She unfastened the buckle and edged her hands still farther. Her delicate touch brought him to the edge of desire, and he held her in a kiss that stopped time.

Oblivious to everything but each other, they shed their clothes in perfectly shared movements. Clark took Cleo in his arms again, his hands caressing her, thrilling her, stimulating her to indescribable heights. She arched her body toward him as his palm lowered over her stomach. She trembled with urgency at his touch.

Her head swirled in ancient, mysterious rapture. She was Queen Cleopatra herself, offering the valley of the Nile to the royal king of her own choosing, traveling down the river with the surging current to meet him, to join him forever. She was his.

DREAMILY, CLEO LAY in the crook of Clark's arm, her head on his shoulder. In silence, they shared contentment and sips of champagne from a single glass. Cleo floated on the soft music from the radio. All songs were love songs.

Then Clark propped himself on his elbow and flashed the smile of a pirate. He was devilishly handsome. "Still think Francine would want me?"

"Oh, you fiend," Cleo exclaimed, smacking him with a pillow and continuing an offensive attack.

"Be gentle with me," he pleaded, weakly defending himself.

They wrestled playfully, rolling gleefully on the bed. Clark allowed Cleo leverage that she could never hope to have against his powerful body.

"Unfair contest!" he protested. "You've mud-wrestled professionally." Waving a corner of the white sheet, he signaled, "Truce. You win."

Cleo relaxed in triumph, only to cry out in surprise as Clark pinned her to the mattress. "I lied," he said, grinning like a Cheshire cat as he straddled her. "Never trust anything a man says in bed. It could be a ploy for this."

He kissed her lips quickly. "Or this." He kissed the tip of her nose. "Or maybe this." He kissed her chin.

"Well, I'm indebted for the lesson." Cleo spoke coyly to the triumphant face above her. "Until tonight I understood the ploy to be this." She boldly placed her hand against his chest in a circular massage. "Or this." She traced a sensitive path with her fingertips from his chest to his navel. "Or perhaps this." Her touch worked magic below.

The intensity of his arousal was searing. His eyes were on fire. His mouth burned on her lips, and his crushing grip flamed her naked flesh. She felt his desire and matched it with her own as they rocketed across galaxies filled with burning stars, blazing comets and supernovas.

AT EARLY LIGHT Cleo was awake, her body refusing to waste the nearness of Clark in sleep. She was snuggled against him, his arm across her hip. She lay perfectly still except for the smile that flickered on her lips. She would have given anything to be able to phone Cassy. "Cas-sy, I'm in bed with a spy. Does this mean I love him?"

She sighed inwardly. It was dawn, the classic time for truth and revelation. She should be able to discover the truth without help.

Her heart pounded, her blood raced, and she felt lucky, so lucky. Of course she loved him. No, it made no sense. She didn't really know him. He was not a normal everyday person, easily analyzed, easily interpreted. She had been with him for barely three days under crazy circumstances. Naturally, her feelings were inflated, unreliable.

And what about him? How did he feel? Last night he had certainly acted as though he loved her. But it would be a drastic mistake, a conceited presumption, for Cleo to attach much meaning to one night of shared pleasure. She remembered that her looks supposedly suited Clark's taste. Alex knew that. Edmondsen knew that. And others. She represented an attractive image to him. So it would have been easy for Clark to make love to her, to go through the motions. But wait. There was more, more in his touch.... No. She couldn't let herself think that way. She had to stop.

Sighing inwardly, Cleo tilted her head and enjoyed the warmth of Clark's body. She watched him as he slept so innocently, so unaware of his magnificent potential. *I'll love you, if you love me,* she proposed, finding humor in the childish logic.

Cleo checked Clark's travel clock often. At eight o'clock she had to make an official phone call. It was a very small price to pay for Clark.

When it was time, Cleo tried to move without waking him. He stirred. She should have known that she could not hide from his sensory awareness. She placed a hand to his head. "Stay. I have to make the phone call," she said, sitting up against the headboard, the need for subtle movement now gone. Clark murmured a good-morning, snuggled his face into her hip and swung a possessive arm into her lap.

It was exactly eight o'clock when Cleo picked up the phone to place a long distance call to her boss, Porter Franklin. After dialing the number, she put her hand back on Clark's head and stroked his hair.

She heard Porter's voice as clearly as if he were in the next room, but for Cleo, Porter and all of California Investment were light-years away.

"Porter here."

"Good morning, Porter. This is Cleo."

"Cleo, you honeymooner! I've been expecting this call. Francine broke the news early this morning. In fact, anyone who doesn't know about you just isn't here yet."

"Oh, Francine told you?" she repeated for Clark's benefit and felt his head rock with laughter beneath her hand. Her recollection of the office focused on the image of Francine, always a loaded cannon, firing at the first sign of strategic gossip. Today, Cleo loved her for it. After last night, she had no further quarrel with Francine.

"I won't be in for two weeks," Cleo told Porter, her voice questioning in deference to his position.

"No problem," came the answer she expected. "You sound happy, Cleo."

"It's been the greatest weekend of my life," Cleo confessed, running her fingers through Clark's hair.

"Good! See you when you get back. Got to run. Eight-thirty meeting."

"Thank you, Porter. Bye-bye."

"Sounded convincing," said Clark lazily, his eyes still closed.

Cleo patted his head. "Stick with me, kid, I'll buy you breakfast. Maybe even a hot pretzel." She took the leather-bound folio that held the room service menu off the nightstand and placed it across her knees. The breakfast specials were titled and described. She read them aloud, one by one, so that Clark could register his preference.

When the phone rang, Cleo caught it on the first ring. "Hello."

"Cleo. This is Alex."

"Hello, Alex."

Clark was instantly alert. He sat up and took the receiver from Cleo, pulling the phone to his side of the bed and presenting his back to her. Seeing him hunched over the phone, Cleo felt shut out.

His conversation defied competent eavesdropping. It was mostly jargon and numbers, which Clark recorded into a notebook. The tone was serious, and Cleo quickly sensed that Clark was slipping away from her. As the call dragged on, she conceded that the business of the day had altered the mood of the morning. Permanently. She got up to put on her kimono and then waited at the foot of the bed for the call to end.

When Clark finally replaced the receiver, he acted as if it were a heavy stone. He reflected for a moment before seeking Cleo. His eyes lingered on the cherry-blossom print of her white kimono as though following the pattern of the branches aided his mental computations.

"Good news, bad news, or all of the above," Cleo prompted.

He smiled reluctantly. "All of the above, but decidedly good news for you. We know you are not a target. The death of Mr. X has been ruled an unassisted suicide. It's confirmed he had no time to contact anyone about you."

"And the CLEOPATRA connection?"

"We still have no clue," he reported painfully.

"Maybe CLEOPATRA is safe, too. What if Mr. X was just a little crazy? Couldn't he have been someone set on self-destruction no matter what my name was?"

"Maybe. But we can't take that chance." Clark's tone softened slightly. "Remember, I saw you, too," he said, starting to reach for her hand, then pulling back in some conscious decision. "There was nothing in you that would have inspired terror. We're running S. Holmes through the computer now for another acronym match. In the meantime, it's still a waiting game. I want to speak to a contact in Reno. He's a magician direct from a European tour."

Cleo's mind flashed to countless billboards throughout the Bay Area advertising the Reno appearance of a renowned magician. "Ian of Intrigue?" she asked in amazement.

Clark nodded. "Alex will meet me there tomorrow night. I'd like to get there as soon as possible."

Cleo cringed. Clark had said "Alex will meet me." He had not said "us." It was a little thing, but it was significant. Last night must have meant nothing.

"Oh, by the way, Alex will be bringing you a passport. We're flying to Paris Wednesday."

Let the adventure roll, Cleo thought as she packed up in record time. Clark was anxious to leave, and she would not stand accused of holding him back like excess luggage, but she was saddened by the feeling of becoming just that.

Soon they were on the road heading for Reno. Clark was preoccupied and distant. This kind of silence must be habitual with him, Cleo noted. They had not spoken much since Alex's phone call. Breakfast, which could have been so romantic, became lukewarm coffee and cold Danish on the road.

Cleo was comfortable in the Thunderbird that had brought them to Lake Tahoe two days ago. The ride was smooth, the scenery pretty. She couldn't complain, but she felt isolated and alone—as if she had been liberated from the confines of a conventional life and then left stranded in the middle of nowhere. Nonsense, she thought, trying to reason away the sensation in the face of the wedding bouquet on the dash, dried, but still pretty.

She would not allow herself to become nostalgic. Tahoe consisted of a series of meaningless events, past events, which should not be elevated to the status of memories. She and Clark were not married. She knew that. She had always known that.

She also knew that Clark no longer hovered around her in public. That had been obvious as they had walked through the lobby and out to the car, the distance between them often suggesting they had never met. Cleo's protection was no longer part of Clark's job, and so the constant attention had stopped. His job, his responsibility, and not his particular feelings for her, had governed his actions over the weekend. Cleo knew that. Yes, she told herself, she had always known that.

It was Monday morning back at California Investment. What was going on? Cleo smiled. Everybody would be talking about her. But seriously, Mira had the day off, and since Cleo was gone, Josh would probably make an easy day of it and go home early. Actually, there would be very little to do for the next two weeks. That last prize study had pretty well cleared their agenda. Nothing major would hit Cleo's office until she got back. There was nothing screaming for her attention.

So now she was going to visit a magician, and then fly to Paris. Hoping to generate some enthusiasm, Cleo amused herself by thinking how astounded Josh and Mira would be with the tales she could tell when she got back. Porter would be so impressed to learn that she had been working with Intelnet, he'd authorize another vacation. And Francine would be even more impressed to learn that she had taken Clark Cannell with a grain of salt....

CHAPTER EIGHT

SHORTLY BEFORE NOON, Clark rolled the Thunderbird off the main street onto Intrigue Way, the private road that separated Ian's sprawling ranch from the sleepy residential suburb on the outskirts of Reno.

Cleo was ready to meet Ian of Intrigue. During the latter part of the drive, she recalled the articles she had read on this phenomenal young magician who divided his time between Reno and Las Vegas. He had homes at both places to be near the giant casinos that hosted his spectacular act featuring live animals. Annually, a television special was filmed live from Las Vegas. Nowhere had Cleo read that occasionally on European tour he did work for Intelnet. That was her privileged secret in Intelnet service.

Clark parked in front of the house, and a man dressed in jeans and a plaid shirt came out to greet them. He looked too ordinary to be Ian of Intrigue, the master of magic and mystery. But he was.

"Clark!" Ian exclaimed, shaking Clark's hand and slapping him on the back. "You made good time. Alex called this morning. Said you were coming." Without his costume and stage makeup, Ian looked much younger than his actual age. Cleo felt maternal in comparison.

Smiling broadly, Clark ran the length of a finger down Ian's cheek. "By golly, I do believe you're shaving now," he teased. Cleo was surprised how quickly Clark had perked up. He was dynamic and enthused again, no longer sullen as he had been on the drive.

"Give me a break, old man," Ian retorted, punching Clark's shoulder.

Clark turned gracefully into the punch. "Well, say hello to an old man's wife. This is Cleo," he said.

"You son of a gun. I thought Alex was pulling my leg. Welcome to my ranch, Cleo. It's not fancy like my Vegas spread, but I hope you won't find this too miserable a pit stop on your honeymoon." He shook her hand grandly.

"Oh, no," Cleo replied. "The pleasure is all mine. Had Clark told me that he was a friend of the greatest illusionist of our time, I'd have married him sooner."

"Clarkie, I like this girl," he trilled. "Come on. Let's get Nareen and have lunch. She's out in critter land."

They started to walk to the kennels and training area. Already, Cleo could hear the chatter of chimpanzees and the chirping of birds.

"We passed quite a bit of traffic on your road, Ian. What do you have going on here?" Clark asked.

"I'm letting a community group do their annual carnival on the west acreage. You'll see it when we get past the house. There." He pointed down the slope to a collection of fair booths and portable amusement rides in the distance. "Since I'm a local celebrity, I endear myself in many ways."

"And get a percentage on the soft drinks, no doubt."

"*Moi*, Clarkie?"

Cleo weighed the ego of this energetic, boyish magician as a necessary ingredient for international success at such an early age. And ego seemed to play a large part in Intelnet. Very much aloof, Cleo could see Intelnet as a sort of magnet, tapping talented individuals and allowing them to thrive on feelings of elitism. Was there really a common good in all of this? Or was it just a game? She would dwell on it later. Right now she was the guest of a famous magician.

Critter land, as Ian called it, was a carefully land-scaped area for a group of tigers, two sleeping lions, a family of chimpanzees, ostriches, peacocks and colorful birds of every type—a virtual zoo, only these animals weren't on display. They were home. Happy, contented and friendly to people. The big cats must have been re-sponding to Ian when they looked up, slapped a tail or twitched an ear, but Cleo also felt they bade her wel-come. Engrossed in the animals, Cleo barely kept track of the conversation.

"No rumbling on the continent?" Clark asked.

Ian shook his head.

"I understand Frank Cordoba is back in town," Clark continued. Even Cleo knew that Frank Cordoba was an international mogul in import and export shipping. His home remained in Reno, the source of his original wealth, generated from controlling interest in casinos on the strip.

Ian grinned. "It just so happens I'm doing a perfor-mance at his estate. He's opening his art collection for a private showing and throwing a gala to benefit the arts."

"When?"

"Tomorrow evening."

"Guest list?"

"Art lovers and fat cats interested in the tax deduction or points in the social register. It'll be basically your who's who from west coast society plus some European money."

"Get me an invitation."

Cleo perked her ears.

"What's the cover?" Ian asked.

"Put my wife in the act."

Cleo glanced up in disbelief. Then came a shrill whistle, which made them all turn.

It came from a woman in jeans and a plaid shirt like Ian's. She waved energetically. It was Ian's wife, Nareen. On approach, Cleo could see that she was noticeably older than Ian, and she had freckles, both facts apparent only in the absence of stage makeup. With a bandanna on her head, Nareen looked like any suburban homemaker watering the lawn, except that she was washing down a cage for two giant pythons, writhing around a dead tree.

"Clark Cannell! I knew you'd be along soon," she said when they got closer. "Well, get over here," she demanded. "The hose doesn't reach that far."

"Hiya, Nareen." Clark stepped forward and gave her a hug. She gave him a polar bear squeeze. "My wife, Cleo," he announced after nudging Cleo to the forefront.

"Well, you went and did it!" Nareen exclaimed. "Nice to meet you, Cleo."

"Nice to meet *you*," Cleo returned with emphasis. "I'm a big fan." She waved her hand in an encompassing gesture. "The animals are all so wonderful."

"They're my family," Nareen said proudly.

"Are they all in the show?" Cleo asked.

"Some are, some aren't." Nareen pointed to a tiger lying alone in an enclosure. "Timmy was found abused in a carnival. We just adopted him last week."

As Nareen spoke, one of the trainers stepped into Timmy's cage with a bucket. Seeing Nareen and Ian with their two guests, he raised his hand in a wave. The move was just enough to ignite the suspicious tiger. The huge animal lunged, dropping upon the unwary trainer.

"No!" Cleo screamed, powerless in all but voice.

There was panic, chaos all around. And then there was a deafening, piercing noise, which grabbed the tiger's attention and sent him into retreat.

It was over as quickly as it had started and time stood still for Cleo in a freeze-frame of action as she assembled pieces of what had happened. Her hands were covering her mouth. She had taken a useless step forward. Nareen was on her way to the cage, her hands in the air. Ian was on the ground grabbing for the hose Nareen had dropped—presumably in an attempt to aim a water spray. Kennel staff appeared from every direction. Only Clark stood collected and cool, holding a gun that had been fired into the air.

Cleo was aware of the next events in a haze. The victim of the attack was shaken but unhurt. Nareen examined his shoulder, as did other trainers. There were jokes to break the tension. There was relief. And there was Clark. Someone must have thanked him. Everyone must have thanked him.

"You gotta get me one of those, Clarkie," Cleo heard Ian say about the revolver.

"Stay away from this stuff, Ian. Trust me. You don't want it."

"Lunch!" Nareen said, exhaling with relief. "Let's have lunch!" She gathered Cleo and Clark with an arm about each of their waists.

LUNCH CONSISTED of cold cuts and cheese directly from the refrigerator. They sat at a round wooden table in a den filled with colonial furniture. Having expected Ian's home to be as glitzy and contemporary as his stage show, Cleo was surprised to be sitting in an inglenook of Early Americana, lacking only the original signers of the constitution for authenticity.

There was no one else in the house, but Ian secured the door to the den anyway, and voices sought a low conspiratorial level. The discussion concerned Clark's access to the Cordoba estate, secured by Cleo's participation in Ian's benefit performance.

Cleo was accepting of the situation. "How can I be in the act?" she had asked Clark earlier when they were alone washing up for lunch in the guest room. "I don't know magic."

"They won't make you do anything that requires guild secrets," Clark had explained. "All you have to do is look good. Be a good-looking piece of fluff. You can do that."

He had said it easily. He might have meant it as a compliment; Cleo had read it as a horse's mouth interpretation of what she had meant to him last night. She had felt an anger inside, but dismissed it as injured pride, foolishness, and continued. "Why can't you just attend Ian's benefit?" she had asked.

"The affair is private. For select invited guests. Ian will have to go to a lot of trouble to secure a complimentary invitation on my behalf. He needs a good reason. What could be better than letting a guy see his wife perform?"

"Why can't you be in the show, part of the crew?"

"Because a lot of the guests know me, and I can't be linked to Ian." Clark lifted his eyebrows. "Ian got started doing small clubs in Berkeley about the same time you were in school there."

"Yes, I know that."

"We are going to say that you two are old friends. That you helped him in his act. And that this is a nostalgic reunion for you two."

"I see," Cleo responded. She had admitted only to herself that the prospect was exciting.

"And there's a side benefit," Clark had added. "I will get to showcase you as my wife before an international crowd, to show you off as a flesh and blood Cleopatra. So we get a lot of visibility in the process. What do you think?"

"I think you're crazy," Cleo had replied coolly. She would play along with the game, but she wouldn't enjoy it.

But her feelings changed dramatically during lunch. She was sharing food and secrets with the famous Ian of Intrigue and Nareen. She felt privileged. It was a once-in-a-lifetime experience for her, and they treated her as an equal colleague. There was some merit in being Clark's wife, Cleo decided.

"We'll give you Nareen's role," Ian said. "It's got star quality, and we can tailor it so you won't need to know about illusion."

"I'll pretend to have the flu," Nareen added. "That way we can say you were here visiting on your honeymoon, and you volunteered to fill in for me at the performance." She paused to receive Ian and Clark's nod of approval. "The costume is no problem. What's your shoe size, Cleo?"

"Six."

"Great. So's mine."

WHILE IAN AND CLARK continued the discussion, Cleo and Nareen adjourned to a large practice room with floor-to-ceiling mirrors, much like a dance studio. Nareen pulled a wooden chair up to a video recorder and inserted a cassette of a prior performance as a prelude to training.

"Never expected to work on your honeymoon, did you," she said, as Cleo sat down. "But I know how much you love him."

Cleo was startled, shocked to the very core. Fortunately, she managed to appear only a little surprised.

"I saw the way you were looking at him in front of the tiger cage," Nareen explained warmly.

Yes, Nareen, you must have seen it, Cleo answered silently. *It must have looked like downright adoration*. Cleo had been so very impressed with Clark, but she had refused to admit it at the time. Now it flooded back. How could she keep denying her feelings for him when they existed as plain as day? Cleo smiled sweetly for Nareen's benefit, covering her turmoil.

"He's quite a guy," Nareen continued. "I feel safe when he's around." She pulled up a chair for herself and sat down. "I didn't think Clark would ever marry. Alex's engagement probably had a lot to do with it. Have you met Megan yet?"

Cleo shook her head shyly.

"Neither have I," Nareen said. She let out a sigh. "You know, I believe people come into your life when you're ready for them." She laughed. "I don't believe in coincidence anymore."

Nareen hit another nerve. Cleo was catapulted back to the BART train. Last Friday she was wallowing in the emptiness of her life. Did Clark come into her life because she was ready for him?

Nareen switched on the VCR. "Ready?" she asked cheerfully. "Pay special attention to what I'm doing in this routine."

Cleo studied Nareen's movements with the same determination she had mustered in the wee hours of Saturday morning when she traded life histories with Clark. Bring-

ing all her concentration to bear, she studied Nareen's role
as a magician's assistant. She analyzed the trademark
elements of Nareen's sexy and chic manner. She wanted
to prove to Nareen that she was a quick study, that she
could, by right, be married to Clark Cannell.

After two runs of the tape, Nareen placed a script book
of the evening performance in Cleo's lap and explained
each function in detail. Cleo concentrated on her peripheral role, never digressing to ask how the illusions were
actually performed.

Then Nareen told Cleo to take a break while she stepped
out to collect some animals. Instead, Cleo watched the
videotape again.

When Nareen returned, she had an Amazon parrot on
her shoulder, a large white rabbit on her arm and five
parakeets in a cage. Cleo was delighted to learn the animal handling techniques. She was overjoyed with each
unexpected wiggle of the rabbit or flutter of birds.

Next, Nareen played the part of Ian, and walked Cleo
through the movements, drilling her on how to smile,
stand, walk, glide, pivot.

"Good, Cleo. Good!" Nareen praised.

Cleo watched her reflection in the mirrors, and her
confidence grew. She was having fun. Real fun. And soon
she would allow herself the luxury of stray thoughts, the
contemplation of her good fortune, magic and Clark.
Mostly Clark.

IT WAS ALMOST seven o'clock when Ian poked his head
into the studio. "Dinner is on," he announced. "Clark
hopped over to Stead Air Force Base, Cleo. He'll be back
late tonight. You're not supposed to wait up for him."

Nareen took a breath, put an understanding arm
around Cleo and together they walked to the kitchen.

Ian had warmed up a leftover casserole.

"Honey, is this what you're going to feed Cleo?" Nareen chided, wrinkling her brow.

"I'm only a magician," he said, kissing her cheek.

Nareen opened the refrigerator and took out a salad that had been prepared earlier. "Cleo, I can heat up some soup if you don't like my eggplant casserole."

"Oh, no. It smells wonderful," Cleo assured her, sitting down at the table.

"How's the practice coming?" Ian asked Cleo when they were all settled.

"Okay," Cleo answered, looking to Nareen's smiling face for confirmation. "I'm having fun. I've always loved magic. I've always loved watching you."

"Do you know how I do it?"

"No." Cleo's eyes were bright.

"Years of practice. Gobs of talent. But mostly years of practice." He leaned back and held up an index finger. "Nareen, one orange."

"Oh, not the orange. Cleo, he does this for everyone who sits at this table and pays him any attention," Nareen informed her, going to the refrigerator and tossing Ian an orange.

Ian reached into his pocket for a dollar bill and handed it to Cleo. "Write your initials on it so you'll know it's your bill." Nareen put a pen on the table.

Then Ian launched into some distracting patter, and at the conclusion of the standard trick, produced Cleo's dollar bill from the center of the orange.

"Bravo!" Cleo cheered.

"Now," Ian surmised, "you want to see how it's done."

"Yes!" Cleo enthused, nodding her head.

Ian smiled. "You will be impressed, but I give you fair warning—it ruins the magic forever."

Nareen tossed Ian another orange, and Ian went through the trick again. This time he did a running commentary on his method, pointing out to Cleo when he diverted her attention, how he did his sleight of hand. Cleo watched attentively. She was enlightened, she was impressed. But Ian was right. When the trick was reduced to a mechanical process, the magic was spoiled in a way she would not have expected.

"Bravo for years of practice!" Cleo said at the conclusion.

Ian took a bow. "Now as a guest in my house, dear Cleo, I'll demystify anything you want. What's your favorite magic routine?"

"Levitation," Cleo answered without hesitation. This was a dream come true. She was, however, quite shocked by Ian. Magicians were not supposed to publicize their secrets.

"Now do you really want to know? Really? Really?"

"Oh, forgive my husband the child," Nareen said.

Cleo gave Ian's offer some thought. "No, I really don't. I suppose I don't want it ruined."

"Do you mean that, or are you just satisfying this one?" Nareen asked, tugging Ian's sleeve.

"I mean it." Cleo was positive.

Ian looked pleased with himself, but he did heed Nareen's slight frown. "Well, Cleo, if you change your mind later, you can ask Clark how I do it."

Cleo lit up with interest. "Does Clark know?"

"He gets some of my methods out of me. That sly bum! But he can't do 'em."

Cleo laughed with Ian, but inwardly she was thinking about Clark's manipulative skill. It really bothered her.

How could she trust someone who had it? How could she love him?

After dinner Ian walked through the act several times with Cleo in the practice room.

"You're a natural," he told her at the end of the session. "No wonder Clark couldn't let you go."

And suddenly Cleo was tired. Very tired and emotionally drained.

NAREEN WAS WEARING a Snoopy nightshirt and fuzzy red slippers when she brought tea to Cleo in the living room.

"Did Ian behave himself?" Nareen teased.

Cleo laughed. "How did you two meet?" she asked, settling back on the sofa with her tea.

"We met when my name was Nadeen—Ian thought Nareen was more mysterious. Anyway, it was right after his gigs in Berkeley, when he was booked as an opening lounge act in Vegas, and before he got his big break." Nareen got comfortable on the sofa. "I was working in a twenty-four hour coffee shop, a real greasy spoon, and Ian came in every night at 1:00 a.m. for dinner for almost a year. He told me his problems. I listened. Then he started getting famous, and he asked me to marry him. I had just saved the money I needed to go to college like I planned. I said, 'No way.' He said, 'I need you.' I said, 'Look, I'm six years older than you and you're an egotistical kid.'" Nareen started to get excited with her own story. "Then he asked me what I wanted out of life, what I'd do with a college education. I said I had dreams. I said I didn't want to ever have to worry about money. I wanted to travel. I wanted to be able to keep animals, wanted to learn to dance. He promised me all those things, and you know what?"

"What?" Cleo said, her eyes bright with enjoyment.

"He kept all his promises!"

Cleo marveled. "That's a love story, Nareen. A real love story." She gazed around the room. "You have a wonderful life together. Everything you want..." She frowned. "Why...how did you get involved with Intelnet?"

"Oh, let me tell you. I didn't want to be. We were in Germany on tour, and they asked if Ian would pass information into the audience by sleight of hand. Ian was pretty excited about the whole thing. Loved the idea of proving himself, you know, of being the best. I told him he was behaving like a kid. And then I found out that the information he passed saved four people who were being tortured in prison."

Nareen poured herself another cup of tea. "So I figured it was worthwhile. But I never let Ian do anything dangerous. You know what I'm talking about, Cleo. I don't know how you and Megan stand it."

Cleo focused on her finger circling the rim of her teacup. "Well, Alex is stepping down to administrative status soon," she mentioned softly.

"Oh, I'm happy for him." Nareen squinted. "I don't think Clark will ever give it up."

"I agree, Nareen." Cleo smiled wryly. "You're absolutely right."

CLEO COULDN'T SLEEP. She was lying alone in a four-poster bed in the guest room. Clark had not returned. She was wearing her old flannel nightgown, feeling very much like herself, feeling very out of place, and feeling a creeping fear about failing on stage tomorrow. *Don't just lie here and worry. Do something about it,* she told herself as she threw off the covers and got out of bed.

She walked down the hall, past the den, past the living room, to the practice room, making every effort to be silent. She opened the door, and carefully shut it behind her. She flipped the switches and brought the three rows of ceiling lights to life over the wood floor of the mirrored room. Too bright. She flipped the switches again until only the lights over the center of the studio remained. The room seemed more private that way, more secure.

Cleo carried a wooden chair to the spot of light. She situated the portable tape recorder at the foot of the chair and sat down with the script book opened on her lap. Alone, she studied, or tried to.

She switched on the music that was to be used in one of the magic sequences. It was a rich instrumental arrangement of her favorite song. This afternoon she had taken it as a happy coincidence. Right now it was a beautiful and haunting flight for the senses, very personal and very stirring.

She looked at her reflection in the mirrors all around. She had never been in such a room before. A truly mesmerizing room, built by the magic of Ian and Nareen, together. The things that Ian had promised a reluctant Nareen were the very things he had given her. And Cleo was sitting right in the middle of it.

Could she have a life like this with Clark? Impossible. Had he made her any promises? He had promised to keep her alive. Well, she was alive, but that didn't count. That was his job. He was taking her to Paris. Just a vacation, he had said. Yes, maybe that was a promise. She rewound the tape and floated on the music again, shivering with the orchestral crescendos. Was it so terrible to love a man who didn't love her? Was it so terrible to admit?

Miraculously, she managed to focus on the script book. And then the door opened in the fuzzy shadows at the edge of the room.

"Clark?"

"Cleo. It's 2:00 a.m. What are you doing up?"

"I'm scared. I don't want to fail, Clark." Her presence was waiflike in the middle of the room.

"Scared?" he said, sauntering toward her, picking up a chair on the way. "Aren't you the one who runs California Investment single-handedly?" He set the chair in front of her and swung his leg over the seat, sitting down with his arms folded on the chair back. "I wouldn't be scared if I had a pen set on my desk—an award for outstanding service...."

God, he made her feel good.

"I never got a briefcase with my name in gold as an award." He shrugged. "I don't even have a briefcase."

Cleo was smiling. *Stop, you lovable doll,* she addressed him silently. She shook her head lightly. "Clark, I'm not you."

He gave a polite little snort and began to survey the room, relaxing his folded arms over the back of the chair. And as Cleo looked at him, drinking in his fine profile, the music of the song rose around her and the unsung lyric carried a powerful meaning. *Do you know what it is you do to me?* she asked Clark silently, carried away by her senses, casting away her sensibilities.

"Pretty music," Clark said to her reflection in a mirror.

"Can you read my mind?" Cleo whispered.

"What?" He turned to her.

"The name of the song," Cleo said. "It's the love theme to *Superman*—the movie." She glanced down shyly.

"Ohh," he said, stretching out the word knowingly. "Lyrics by Leslie Bricusse, music by John Williams."

"Clark, how do you know that!" she exclaimed. It was her favorite song, and she could not credit its origin.

"I saw it on the sheet music you have on your piano."

"Oh, Clark, you are amazing." A truly special man, she thought.

"So what are you working on?" he asked, indicating the script book.

"This is sort of a dream segment," Cleo explained. "Ian stands there."

Clark got up and stepped to the masking tape marker on the floor. "Right here?"

"Yeah. And then there's blue smoke swirling at his feet."

"Ah," he said, pretending to see the smoke. "And what do you do?"

"And then I get up—" Cleo rose "—make a twirl here. Then you extend your hand, yes, like that, and I reach out, and take your hand...."

The movements came naturally to Clark on the mere suggestion from Cleo. He whirled her around the floor, and Cleo danced in a dream, in the arms of the man who had stepped into her life and into the tingling orchestration of the music that carried everything she wanted to say to him.

He seemed to enjoy the music, their reflection in the mirrors, as they danced within the ring of light surrounded by shadow. *Can he read my mind?* Cleo thought. *Does he know the lyrics, too?*

"By the way, we're not going to Paris."

Cleo came back to earth. Clark was not thinking of the lyrics. And he had just broken the promise to her.

"Are you disappointed?" he asked, feeling the change in her.

"No." She was stable, withdrawing from him gently. There had been no promise, could never be a promise. She sat down in the chair.

"I'm flying back to San Francisco in the morning."

Cleo looked up at him in a panic. "Are you coming back?" she blurted.

Clark seemed a little perplexed. "Cleo, you aren't in danger anymore," he told her, studying her. "I'll be back in time for the show, of course."

"Gee, busy day," Cleo muttered, sitting properly in the chair. "You'd better get some sleep."

Clark nodded but seemed reluctant to leave her. "Anything I can do to help?" he asked.

"No, I have to do this alone." Cleo was already looking into the script book seriously.

"I understand," he said, leaving quietly.

"Oh, I know you do, Clark Cannell," Cleo whispered when he closed the door. "I wish with all my heart you didn't."

IN THE MORNING, Nareen and Cleo went through the entire routine. Quite a bit of time was devoted to the execution of stylized maneuvers with a two-foot wand. Cleo practiced under Nareen's critical eye: the drumroll stance, wand held out to the side; the curtain stance, wand held high in the air; and the grand stance, wand cradled in the crook of the arm like a majorette.

By midmorning the other preparations had gotten under way. Ian's mechanical crew left for the Cordoba estate to assemble the portable stage. Cleo met briefly with Ian's veteran crew of nine—five prop assistants, the lighting specialist, the sound technician and two dancers who would perform a Jack and Jill magic vignette. Cleo was introduced as Ian's old friend. There were no questions asked.

By late afternoon, Cleo was ready for her costume. She followed Nareen through a side door of the practice room into the wardrobe room. It had already been determined that Cleo could manage Nareen's costume. Padding would be used where necessary, as Nareen was heavier.

First came the glittered black stockings, then the strapless black taffeta bodysuit, shirred at the bust and hips, fitting tightly and displaying the full leg. The sequined bow tie followed, then the black elbow-length gloves, the black spike heels. Next Nareen troweled on the stage makeup over a heavy oil-base foundation. She highlighted Cleo's eyes to mysterious perfection with purple eyeliner and violet and silver glitter. She painted Cleo's lips a cherry-red and added rouge and rose glitter to her cheeks. Last, Nareen expertly put Cleo's hair up with a hairpiece and a rhinestone tiara. The effect was dramatic.

When Cleo took her place in the mirrored practice room again for the dress rehearsal, the look of the costume chased away any inhibition and a new confidence propelled her to a stunning performance. The lesson was complete.

With a slap to the fanny, Nareen dispatched Cleo to the guest room to rest before dinner. That proved to be Nareen's tallest order.

Cleo posed before the freestanding framed mirror. She couldn't believe her reflection. Soon she would be the ravishing assistant to a world-renowned magician. She knew no stronger potion than three days in the life of Clark Cannell. It was the first time today she had allowed herself to think of him.

And as if she had conjured up his being with that thought, Clark appeared magically in the mirror behind her. He was dressed in his dark suit, so sophisticated and suave, and his eyes telegraphed his message before the words were spoken. "You're beautiful."

Cleo spun around, glowing more than radioactive uranium. Approval from him was everything. She pressed a finger to her lips to prepare the hush for the most scandalous of secrets. "Only half of this bosom is really me."

Smiling, he placed both hands firmly on her shoulders. "How do you feel?"

"Like I'm in show business!" she exclaimed, fluttering her hands at each side of her face, palms forward, fingers spread apart. "But I'm nervous," she confessed.

Clark tightened his hands on her shoulders. "The most important thing, Cleo, is not to be nervous. You can do it. You know it. Ham it up. Act as if you were born on that stage, and that every person on this earth would gladly fall to his knees before you."

"Including you?" Cleo asked, toying with his tie. It was okay to flirt with him. She was in costume, not herself. Besides, she had her feelings under control.

"Especially me," he answered quietly, bringing goose bumps to her flesh.

She looked up jauntily for a kiss. Clark lowered his head, then stopped short, puzzling over the generous application of makeup, the cherry lipstick, the glitter oiled into her cheeks. "Where can I kiss you?" The question was rhetorical. He lightly kissed one ear, turned her head and kissed the other.

Cleo blew him a kiss, which he caught at the door. He winked. "Break a leg, kid."

Cleo stared after him, vowing to give him the performance of his life. She was going to make sure he remembered her.

IT WAS NOW FIVE O'CLOCK. Clark would arrive at the
Cordoba estate with the throng of invited guests, sample
the hors d'oeuvres, view Cordoba's art collection and, of
course, wait for Ian's curtain at seven. Of course, he
would be doing all his spy things, Cleo thought. But it was
for a good cause. She trusted him in that.

Clutching her wand, her black velvet cape draped over
her arm, Cleo joined Ian and Nareen, on schedule, in the
kitchen. Ian in stage makeup, his eyebrows heavy and
mysterious, eating a TV dinner in a colonial kitchen was
a curious sight. He smiled and motioned for Cleo to be
seated.

"Cleo! We haven't had much time together today. I
have your wand. Are you going to be all right?" he asked
as he reached over to remove the wand she carried to the
table and make her a present of the new one.

"I'm fine! I'm going to do everything Nareen taught
me," Cleo said cheerfully, acknowledging Nareen, who
pulled a dinner out of the microwave with a big smile and
set it before Cleo.

It was meatballs, and Cleo cut each of them, already
small, into six dainty pieces so not to mess up her lipstick. Nareen groaned at her own oversight and quickly
slipped a straw into Cleo's iced coffee.

They ate in polite and efficient silence. Then Ian rose
from the table, and Nareen helped him secure his cape.

"When I bring the van up to the door, Cleo, I'll honk
the horn for you," Ian said and left.

Nareen watched him go. After a moment, she turned to Cleo. "You tell Clark to take care of him, won't you? He's all I really have."

Cleo was brimming with emotion. "I promise you he will be safe," she said, getting up and kissing Nareen lightly on the cheek, spending a little lipstick for a very good cause.

When she heard the horn, Cleo joined the troupe in the commuter van. She shunned conversation by studying the script book open in her lap. If anything appeared amiss, the troupe gave no indication.

CHAPTER NINE

EVEN THE WROUGHT-IRON GATE to the Cordoba estate was impressive, with its ornate castings at the crown. Blatant wealth, Cleo breathed silently to herself as the gates were pulled open by grounds security. Like a huge horseshoe resting on a green slope, the road led from the gate to the front of a stately, three-story mansion. At the hub of the driveway was a marble fountain in full water blossom.

The van pulled off the main driveway onto a cobblestone service road, which led behind the mansion, and parked at the garden cottage. Parked up ahead on the grass were two moving vans bearing Ian's logo, a black panther in tuxedo leaping a crescent moon. One van had carried the platform stage, which had been assembled on the grounds that afternoon, the other had transported the animals, the props and special-effects apparatus.

Cleo walked with Ian and the dancers, who were dressed as Jack and Jill, along a hedge of rosebushes from the garden cottage to the stage. The pool on the other side of the rose garden was reminiscent of the reflecting pools of the Roman aristocracy. It lay like glass at the base of a three-tiered terrace rolling out from the colonnaded mansion. Elegantly dressed guests filled the terrace and walked down to poolside, enjoying the warm summer evening, with the help of free-flowing champagne, and hors d'oeuvres from the caterers' tables. Cleo wondered if Clark had been successful, whether he had accomplished his purpose.

At the far end of the pool, under an arbor covered with lilac wisteria, thirty rows of white café chairs had been placed in front of Ian's platform stage. The stage itself was assembled at the arbor's outside edge, within the mouth of a royal-blue tent. The tent provided a backstage area and a curtained corridor within which the crew was able to wheel equipment on rollers around and beneath the platform.

Cleo took her assigned place in the corridor, out of the crew's way, and waited quietly. Ian was coordinating with the technicians and doing last-minute blocking. Through a vent in the tent, Cleo could see children filing into the front rows—little girls in party dresses with starchy crinolines and little boys in three-piece suits, looking like miniature men.

Soon all the chairs had been filled, along with Cleo's anxiety quota. She wasn't a performer, just an ordinary person set up by a man who could do anything. And as such, had he misjudged her capabilities? Where was he? She was panicking. She had to see him.

She searched the sea of faces until she located him. Clark was standing behind the last row of chairs in the company of another man. But Cleo saw only Clark. He seemed so relaxed, one hand thrust casually into his trouser pocket, the other holding a glass of champagne. She saw him being introduced to another couple and making a fine impression. He could do anything. But he couldn't help her now. She was on her own.

The ready signal was given backstage. The stage went dark. And then it came, the reverberating, deep-voiced announcement, "Ladies and gentlemen...presenting Ian of Intrigue." A chill ran down Cleo's spine.

Spotlights turned blue, theme music came up, blue smoke was released and Ian appeared, flaring his cape to solid applause. There was no turning back.

Ian's words onstage were just syllables that washed over Cleo like a foreign language as she awaited the sound of her cue line. "Where is my alter ego?" There it was. Those key unintelligible syllables. Blocking out all emotional fluttering, Cleo walked out onstage to Ian's outstretched hand.

She could not have anticipated either the tremendous applause or its effect on her. The affirmation was so powerful that she greeted the audience with real and not rehearsed enthusiasm. She was part of the show. The audience didn't know, didn't care that she wasn't born to showmanship. Tonight she was a star.

Her eyes found Clark, who toasted her and blew her a kiss in no discreet gesture. Ham it up, Clark had told her, so she made an ostentatious greeting part of the show. The audience loved it. They saw a fresh personality caught up in a love story with the handsome man in the back, which did not interfere with any fan loyalty to Nareen.

And so Ian's trademark scenarios went off without a hitch, including the Superman sequence where Ian conjured up globes of light, which swirled the stage to his command. And then the show took the turn requested by Frank Cordoba. It was geared to the children in the audience.

"Let us take a trip," Ian said at the beginning of the scenario. A canvas backdrop was retracted to reveal a bright red biplane with shortened fuselage and wings. Taking Cleo's hand, Ian closely inspected the craft, which moved slowly on a rotating base.

"I feel strangely like I could fly away on my own wings," Ian recited from the script. On that line, he produced a blue parakeet from within the inner pocket of his tuxedo. Cleo allowed the parakeet to perch on her wand and then transferred it to one of the seven trapeze swings that descended in a row from the curtained heights. As the show continued, Cleo delivered twelve parakeets to the swings. An Amazon parrot was the finale of the sequence, and Ian bowed to applause while the trapezes were raised into the top of the tent by crewmen, who reeled the birds in like laundry on a clothesline pulley.

Then Ian resumed checking the biplane for airworthiness, exposing the cutaway compartments to the audience. He talked of stowaways and then rabbits appeared—big white rabbits with American Express cards tied around their necks.

Cleo took each rabbit from Ian, hugged it and put it in the hands of one of the children whom the dancers had assembled onstage. Then the children put the rabbits into a trunk, and Ian made the animals disappear.

For the grand finale of the scene, Ian brought in a pilot, a chimpanzee in a World War I flying-ace uniform, who magically flew the plane away. The curtains closed as Ian and Cleo waved bon voyage.

Cleo's role in the Jack and Jill vignette was to escort two children to special spots on the stage where they could sprinkle magic dust on cue from Ian.

Jack and Jill danced up the hill, encountering problems with the proverbial pail of water, which Ian magically remedied. In the climax, Ian disappeared into the well, only to reappear as Jack, who had supposedly at no time left the stage.

When the show was over, the entire troupe held hands to furious applause in a curtain call with blue smoke swirling at their feet. Red smoke was released next, and the stage turned orchid. Cleo was exhilarated, holding on to Ian's hand, Jill's hand. There were cheers from the audience and a spray of bravos. In the distance Cleo could see Clark smiling. He was pleased. She was ecstatic. Maybe she could be the wife of an intelligence agent, his excellent copartner.

When the curtain came down, the crew began dismantling right away. Ian stepped off the platform into a cluster of autograph seekers. Cleo was caught in the shuffle until Clark collected her, steering her away from the crowd.

Dizzily, Cleo clung to his arm. He took her down the length of the pool to a caterers' table. There in exaggerated clumsiness, he spread caviar on a cracker and fed it to her. Cleo played to his behavior, sensing that he was making a spectacle of himself in prelude to some strategic move.

"There's someone I'd like you to meet," he said when the time was right. The gala was breaking up. Guests were starting to leave.

He steered her to the foot of the terrace, to the short, easygoing man he had been standing with during the performance. "Cleo, this is a longtime acquaintance of mine, Hallaran Mayor."

"Mrs. Cannell, you have a fan," Hal Mayor said, taking her hand.

"Hal, would you mind standing over here a minute? I want a picture of my wife on the terrace," said Clark, positioning his pocket camera. "Ham it up, Cleo. Let's see a drumroll stance." Cleo happily obliged. "Once more, Cleo, hold it higher."

So this would be the climax of her masquerade, Cleo thought, as Clark's camera flashed in the twilight. Her euphoria was interrupted by the sudden appearance of a formidable, humorless man who tapped Clark's shoulder.

"There are no photographs. Photography is forbidden in interest of Mr. Cordoba's privacy."

"But we are not facing Mr. Cordoba's estate," Clark told the private security agent calmly.

"I must ask for your film."

Hal tried to intercede. "Now wait a minute. Frank won't mind. This man is on his honeymoon."

"I must insist."

"Very well." Clark reluctantly allowed the man to open the camera and remove the roll of film. "My apology for the intrusion."

Cleo's heart crashed to earth and shattered into pieces. This mission had to be a success. She had been the weakest link, but she had been magnificent. And now, events beyond her control had claimed her effort, rendering her accomplishment meaningless. Clark needed this success. What was more, Cleo needed this success, needed to be a functioning part of his life. Clouded by hopeless, helpless misery, Cleo barely felt the quick kiss Clark gave her. "I'll see you at the ranch, Cleo," he said as he left with Hal.

Preoccupied in dismay, Cleo walked the edge of the pool toward the stage. Why had Clark given up so easily? Her eyes moistened with disappointment. It was just like working at California Investment. She had done everything and accomplished nothing. She was all made-up and dressed up, with nowhere to go.

"Bunny lady!" a little girl exclaimed, throwing herself into an embrace of Cleo's knees.

Momentarily losing her balance, Cleo dropped the wand, which clattered on the cement and rolled to the edge of the pool.

"Allison Alicia!" shouted the little girl's blue-blooded mother, peeling the child away.

Smiling and waving goodbye in character, Cleo picked up her wand and continued on her way. She noticed the wand to be lighter and discovered the cap was missing. She was looking into a hollow tube. Oh, well, she thought, without missing a step, wands were a standard item. Ian had spares. He and Nareen had such a storybook life. They probably grew wands in the garden.

She approached Ian, who was supervising the load-up. He was jubilant. The stage had been collapsed, and he stood among the remaining stage boxes, waiting for the forklift truck to return. "Hi there. You were great. Hey, why so morbid?"

Moving close, Cleo whispered, "Clark didn't get the pictures."

Ian beamed. "Perfect, kiddo. You took the pictures. Clark activated the camera tip on the wand. I installed it myself."

Cleo's eyes flew open. The wand. The wand was empty. She held it up to Ian. His face turned ghostly. If the camera was found, the consequences would embroil both Ian and Clark.

Impulsively, Cleo leaped to correct the accident. "I'll find it," she promised, running off, not wanting to waste time in conference.

"Cleo, don't get caught," Ian whispered hoarsely after her.

Cleo hurried back to the pool, walking quickly but trying to appear casual. Thankfully, the area was deserted. All the lights around the pool had been dimmed. The caterers were gone, and the hosts were bidding the guests farewell at the front entrance of the house.

Cleo frantically searched the rim of the pool. She couldn't find the cap, the camera, the whatever. She shouldn't have run off without Ian. Suppose it had already been discovered? She was on the verge of silent hysteria when she spotted the wand cap at the bottom of the pool. The deep end.

Cleo could swim but had never been able to dive or open her eyes underwater. And if she'd thought about it longer, she might have come up with a million more reasons for not being able to retrieve the camera quickly. But she couldn't let the water be a barrier. She had to get that camera. Fast.

Immediately, she stepped out of her shoes and yanked off her tiara. She looked around fervently, sat on the edge of the pool and then slipped into the water. She filled her lungs with air and plunged beneath the surface. Once submerged, she forced her eyes open, inverted herself and frog-kicked to the bottom of the pool, where her flailing arms reached for the camera. She grasped it and shot upward in a surge of panic.

Her head above water, she looked around anxiously to see if she had been observed. Clear coast. Good. She swam to the side of the pool and hauled herself out. Dripping wet, she made sure her hairpiece was still secure, inserted the tiara and stepped into her shoes. Clutching the camera in a tight fist, she made her way along the rosebushes. She glanced furtively in all directions. Still clear. Great. She must not get caught. She could explain being wet. She had been at the pool. She fell in. But explaining the camera would be hard. She couldn't hide it. There was too much foam rubber in her bosom.

She sprinted into the shadows of the arbor, praying for just a little more of the luck that seemed to be with her. She considered making a dash for one of Ian's trucks, but knew she must make contact with Ian, who was stalling the transport operation until she returned. She approached what was left of the stage, just two crates on the lawn.

Ian saw her. She signaled victory. Greatly relieved, he started toward her but halted when Frank Cordoba walked up from the service road. "Ian, I appreciate the performance," he said, brandishing his pipe. "You really know how to make kids happy. I just saw the last of them drive away."

Cleo quickly crouched behind the closest crate. It was shoulder high, about the size of a compact car.

"I'm always happy to do magic, Frank," Ian replied.

"I see you're all loaded except for these." Cordoba tapped his pipe on the crate near him and began strolling toward the crate that shielded Cleo. "These are custom crates, aren't they? I like your logo," he added, walking with Ian closer to Cleo's hideaway.

Praying for one last nod of fortune, Cleo's fingers flew to the metal latch of the plastic travel crate. She opened the side of the crate and crawled into the dark recess. There was just enough space to wedge in with her legs stretched straight in front of her. She closed the panel just as Cordoba and Ian arrived, holding it shut against her shoulder. Ian casually leaned against the panel, acknowledging her presence, and sealing her against discovery. The click was the tonal grace of heaven. Cleo was safe. They had done it.

Sitting in the corner in the dark, Cleo leaned back and rejoiced in the conversation of the men outside. It was over. She had done it. Saved the show. Saved it all. God, she was good. She laughed inwardly at her own ego, but enjoyed it, reveled in it, fed it. It felt good. Was this why Clark didn't mind living as he did?

It was a warm evening, and Cleo was warmer still inside the crate. Warm in body, warm in spirit. Happily she braced herself as the forklift maneuvered into position and raised the crate off the ground for the short ride to the van.

"Do ya want this crate over there?" Cleo heard one of the crewmen yell.

"Naw, we got the animals nice and cozy with us. You keep it."

The crate was hoisted into position and shoved deep into the cargo hold. This van must be half empty, Cleo thought. Then the cargo door was lowered on squeaky ratchets. It slammed shut with a resounding thud to be followed by the sound of the van's engine turning over. Cleo prepared to spend another fifteen minutes in hiding. It would take at least that long to drive to Ian's ranch by freeway, longer on a local route. She settled back into a relatively comfortable position, secure in the privacy of darkness, the prized camera on her lap, a smile on her lips.

The van came to a stop after a reasonable time. Cleo heard the brakes squeal and the driver's door slam. Then it was quiet. Cleo waited. Nothing happened. Apparently, the crew would not unload this van until later. Cleo was patient. Of course, Ian was the only one who knew where she was. He would be along any moment to liberate her and to heap praises on her. She had to be patient. This was nothing like California Investment.

But time dragged on until Cleo was sure almost an hour had passed. It was getting hot in the crate. The air smelled stale. Her costume was still soggy in places, but her hair was dry. She felt no more joy, just uneasiness and nagging worry. Where was she? She had assumed she was parked at Ian's ranch. She could be anywhere. Where was

Ian? Had something happened to him? Had something happened to Clark?

And in the darkness Cleo came to understand what it really meant to be part of Clark's life, to be Clark's wife, waiting, worrying. Oh, where was he, she agonized, thinking up every horrid possibility. She didn't know enough about his work to think logically. She would always be sitting alone in the darkness when it came to his work. And then another unsettling thought hit. What if neither Ian nor Clark cared where she was or how long she waited because film damaged by water was useless? And here she had been basking in her own ego when the mission had actually failed at her hands.

Suddenly, the squeaky ratchets of the door were singing. Cleo did not hear any voices, and she kept silent, maintaining secrecy in the face of the unknown.

Still no sound. Cleo was fearful. She could feel someone enter the cargo hold. She was not alone. She was scared.

She jumped when someone tapped the side of the crate, and she barely suppressed an audible gasp. Who was outside? Who had discovered her? Then she heard, "S'cuse me, ma'am. I'm lookin' for a quick-thinkin' lady," and she nearly choked on relief. Clark, her Clark, was outside—safe, sound and obviously happy in a western fantasy.

"Are you a good guy?" she demanded, as she heard him unfastening the latch. And then the panel swung open, and he was crouched beside her. "Where have you been, good guy?" she said, restraining herself.

"It's a big range, ma'am," he drawled.

"Oh, you crazy fool!" She laughed, throwing her arms around his neck.

He eased her out of hiding, and clasping her waist, hoisted her to a seat on top of the crate.

"I have a bone to pick with you, good guy," she said, holding out the camera in her hand. "Why didn't you tell me about the camera? We could have avoided all this."

"Tell me, quick-thinkin' lady, would you have been scared if you knew?"

Cleo looked at the easygoing figure before her. He was so comfortable in his belief and so right. "Okay, good guy, you win. But this is my western and you get the girl." She pointed a finger in his face.

"Is that so?" he snickered. "Hang on to the camera."

"Hey," Cleo protested as he closed in on her and threw her over his shoulder. "Clark! What are you doing? Clark!"

He carried her, laughing and flapping, across the driveway to the house, where Ian and Nareen were waiting, ready to join the celebration.

"Give Ian the camera," Clark instructed, turning so that Cleo could face Ian.

"Atta girl," Ian said, taking the camera. "I'll have the film developed before Alex gets here. Should be around midnight."

"Did Clark tell you what happened?" Nareen asked Cleo, her eyes dancing in merriment.

"No, what happened? Clark, put me down."

"The commuter van had a flat tire on the freeway, and my husband, the magician, didn't have a jack. Clark had to go out and find him."

Everyone was laughing.

"Clark, put me down," Cleo chimed.

"Now will you two go on an honest honeymoon?" Nareen scolded. "Come on, Clark, you've made Cleo work enough. Take a vacation. You said you were going to Paris.''

"Did you really want to go, Cleo?" Clark asked, glancing over his shoulder at her.

"Clark, put me down," Cleo wailed, spanking him.

Clark looked thoughtful. "Well, Hallaran Mayor invited me to his summer home in Acapulco tonight. Aboard his private jet. I told him I didn't have time. I should have told him I had to change a tire." He smirked at Ian.

"Watch it, Clarkie. You want these pictures developed right," Ian joked. "Seriously, why not take a few days on the beach before you go home?"

Clark considered. "What do you think?" he asked Cleo, patting the back of her thighs.

"Clark, I don't even have a bathing suit."

Ian spoke. "Like I said, Clark, why not take a few days on the beach?" He grinned comically.

Clark eased Cleo off his shoulder. "Okay, quick-thinkin' lady, a day or two in Acapulco. I'll call Hal before he takes off and tell him to expect us tomorrow afternoon. Why don't you take a shower and meet me at the front door in fifteen minutes. We'll kill some time while a magician develops some film." He looked at Ian, breaking into a laugh. "No jack. Geez, Ian."

So Cleo ran into the guest room with Nareen close behind to help undo the costume. It wasn't so bad being Clark's wife, Cleo decided. She could handle it.

EXACTLY FIFTEEN MINUTES LATER, Cleo appeared at the door wearing a plain, long-sleeved blue shirt and the same white skirt from the day before, her shampooed hair in a tight bun. Clark spirited her out of the house and down the back lane. They walked arm in arm beneath a parade of stars toward the carnival on the far acreage of Ian's property. The collection of booths and small rides wreathed with pulsating light bulbs lay in the distance like a magic village.

Cleo was excited, happy and deeply content. She considered it her right to feel this way. She had earned it. She had been a part of Clark's life, and she had not failed. They worked well together. It was obvious to her. It must certainly be obvious to Clark.

Cleo was happier still at the carnival. Beaming with pride, she strolled with Clark like a girl with her best beau at the state fair. He indulged her like a child, solicitous of her every whim. He bought her every fast snack sold. He carried her voluminous cloud of cotton candy, he wiped her fingers, he held her Coke while she ate pepperoni pizza messily with both hands.

It was all uninhibited, adolescent fun. This was the second time Clark had fashioned a holiday for her. He might simply have been rewarding her for service to Intelnet, but Cleo was convinced that his attention far exceeded that of an ambassador for his agency. He did care about her. Maybe he even loved her.

"Look at the Ferris wheel, good guy," Cleo said, pointing.

That was all it took. Clark bought a roll of tickets, and in a rickety, open gondola that creaked its way toward the full moon, Cleo found heaven, snuggled against Clark. There were no confines on her enjoyment, no glass windows. She was free to touch the sky—to touch Clark. This was reality, she thought. They could make a life out of this.

It was an exceptionally dissonant creak that caused both Clark and Cleo to start. Clark looked over the side to judge the hazard of height. Unconcerned, he turned to Cleo with a smile. "Scared?" he asked.

Cleo wound her arms casually about his neck. "How can I be scared if I'm with you?"

Her answer pleased him. He drew closer. His mouth melted over hers as the Ferris wheel slowed, then stopped, their gondola on the very top of the wheel.

"Some kiss," Clark marveled. "Witchcraft."

"No pins." Cleo smiled. Her eyes spoke to him in a tranquil moment and then a bullhorn rasped over the calliope music. "No need to worry, folks. We're having a little problem with the generator. It'll take a few minutes. This only happens once in a blue moon."

Suddenly Clark shifted uncomfortably. Cleo simply leaned against him. There was no hurry. She was suspended in a sea of stars, on top of the world, with Clark by her side in the moonlight. "I don't think that's a blue moon," Cleo mused. She looked up at Clark. He was intent on the moon, the big, luminous ball above.

"Actually, it's an orchid moon," he said, staring solemnly.

Smiling, Cleo rested her head on his shoulder. "Call it an orchid moon, any color you like. When I'm with you, I'm color-blind. And if you don't believe it's a cream cheese moon, I'll agree with you. All I know is that I could stay here forever under your orchid moon."

Clark shot away from her instantly, as if her words were delivered on a branding iron. It was a stranger's face that turned to her, cold and serious, speaking the words that would burn in her brain many times later. "Sooner or later, we have to get off."

Cleo looked at him questioningly, but before she could comprehend his reaction, which grated so against the frolic of the night, he wrested her toward him and kissed her. Something was different in his kiss, his rough manner. Cleo knew it, but didn't understand, didn't try. She held him, loved him, nothing more. The moment he released her, the Ferris wheel moved again.

"Forget the witchcraft," Cleo breathed. "You're the one that's disrupting the generator. But even if you couldn't control electricity, I'd still love you." There she had said it. Her longing found gratification in her penchant for honesty. Her love for him was strong enough to demand this shameless admission, whether it was shared or not.

There was struggle in Clark's face, but it was brief. His words were objective, his delivery detached. "It eases my mind that you are holding up so well in this inconvenience. Fortunately, it's all downhill from here. After Acapulco, I'll take you back to Washington to wait for the end. Next Friday, at the latest, you'll be back in San Francisco."

No words were spoken as the Ferris wheel continued its circle between the earth and the full moon. In the silence, the terrible void, Cleo, neither embarrassed nor ashamed, understood the preview of their future together better than she wanted to. Clark had been very clear, had even resorted to his crisp, detached agency voice. He had sounded more like Edmondsen than Edmondsen.

As the Ferris wheel went around for the final time, the last run before closing, Cleo felt the ring on her finger. She recalled a portion of the wedding ceremony that grew more and more beautiful in memory—"life together goes around and around." But sooner or later they had to get off.

The gondola creaked in its spastic approach to the landing platform as riders disembarked. Cleo watched pairs of carefree people walking away, leaving empty gondolas rocking in their wake. Now it was their turn. Sooner or later they had to get off. This was the unavoidable truth fashioned in Clark's own words. How appropriate. When had she known Clark to do less than what was appropriate?

Cleo held on to Clark's arm on the walk back to Ian's ranch. He did not return her affection, but she clung to him in defiance, proving to him and to herself that it was no crime to love someone who didn't love you. Clark took her hand only when Nareen welcomed them at the door.

"Alex is here," Nareen said amid greetings.

Clark went directly to the den for a conference on the pictures from the Cordoba estate. Cleo saw him walk away from her. Probably forever.

A loneliness came to Cleo as she prepared for bed. The job was simply coming to an end, she reasoned. Maybe Clark had enjoyed her company, even loved her a little...or even a lot. Still it meant nothing. He would never give up his career. What had he called Alex? A sentimentalist. Clark was a man of steel by his own definition. And Cleo would simply have to go back to California Investment and pretend that nothing had happened. But that was impossible.

Last Friday she was just another discontented individual, afraid that life was passing her by. Saturday and Sunday she'd fallen in love, and on Monday and Tuesday she had been promised another life. But sooner or later she had to get off. Be happy, Cleo told herself. She had packed more living in this short time than in years. She had gotten the adventure she had wanted. She became very rational in her thinking, but could not shake off the feeling of being stranded. How could she have come so far and still be nowhere?

CHAPTER TEN

CLARK TURNED the doorknob gently. He knew Cleo would be sleeping. There was a light on. Was she awake? No, fast asleep. She must have left the lamp on for him, or maybe she fell asleep waiting.

He stepped into the room quietly. He needed his code book. He had papers to translate, work to do. But he looked at his Cleopatra, waiflike in the mighty four-poster bed and stopped. He couldn't help it.

She was wearing her cozy flannel nightgown, her face angelic. He wanted more than anything to take her in his arms. She was so precious to him. Would it hurt to tell her? Yes. God, yes.

Suddenly he was aware of how tired he was. He dropped into a wing chair beside the bed without taking his eyes from Cleo. He pressed his fingers together forming a tent for his nose. He must be getting old, he thought. He wasn't sure of anything anymore except that Cleo was beautiful, and he continued to watch her steadily. Actually, he had told her how he felt—on the shore of Lake Tahoe—in a disguised, clever fashion: "Every day Cleopatra means more to me."

How could he have said it and meant it about a woman he had known barely two days? Easy. She was special. And she was no stranger. He had researched her life history, inspected her home and listened to her pour out her heart in earnest the night they drove to Tahoe. Yes, he had done a good job of probing during that ride, trampling on her privacy. She had not even realized that his questions were motivated as much by interest as by professional duty. God, he did his job well.

His mind jumped back to the hours in the car, on the way to Tahoe, in the dark, just before they were married. Geez, he had married her, hadn't he? He could hear her talking, could produce her speech on a transcript. He listened to her sweet little voice again, the honesty, the faith. They were alike in so many ways. He wondered if she sensed that. Probably not. She didn't seem to have much confidence outside her job.

It was a shame she didn't have someone to love her, to take care of her, to make her happy, to share her life. It would be unfair to let her think he could.

So he would let this woman with orchids in her hair go. He owed her for exposing a possible leak in CLEOPATRA, for pulling off the show at the Cordoba estate...for loving him. And he would pay his debt by saying goodbye, remembering her each time he saw an orchid. Thank God where he traveled orchids were rare.

For now, he would let her sleep.

"WAKE UP, CLEO. We have a plane to Acapulco in an hour. I let you sleep to the last minute."

Her eyes opened easily, eager to see Clark. But she caught only a glimpse. Once he was sure that she was awake, he withdrew into the bathroom with his electric shaver. He didn't bother to say good-morning. Cleo saw that his side of the bed was untouched. Undoubtedly, he had been working all night. Of course he was tired, troubled and preoccupied, and had no time for small talk. Still, it hurt that he could not spare her a minute.

Obediently, Cleo sprang from bed to get dressed. Clark had crafted another hasty departure, and she knew her role well. Clark wore a polo shirt, so Cleo also dressed casually. She hurriedly matched a navy-blue wraparound skirt to the blue shirt she had worn last night. She wore the shirt unbuttoned at the throat to show off a shell necklace that might have begun its life in Acapulco. She ran a brush through her hair, then studied her look pointedly. Instinctively, she wound her hair into an efficient knot, the way she wore it to work. The result served her need to control her life again, to reclaim what had been orderly and right from before she'd met the man in the next room.

On course to the Reno airport, the rented Thunderbird cruised over deserted, early morning streets. Alex at the wheel, and Cleo beside him, sat as lifeless as a pair of store mannequins. The silence was stiff and depressing. In deference to Clark, who slumped in the back seat, his eyes closed, Alex did not speak. Judging from Alex's expression, Cleo guessed that the mission was not going well.

She found it easy to conform to the mood. The wedding bouquet, long forgotten, was still on the dash, its withered roses dry, brittle and dead. Cleo began to get angry that she had not been given the chance to say goodbye to Nareen or Ian. She resented being carted around without knowing what was happening. But she couldn't complain. She had agreed to the circumstances. She was getting a free trip to Acapulco. What more could she ask?

Alex double-parked in front of the air terminal, and Clark sprang from the car before it stopped completely to unload the suitcases from the trunk. For an instant, Cleo considered saving the wedding bouquet, but resisted the impulse to snatch it off the dash. It was dead, she told herself. Let it lie. "Goodbye, Alex," she said, releasing the door handle.

She turned in surprise when Alex leaned across the gearshift and caught her elbow. His face was as kind and genuine as she remembered.

"I haven't apologized to you recently," he confided. "What do you say to someone who's more than a good sport? I'm awfully glad I found you."

Oh, to love a sentimentalist. How she wished Clark could speak those words.

Once on the plane, Cleo sought refuge in the infinity of blue sky outside the window. Immersed in a folder of official reading, Clark ignored her from the center of his exclusive world. Cleo knew she could not compete for his attention against Intelnet, which nourished him and gave him life just as California Investment had done for her. It was Wednesday, and Cleo counted nine days remaining on her lease. Eight words rolled over and over in her head. *Sooner or later we have to get off.*

A white Rolls-Royce was waiting at the Acapulco airport to take them down the coast to Hal Mayor's vacation retreat. Clark was still distant on the ride. And again, a window of picturesque scenery, this time drenched with Latin culture, served as Cleo's solace.

Hal's retreat, with tile roof cabanas and palm trees, looked like the grounds of a commercial resort. The foliage was lush and green. The chatter of birds was incessant, and the sea breeze spoke of pounding surf at the ocean's edge.

A stocky gentleman in a ruffled shirt worn over black trousers met the Rolls as it pulled in front of the main house. "*Buenos días, señor, señora. Señor Mayor waits for you. This way, please.*"

They were led through the cool interior of the foyer and through an outdoor passageway to a terrace that overlooked the lawn extending to the stables. Hal Mayor, their affable host, sat beneath the umbrella shade of a patio table like a wealthy tropical plantation owner.

Throwing his newspaper on an empty chair, he rose in greeting, speaking with the slight drawl of his Texas oil background. "Well, Mr. and Mrs. Cannell, how was the flight? I just got out of bed myself. Bring on lunch, Juan. We're all here now."

Hal seated Cleo in the chair that faced the stable yard. "I'm glad I could talk your husband into coming down here," he told her. "He and I have been trading favors for years now in Washington, but I've never had him down for a visit. And I want you to come back, so enjoy yourself, hear? I've got tennis courts, a golf course, beachfront, horses."

Cleo smiled in false appreciation. Possessions were no measure of a man, but men always seemed to think so.

"You have quite a collection of palominos, I see," said Clark, scanning the stables.

"Yes. It's easy to get horses," said Hal. "It's stable help that's hard to come by. When they're not soused in tequila, they're off serenading some sweetheart. I just found out that my man, Miguel, who wouldn't so much as say boo to a goose, let alone a woman, headed up to San Francisco for the weekend and hasn't shown up for work yet."

Cleo wasn't listening to anything Hal said. Her eyes were fixed on a golden-haired figure riding a painted palomino in wide circles in the stable yard. Her heartbeat accelerated through test stages of recognition, and Nareen's philosophy on coincidence overwhelmed her. She could hear Nareen's voice, definite, assured: "People come into your life when you're ready for them." Was it true? Or was it a giant conspiracy of fate that plucked her away from a routine life to orbit the earth with Clark Cannell and fling her back to terra firma at the feet of Perry Paul Spencer III?

"That's my nephew on my sister's side going in circles," Hal explained. "He's an artist. They ride that way, you know. He'll probably join us as soon as he picks up on lunch."

Hal had no sooner spoken, when horse and rider began to gallop toward the terrace. Cleo gripped the table, her heart pounding, her nerves geared for overload. Should she prepare Clark? Hal? Would there be time?

Perry wore eight years nicely, on the body of a man, not a boy, yet he still possessed his poetic quality, his boyish air. Would he recognize her? Should she say something to Clark? Then the sensitive face that had once made her so happy lit up in recognition.

"Cleo Sherlock Holmes!" he said incredulously before dismounting.

What happened next was keenly monitored by Clark. Perry dropped the reins on a hibiscus bush and climbed over the terrace railing, calling out, "Nobody wake me from this dream. A goddess is at hand."

Cleo stood to receive his exuberant greeting, hesitant, embarrassed. A part of her past was running toward her, and she wasn't certain how she should react, how to merge the past with the present, especially since she had no reason of her own to be sitting on Hal Mayor's patio.

Perry lifted her straight up into the air. "Quick, somebody get me a pedestal."

"Perry, you haven't changed!" Cleo exclaimed joyfully.

Setting her to the ground, he took both of her hands. "Whoops. I think I'm in trouble here. I doubt if that ring came from a cereal box."

Clark stood, extending his hand. "Clark Cannell. Cleo's husband," came the voice, firm and possessive.

Cleo immediately felt guilty for more than just her failure to make the introduction. "This is Perry Spencer, Clark. We went to school together."

Perry took the chair opposite Cleo, and when all the grinning excitement subsided, Clark seized control of the conversation. "So you and Cleo were at Berkeley together? Did you know Ian of Intrigue, too?"

Cleo caught Clark's purpose. "Perry was a transfer student," she explained. "Ian had moved on before Perry came to Berkeley." Her answer was chronologically correct, but she knew she was on thin ice. Fortunately, Perry was much too engrossed in the sight of her to question what was to him meaningless.

"I'm beginning to think my wife knew everyone," Clark quipped, winking at Hal.

"You always find out after the wedding, old boy," Hal bellowed, and the subject was closed.

Throughout lunch, Clark and Hal talked of international politics. Though she smiled and nodded her head appropriately, Cleo paid no attention to what was being said. Perry, too, was not following the conversation. They both went through the motions of eating while contemplating each other.

Perry's eyes never left Cleo. Whenever she looked at him, which was infrequently because she could not handle his stare, he smiled as if his fondest wish had come true. When their eyes connected, electricity would pass between them, and Cleo would smile shyly and blush. Eventually, Hal became uncomfortable with his nephew's infatuation with the wife of a guest and began to force Perry into the conversation.

Cleo learned that Perry managed a string of art dealerships for Hal, traveled a good deal, but made his home on the estate in Acapulco. Cleo had known there was wealth in Perry's family, but with no detail. Perry had never gotten along with his father, and this close association with his uncle told her that the rift was now permanent.

After the fruit compote had been cleared from the table, Perry said, "You still don't know who Cleo is, do you, uncle? Look at her."

Cleo tensed under Hal's scrutiny. She felt Clark's knee press against hers. What was happening?

Slowly, Hal's belly began to bounce. "Well, well, so it is. You fooled me with the upswept hair. Well, honey, I'd say we've been good friends for about six years now."

Cleo was at a loss. She looked at Hal with sweet ignorance, resisting the urge to turn to Clark for guidance.

"I painted a mural for Uncle Hal's den," Perry explained, and Cleo hid her relief. Clark withdrew his knee.

"It's funny how the hair makes such a difference," Hal remarked, still studying Cleo. "Come, honey, I'll show it to you." He took her hand.

Perry jumped up to take her other hand, saying enthusiastically, "You'll like it, Cleo. It's not a nude."

Clark had no choice but to tag along behind.

The den was cool and dark. The only light came from the aquarium tanks built into the walls. The mural was behind Hal's desk. It was a collection of nymphs gathered around a bathing pool. The nymph in the foreground was almost lifesize. She wore a white toga, had purple wisteria in her hair and carried a tray of globular yellow fruit. Other than the artist's pleasure at ripe breasts to complement the ripe fruit, the nymph was Cleo.

"You've watched over my shoulder on every deal I've made, honey," Hal teased.

"It's a spectacular painting, Perry," Cleo exclaimed without exaggeration. "What should I thank you for first, leaving my clothes on or the silicone implants?"

Hal led the round of laughs, but Perry put in quickly, "Cleo, will you have time to see my studio before you leave?"

"This afternoon would be good," said Clark soberly from the back of the room. "I'm going to persuade Hal to show me the rest of his horses."

Hal beamed with pride.

PERRY'S STUDIO was the only structure on the estate not of Spanish architecture. About five hundred yards behind the main hacienda, it was perched like a Malibu beach house on the edge of a promontory, which presided over the rocky shoreline and buttressed a long stretch of sandy beach.

"You certainly have no shortage of inspiration here," Cleo observed, her hand sweeping the ocean view.

Perry nodded his head, his golden curls shining in the sun. He opened the sliding glass doors to let the sea breeze and unfiltered sun into the studio. "Scenery is cheap, Cleo. The people I care about are the best inspiration, the people I know now—" he paused "—and the people I used to know."

It was a nostalgic remark, placing Cleo on guard. She had been studiously avoiding Perry's eyes, which constantly looked at her in awe. Smiling, she involved herself in Perry's paintings, some completed, but most in progress, on a series of easels. The colors were bright, the moods lively. As always, the painting encouraged a happiness as natural as a handful of wildflowers picked by a child. This was Perry, full of childlike qualities, impish, innocent, spontaneous. When he walked out of her life, he had taken his sunshine with him. By studying the paint-dashed canvases, Cleo found a vista in which to view the past and all the wonderful memories of being with Perry, while avoiding all of the complications of being in the room with him.

"Is that Sather Gate?" Cleo paused before an abstract.

"Yes, and that's you," he answered pointing to a little blob of purple. He was still a promoter of whimsical fantasy.

"Uncanny resemblance," Cleo remarked. She wondered if that purple blob had been the moment's invention, or if it had been painted with her in mind. Should she flatter herself into believing that after all these years she still influenced his work? In a moment she had no doubt.

"I've missed you," she heard him say sincerely. That was Perry. No false pretenses. Not afraid of honest emotion. "I told myself if I ever saw you again, I'd beg you to spend your life with me."

The safe bubble from which Cleo viewed the past was broken. The memory was no longer pasted to the canvas but standing right beside her. Not now, Perry, she groaned inwardly. Not here and not now. How could she relate to him honestly when she had no true identity?

Reading the discomfort on Cleo's face, Perry easily shifted the conversation. She was grateful for his sensitivity. "Well, Cleo Sherlock—" his name for her since he had seen C.S. Holmes on her mailbox "—so you married a guy from Intelnet this weekend. Intelnet is pretty heavy stuff. Sometimes spy stuff. Do you have his and hers trench coats?''

Cleo laughed, as always. Corny humor. She loved it.

''I'm very happy for you, Cleo Sherlock. I know first-hand how hard it was to convert an accounting student into a connoisseur of life. So if a guy can blast you out of your regimen in one week, straight to a Reno quickie, he must be the right guy for you. Just one thing bothers me. Why should I know Ian of Intrigue?''

Cleo tensed, her mind turning furiously. Perry was no fool. He had been cognizant at the lunch table, but comment had not been a priority with him.

''I knew every friend you had in school,'' he continued softly, ''and Ian of Intrigue was not one of them. Believe me, I'd have remembered him.''

Cleo was caught. What could she do? She couldn't manufacture a suitable lie. And if she held to her story there would be no end to Perry's skepticism. She swallowed hard. ''Perry, as one of my dearest friends, let this lie between us. I may have known Ian. You were not at Berkeley when he was around. It's important that you accept what I say.'' She searched Perry's face as he reflected on her words.

He nodded cooperatively. ''Okay, if it's important to you, then you have my word I'll never bring it up again. That much I can do for you. Never doubt that I care for you.'' He lowered his gaze to the floor, signaling the subject was closed, then switched topics cheerfully. ''Let me make you a drink. How about my old Palette Sunrise? Bet you don't remember it.''

Enthusiastically, Cleo recited as Perry nodded his head, ''The orangiest of oranges, ah...the reddest of tomatoes, the yellowest of bananas in the...in the...''

''Clearest...''

"Clearest of mineral waters!"

"But it's better now. I own a blender."

Laughing, they were nineteen years old again.

PERRY WALKED CLEO back to the main house at seven-thirty, the appointed time for dinner. He did not stay. He had a prior engagement with a friend in Acapulco. Cleo did not ask the gender of his friend, but found herself speculating as to the type of relationship he might have, feeling both guilty and jealous.

Juan greeted Cleo in the hallway. "*Señora*, we have dinner for you. Señor Mayor and your husband eat to-night in Acapulco City."

The announcement surprised her, and her pride was stung that Clark had excluded her. Then she realized it was a godsend to spend some time alone. She needed privacy to sort out her jumbled feelings.

But it was not easy to think at dinner. She sat alone at a long table set formally for one. The silence in the dining room hung as heavily as the large iron chandeliers over the table. House servants, in stilted attendance, made her uncomfortable. She would have been happier sitting on a stool in the kitchen, listening to the clang of pots and pans and unhushed speech.

A waiter was stationed formally in the archway as liaison to the kitchen. When Cleo's napkin slipped from her lap, he retrieved it from the tiled floor in an instant. In another instant the woman in charge of the table emerged from the kitchen with a new one. Cleo felt conspicuous with all this attention, developing the impression from the whispers in Spanish that the staff pitied the abandoned wife. It was, admittedly, nothing but foolish self-consciousness, but it bothered her. Perry would chide her for it. What would Clark do?

She had grown accustomed to the fact that Perry lived here. Spending time with him in the studio had smoothed her acceptance of this blessing in seeing him again. But coming to terms with all the events that had brought her to this reunion boggled the mind. It had to be some quirk in the position of the moon and stars that they should meet again after all this time...here...and now. And it was certainly some quirk that Cleo found she was torn emotionally between two men. Both special. One from the past, one from...the future? Oh, where would it all lead?

Plates arrived and plates were carried away. Cleo ate at a dignified pace, judging it improper to swallow each course at breakneck pace when such effort and ceremony had gone into preparation and presentation.

The finale, a tapioca flan, took her a while to eat. It was a compulsion with her to chew every bead of gelatin. She smiled to herself. Perry understood that compulsion. In fact, Perry understood every facet of her personality. How could she have thought that she and Clark could be a natural pair? If she had known that Perry would slip back into her future, would she have fallen in love with Clark last weekend?

IT WAS CLOSE to nine o'clock when Cleo went up to the guest suite in the east wing. There was light visible from under the door. Cleo entered expectantly and was happy to find Clark reading a newspaper. He was already comfortable in the twin bed closest to the balcony. He was certainly adept at filling a room with his casual presence, conquering a foreign space by his dominance, she decided. The twin beds, however, were a dismay, and Clark's response to her greeting, a grunt from behind the newspaper, even more dismal. Conversation was out of the question.

Cleo moved unobtrusively about the room before retreating to the shower. She noticed, too, that Clark had left her suitcase untouched. It was to be separate closets. Separate beds.

She dallied in the bathroom as long as she could in hopes that Clark's mood would change. However, Clark was no more sociable when she emerged. He was still nursing a sour disposition.

Resigned, Cleo turned down the bright floral bedspread, slipped into bed and began to study the ceiling. She had seen Clark moody and withdrawn before, but this time, she felt hostility on brew. Why? He was obviously tired, but fatigue would not explain this brand of crankiness.

Knowing that Cleo had slipped into bed, Clark folded his newspaper into a tight rectangle and slapped it on the nightstand. It was time for him to speak. He wanted an ugly scene. Cleo wouldn't understand. Maybe someday she would. Either way, it wouldn't matter. In one week he'd never see her again.

"I trust you had fun with Perry today," he said, a chilly sarcasm injected into his already cold tone.

So that was the key to his sulking, Cleo thought. Jealousy. A macho reaction to encroachment on affection. She might have been flattered if it had not been for the condescending tone he employed. He used it, that hulk Edmondsen had used it. She hated the pompousness of the Intelnet delivery. Even Alex eased in and out of a British accent to serve his purpose.

At Cleo's silence, Clark made a demanding inquiry, "What did you do?"

Cleo raged inside. He had suggested, no, *insisted* that she and Perry go to the studio together. Still, Cleo knew she owed him a report in as much detail as he would require for the sake of their official purpose.

"We just spent the afternoon at his studio and talked over old times," she answered. "Needless to say, I'm shocked to find him here." Clark said nothing. "Small world," Cleo added for lack of anything better to say, trying to pull Clark into conversation, wishing to unburden herself, reaching to him so that he might help her sort out her feelings.

"Small world for you, at least," Clark mocked.

Cleo was shocked, angry. How had their relationship deteriorated so badly? What had she done? They were back in the antagonistic pattern set the night they first met. And as with that night, Cleo held her tongue, pretending to be unscathed by the verbal stab.

She wondered if she should report to him how she had handled Perry's question on Ian of Intrigue. No, she decided. Why should she hold a friend's word of honor up for inspection by Clark Cannell? Let him believe he had laid the issue to rest with his quick thinking at the table. Why should she inform him that some people weren't fooled by the expert smoothness of a Clark Cannell?

While she was feeling powerful in her defiance, Clark switched off the lights, and the darkness took her by surprise. She didn't think their conversation, if it could be called that, was over. "Good night," she said, after a few moments, more as a reflex than anything.

There was no response. Had he fallen asleep already? Jealousy aside, Cleo seriously wondered what was bothering him, what his problem was.

"By the way." His voice shot across the darkness. "We'll be staying here until Sunday, so be sure to use the time to your advantage."

Cleo was enraged, but too absorbed to fight. Clark had thrown the information to her as an afterthought. He could have spared her the courtesy of a discussion. Suddenly, she couldn't care less what was bothering him. It was his problem, a problem of a rude, self-centered man. She rolled over and let sleep embrace her vigorously.

CHAPTER ELEVEN

THE NEXT MORNING Cleo awoke alone. It was Thursday, she noted on her mental calendar. Eight more days to go. She wasn't sure this morning whether she was counting the days in celebration or in dread. She dressed quickly and went down to the dining room, certain of catching up with Clark at breakfast. His mood would determine her day. She was ready to forget last night.

But Clark was not at breakfast. Juan informed her that Clark and Hal had gone deep-sea fishing early that morning with no specified time of return. Juan pointed out the assorted Danish pastries and fruit on the buffet table and asked if she had an order for the kitchen while a waiter poured her a cup of coffee.

Declining anything further, Cleo sat to breakfast, embarrassed that she could not keep track of her husband, imagining anew that Hal's servants were twittering. The pastry was sweet and flaky, but with each bite, Cleo felt more self-conscious and more foolish.

"Hello. I don't blame you for not going fishing." It was Perry standing in the archway, appearing as he always had, to free her from her conventional worries. He selected a cluster of grapes from the buffet and joined her at the table. "Let me show you Acapulco," he offered, popping a grape into his mouth while the waiter poured his coffee. "I've single-handedly set tourism ten years ahead in Acapulco."

Cleo didn't doubt it.

"WE'LL BE CRUISING at a speed of forty-five miles per hour at an altitude of about a foot," he told her as his fiery red Alfa Romeo convertible headed to the city. He drove along Costera Miguel Aleman, the scenic coastal highway, pointing out the ultramodern luxury hotels and beaches along the way. Cleo liked the melodic sound of *playa*, the Spanish word for beach, and when she told Perry that Playa Condesa sounded much better than Condesa Beach, he promised to take her to all the *playas* on the peninsula. What was more, he began to replace English words with Spanish words, and by the time Perry parked his *carro* at the city center, Cleo had acquired a vocabulary large enough for prime-time Spanish TV.

Perry led Cleo on a walking tour of downtown Acapulco. He was a lively guide to local custom and history. Of course, he embellished each tourist attraction for interest. His imagination knew no bounds. For Cleo, it was just like old times.

"See that Moorish-looking cathedral in the square?" he asked.

"Yes."

"It's actually constructed from parts of a scrapped movie theater."

"Really, Perry. And I suppose the first mass of the day is shown at a discount with popcorn."

"*¿No lo crees?* You don't believe me? *Señora*, I speak the truth. I'll prove it." He stopped several people on the square, who confirmed his story. Perry was a natural sidewalk comedian. He made everyone laugh. Cleo noted that his humor was very different from Clark's. Perry put on a show for the world, whereas Clark stood back, reserved, urbane.

Cleo's analytical mind worked overtime. In addition to keeping pace with Perry's colorful narration, learning Spanish, absorbing sights and sounds, Cleo could not stop comparing Perry to Clark. It became a frustrating obsession. To what end, she scolded herself. Still, she could not stop.

They walked the busy streets, dodging the *calandrias*, decorated horse-drawn carriages, and wandering through narrow side lanes lined with curio shops and merchandise stalls. Perry did the trailblazing. It would have been so natural to take his hand, but Cleo was not free to do so. And if she were free, could she take his carefree hand and forget the strength and power she felt in Clark's?

All around tourists were bug-eyed, pointing, examining merchandise and whispering haggling strategies to one another. Cleo did not find the shopping compelling. She merely scanned the merchandise with little interest. She was juggling too many things in her mind to consider buying. Besides, she wasn't sure she wanted something tangible from Acapulco. She was just walking through, as one-dimensional as a travel poster, lulled by the comfort of the past, while living a lie in the present.

She did, however, think of Josh and Mira when she came upon souvenir pencil cups. They were perfect for the office. She must have mumbled out loud.

"What?" Perry asked. "Are you keeping your job?"

"Ah, yes. I'll probably just do consulting on a project-by-project basis. I haven't worked out the details," Cleo fabricated breezily.

Perry's face was alive with humor. "I've got a detail for you, kiddo. You married a guy who lives on the east coast. Your job is on the west coast. There's a lot of country in between."

It's a big range, ma'am, Cleo heard Clark say.

"It'll work out," Cleo said casually, examining a pencil cup. "Clark travels a lot." She was not uncomfortable with Perry, so the innocent lies rolled off her tongue easily. He was not with her to judge or punish. She was relaxed.

Perry shook his head in a laugh. "Can't give it up, can you, Cleo Sherlock? You've got too many work genes, spelled g-e-n-e."

"Per-ry." Cleo held up her palm, laughing. "I know what kind of genes you mean." He used to say it all the time.

"Well, I suppose you just can't stop after eight years of breathing all that rarefied air on the twenty-fifth floor."

Cleo threw Perry a bright look. He had remembered.

"Actually, I'm on the fifty-first floor now."

"Oh, oxygen! Oxygen!" he cried. "Hey, don't give me one of those looks." He rested his arm on her shoulder and gave her a brotherly squeeze. "I'm impressed. Really."

"You?"

"Really." He was shaking his head like a big, panting dog.

"Then you're really getting old, kid. I wouldn't expect you to be impressed."

"Heck, yes, I'm impressed. Next you're gonna tell me it's only a forty-five-story building. Right?"

Cleo laughed. He was corny, so corny.

"Do you ride the cable car to work?" he asked.

The cable car. Cleo knew instantly what he was thinking of. Right after she had been hired through a campus interview, she had dragged an unimpressed but amused Perry into San Francisco and reverently pointed out her destiny, the twenty-fifth floor of California Investment, as they rode the cable car up California Street past the building. Great fun.

"You're smiling," Perry noted. "Well, do you take a cable car every morning?"

"No, I walk," she answered truthfully.

Perry threw back his head and guffawed. "You walk," he repeated. "Should have known. More efficient, huh? Cable car too slow for you?" He shrugged. "It's definitely in the genes. Do you take the elevator to the fifty-first floor or do you scale the side of the building to avoid the crowds?"

Cleo gave Perry a comic look of exasperation—just as she used to. It was like old times, only now she related his teasing to something she might say to Clark. If Clark were ever annoyed by a congested elevator, she envisioned him dropping out a window and rappeling down the side of the building.

They had been moving slowly through the shop and on completion of the round, Cleo stepped out the door.

"Hey, aren't you going to get the pencil cups?" Perry reminded her.

"Naw." She shook her head. What's the big deal about the fifty-first floor, she thought. Who needed all that corporate gray when here the midday sun was shining bright, and the earth was warm and golden? No, she would not waste time picking out something to take back to California Investment. "Some other time," she explained.

Perry nodded. His expression told her that he enjoyed her company immensely. "Where are you living these days?" he asked as they passed rows of clothing shops.

"I have a house in Oakland."

Perry grinned. "That's west coast. I mean east coast."

"Clark has a condo in Washington, D.C.—just off the Potomac, I understand," she mentioned casually, stopping to pick up a piece of pottery from an outdoor display.

"You haven't seen it?"

"No. You know we just got married and we're—"

"Yo. I get the picture," he interrupted her. "You're traveling right now to the east coast." He tilted his head quizzically. "So tell me about the west coast. Where in Oakland?"

"The hills."

He broke loudly into a Rodgers and Hammerstein song, "The hills are alive..." Cleo was yanking on his sleeve and he stopped, nodding to the English-speaking tourists who had looked his way.

"I can't take you anywhere," Cleo scolded him jokingly, as they continued a leisurely stroll down the street.

"You have a view of the bay from your house?"

Cleo nodded.

"Can you see the California Investment tower from your window?"

Cleo nodded.

"Aha! Good reason to buy in the hills. That way you can keep an eye on the office. All right. All right! Don't give me that look. Just kidding. Really, it's a great location. You can catch the Fourth of July fireworks without leaving home."

Cleo nodded, not admitting that she had owned the town house through two Fourths of July and had never watched the fireworks displays. Perry would have made an event out of it, cooking up popcorn, maybe wearing a special hat for the occasion. She remembered the time Perry had taken her to see the fireworks on the San Francisco marina. They sat on a blanket on the grass, and

Perry narrated each burst of light, complete with honest "oohs" and "aahs." After the display, the traffic jam was unbelievable, but Perry wasn't disturbed. Instead of inching across the Bay Bridge, he navigated his beat-up Volkswagen to Fisherman's Wharf, and they shared a monstrous ice-cream sundae at the Ghirardelli Chocolate Factory. She could almost taste that ice cream now. Did Clark like ice cream?

"You aren't buying anything," Perry said to her after they had combed through a few more shops. "Don't you want anything for your house? Either coast?" He pointed left and right. "Wrought silver is an excellent buy in Acapulco."

"Some other time, Perry."

"Gee, were you always this anti-souvenir? Don't you have any junk in your house?"

She grinned, looking at him sideways. "I have a piano." She and Perry had frequently clowned over a make-believe piano. She would pretend to be at the keyboard; he would pretend to be the vampy torch singer perched on top.

Perry's eyes got wide. "A piano?" He grabbed an imaginary microphone out of the air.

"No singing!" Cleo commanded with playful authority, grabbing hold of his sleeve again.

"No singing?" he implored meekly. His voice got very tiny. "Not even one itty-bitty little song? Just one?"

"No singing," Cleo repeated, trying very hard to remain in character and not laugh.

"Well, I never liked pianos very much anyway," Perry said. "They're so predictable—eighty-eight keys, some black, some white. You need a purple keyboard."

"Oh, I do declare." Cleo sighed theatrically. "I just don't know how I live without a purple piano." She put her hand to her brow, a long-suffering southern belle.

They laughed together, and Perry's eyes worshiped her. Oh, Perry, she thought. If it had worked out differently, if he hadn't gone to Athens and drifted away, they could have had Fourth of July at her house, popcorn, a purple piano. And California Investment would simply have meant a good job and a good income.

Could she put in a bid for the old days? Perry hadn't changed. But she knew she had. Could she really let him divert her with whimsy as freely as she had done before? They were adults now with adult responsibilities. She imagined Perry turning off her alarm clock someday when she had to be on time for a meeting, just because it suited his latest thoughts on sleep.

Perry was now telling her about a musician friend of his who made custom guitars in all colors for rock singers. He started to describe the process in specifics and Cleo drifted.

"Oh, my goodness," Cleo said suddenly, stopping to admire a pair of Taxco silver candlesticks. They were simple and strong, attracting her attention like a beacon.

Perry sprang into action. "I don't believe it. That look in your eye. I smell a purchase here. I was beginning to worry. I've never brought anyone down here who didn't buy something."

Cleo followed through on her impulse, and Perry, through a long animated discourse, which invigorated the merchant, got her a great bargain.

Continuing to walk through the city, they made lunch out of two bottles of Mexican beer, their appetite destroyed by the heat.

"How's Cassy?" Perry asked.

"Oh, didn't I tell you? She's married and living in San Luis Obispo. Her husband is a dentist. Stan Pring."

Perry's eyes grew wide. "Pring? Painless Pring? That's rich. Oops, sorry."

"Oh, feel free. I don't much like Stan."

"That makes you and Cassy even," Perry concluded. "Cassy never liked me."

"She just didn't know you, Perry. You only saw her when she visited. What? Three weekends?"

"She would tell you three weekends was enough of me. Did Cassy keep her job?"

"Yup. Until the baby. I have a niece who's about six months old now. I only saw her once and didn't get to hold her as much as I wanted. I was on a stopover from a business meeting in L.A. I get pictures and I listen to gurgling on the phone."

Perry was not smiling. "Cleo...go see the kid."

She knew what he meant. He was right. "Cassy expects me at Christmas. I go every year," she explained.

Cleo spoke confidently and Perry backed off. Cleo was married now. He didn't have the right to rearrange her priorities. "What's the kid's name?" he asked. "No, no, wait. Let me guess...." His brow knitted. "I've got it. Cassistania Pring."

"Jane," Cleo stated clearly and waited for his reaction.

His eyebrows shot up. "Jane Pring? Just Jane Pring? Mother Cassandra, Aunt Cleopatra, and just plain Jane Pring?" He shook his head in disbelief. "It must have been Stan's idea."

"It was Cassy's—no more weighty, exotic names. She was tired of lugging around her own name, listening to people tell her how unusual it was."

"Aw," Perry said. He was genuinely disappointed. "I liked the tradition. It never affected you to be Cleo, did it?"

"Never," Cleo said honestly. "But it may have gotten me the role of an Egyptian queen in a fifth grade play. Naw, it was because the teacher trusted me with the long lines. I had the best memory in the class." Her mind momentarily turned to Clark. "I guess I never considered my name unusual." She flashed a smile at Perry and continued. "Remember that TV program when we were kids?"

"Yeah, *The People's Choice*," he chuckled, already picking up on her reference. "Cleo was the name of that basset hound. Long ears." He jiggled Cleo's earlobe. "Smart dog though. Good role model."

Cleo laughed and took a sip of beer. She reconsidered what she had told Perry—that her name had never had a significant effect on her. What a gross misstatement. Her name had brought Clark Cannell to her, and Perry to her once again.

By late afternoon, Perry and Cleo had walked across town. They stood at the cliffs of La Quebrada, the site of Acapulco's famous high-dive attraction. Perry explained that each evening by torchlight, a diver plunged off the cliff into the rocky cove below. More than just a precise dive, the trick was to time the surf so that the water level would be high enough to offer protection against the treacherous rocks.

"Can you imagine, Cleo, leaping off that cliff and hitting the water at close to one hundred miles per hour? To some it's a thrill, to me it's suicide."

Yes, Cleo thought, to some it would be a thrill. She must mention it to Clark.

Later Perry hailed a cab to take them back to his car at city center. Then, Perry drove to the Shangri-La Restaurant. In typical Perry style, he had chosen Chinese cuisine to conclude a tour of Acapulco.

"Are you sure you've set tourism ten years ahead in Acapulco?" Cleo asked him over sizzling rice soup.

"*Sí, señora*, and at least twelve years ahead in Beijing."

Cleo laughed a long, contented laugh. Could she build a life with Perry and be happy? Possibly. But only if she didn't love Clark.

IT WAS AFTER EIGHT O'CLOCK when Perry and Cleo got back to the estate. Hal and Clark were still out and that was fine with Cleo. She entered the guest suite, glad to be alone. She threw her purse on the bed, and herself after it, sprawling crosswise, stretching her legs, her toes. She expected to feel a wave of exhaustion, but her body actually felt invigorated. It was her mind that was tired.

She sought relief by settling into the spa. She did not use the water jets; she wanted peace, calm. She sprinkled bubble bath into the water until there was a thick foam over the surface. Deliberately, she cleared her mind and floated away on the fragrance of crackling bubbles. She would conduct no more feasibility studies on either Clark Cannell or Perry Spencer.

When Cleo was fully relaxed, she heard what she thought was a knock on the door of the suite. If she hadn't left the bathroom door ajar, she would not have heard the intrusive sound. She listened. Yes, it was unmistakably a knock. She considered ignoring it. She was much too comfortable to move.

"Cleo?" a voice called along with the knock.

"I'm in the bath," Cleo shouted to be heard.

"My contact lens solution. In your purse. Can I get it?"

"Come in," she shouted, recognizing Perry's voice and feeling very unrefined in carrying on a conversation by yelling from one room to another.

Perry entered. "Sorry to disturb you," he said, standing out of view of the spa. "I won't peek."

"You better not, kid," Cleo joked. "My purse is on the bed. Help yourself." She settled back.

Just then she remembered the gun in her purse. She did not want Perry to find it. He would want to know what had prompted this strange new habit. "Wait, Perry!" she shouted, shooting out of the tub like reverse lightning.

She didn't know how it happened—it just happened. She fell backward with a resounding splash against the water, and with a small scream, she felt herself go under. Only the generous size of the spa prevented her from cracking her head on the tiled perimeter.

When she surfaced amid the layer of bubble bath, gasping for breath, Perry was crouched at the edge of the spa. "What happened, Cleo?"

"I fell in," she said incredulously, her face bearing the astonished expression of a bathed cat.

"Are you hurt?" Perry asked, urgently placing both hands on her shoulders.

"No, I just fell in," Cleo said in a comical daze. "Take me back to La Quebrada."

They both laughed.

"Forget it." Perry pointed to her reflection in the mirror as the foam on her head descended over her ears. "You look like an outtake from *The Giant Bathtub That Ate Cleveland*." They exploded into large fits of rollicking laughter. They could not have guessed how long Clark had been in the room.

Perry was the first to notice. He stood immediately, extremely conscious of his wet hands. "This is not what it looks like," he ventured sheepishly.

"It's okay, Perry. Hand me that towel," Cleo said quickly.

Clark was silent. He remained as impartial and imposing as a monolith.

"I'll just be going," Perry mumbled with his head down, hoping his swift exit would set the matter straight.

Quickly securing the towel around her in a sarong, Cleo ran after Perry, scooped up her purse and caught up with him at the door. "Your contact solution," she said, giving him the plastic bottle from her purse.

When he was gone, Cleo turned apologetically to Clark. Like Perry, she felt as if she had misbehaved. Clark didn't say anything. He was leaning against the far wall, arms folded across his chest with an air of superiority. Clark could make people so comfortable. He could also make them squirm.

Cleo started to walk toward him in small steps, speaking in a singsong, gesturing constantly. "Perry came up for his contact solution. You see, I carried it in my purse today.... I was in the tub, so I told him the purse was on the bed and to go ahead and get it...." She knew she sounded ridiculous, but she was getting no feedback from Clark. Why didn't he stop her inane chatter? He just stood there staring. He was possibly enjoying her discomfort. "I remembered the gun. So I jumped out of the tub. I lost my footing and I fell in. It was really stupid." Oh, good, she thought. A smile was beginning to curl his lips. "Perry heard the splash and came to see if I was all right and it was all so stupid, well, it was hilarious!"

Her explanation finished, she now stood directly before him, looking up at him. He must be teasing me, Cleo thought. "Clark?" she said, tilting her head.

He was looking at the swell of her breasts above the line of the towel. Slowly, he reached out and traced a finger seductively over the top of her breasts where foam from the bubble bath still clung. Cleo drew a breath in anticipation.

Then he held her gaze as a mocking smile charged with sexual energy spread across his face, and he deposited the dab of foam on the top of her nose. With one eyebrow raised, he said with smooth arrogance, "Did you hear me ask you what happened?"

Standing like a mute clown, Cleo watched him swagger away. She was dumbfounded. Clark unbuttoned his shirt and tossed it to a chair. He was getting ready for bed; the subject was obviously closed.

Finally, Cleo whined in exasperation. "I don't understand you, Clark. You haven't said three words to me since we arrived in Acapulco. What's bothering you? Are you worried that my friendship with Perry is ruining our charade?"

A low laugh rumbled in his throat. He let her stew for a minute. "I'm not worried, Cleo. Have fun with your little schoolboy."

Cleo was enraged. How dare he disparage her dearest friend, and furthermore, stand there parading his remarkable chest, proudly implying that no amount of indiscretion on her part could damage their contrived marriage. In short, he was saying he had no competition. Such arrogance. Ego.

"You are . . . so filled with your own self-importance," Cleo sputtered in anger. Her expression hardened into a cold, accusatory stare. "If I were you, Clark Cannell, I'd worry. I'd sit myself down and ask myself jf anyone ever really loved me. Is there any reason that anyone would?''

He looked a little strange. She didn't stop to figure it out. She went into the bathroom and slammed the door. Seething with fury, she resumed her bath, certain that she caused steam to rise out of the cool water. The bubbles were melting, and she kept pounding the remaining clumps of foam into the water.

Later, as anger subsided, Cleo regretted what she had thrown at Clark. She had wanted to hurt him. Apparently she could be cruel, too. She winced with embarrassment, recalling her words. They were spiteful. They were vindictive. And, worst of all, they were untrue.

CHAPTER TWELVE

FRIDAY PROMISED TO BE a repeat performance of Thursday. Cleo woke to find Clark's bed empty. She knew the routine. Get up. Get dressed. Go see Juan.

But there were no routines in her dizzying travels with Clark Cannell, she conceded, when she found him at the breakfast table with Hal. It was a welcome surprise. She joined them cheerfully, but soon felt like the unsuccessful applicant to an exclusive club, men only. Mayor was congenial enough, but patronizing. His courtesy was overdone. Cleo concluded that she did not like the man. Deep beneath all that good-old-boy affability lay a well of guile that was a long way from depletion.

And though Clark was no clone of Hal Mayor, Cleo soon held him in equal distaste as she watched him mowing across his plate of eggs, ham and potatoes, in lively conversation with Hal. If Clark could thrive in the company of Hal Mayor then he and Hal had to be kindred spirits. But Cleo was not ignorant of the flaw in her reasoning. If she were to measure the man by the friends he kept, then what of Alex? Nareen? Ian? It was apparent that she was just angry at Clark and willing to fault him at any opportunity.

Hal finished his breakfast first and spent a good deal of time appraising Cleo over his coffee cup. He seemed amused.

Then Clark gulped the last of his orange juice and thrust his chair back from the table. He and Hal stood to leave, in unspoken understanding.

"Where are you going?" Cleo heard herself ask, appalled at how pathetic she sounded.

Hal and Clark exchanged glances as if to acknowledge a mutual joke.

"Be a good girl, Cleo," Clark said.

Hal winked. "Perry's at the stables."

Once again, Cleo sat abandoned at the breakfast table under the watchful eyes of the servants.

LATER THAT MORNING, Cleo and Perry were riding horses side by side on the beach. The reins rested loosely and uselessly in Cleo's hands as her docile steed, Marina, plodded at the water's edge, launching into flight the sea gulls that dotted the sand.

The horseback ride had been impromptu. Cleo had flown directly from humiliation at breakfast to Perry. Had she planned the ride she would have worn slacks. Now she was unconcerned that her cotton skirt with its ruffle hem was hiked up around her thighs. It was modest enough for a hot day. The salty sea breezes felt good against her skin, but it was Perry's touch that sparked a stronger sensation.

His hand brushed her thigh as he took hold of her calf. "I didn't adjust the stirrups correctly for you. Your foot isn't resting right," he said with a frown.

"It hardly matters, Perry. I'm only going along for the ride." The nonchalance in Cleo's voice belied her unsettled emotions.

Perry's hand lingered at her ankle as he glanced up, and their eyes met in a way Cleo knew they could not, should not. Her guard was down and surely Perry could see. He was so very near, so very real.

Recovering, Cleo gazed out over the ocean, suddenly very interested in the horizon, but Perry's fingertips found the base of her chin and brought her back. She looked into his face. He was squinting in the sunlight.

"What are you doing here?" he asked seriously.

The sun beat mercilessly upon Cleo, leaving no shade to hide behind, no place to park the truth. Her lips parted as she watched Perry, sweetly, incredulously. Then she stared straight ahead, taking a fresh grip on the useless reins.

"Cleo, I don't buy it," he persisted, and Cleo continued to stare ahead. "What's your connection to Cannell?"

Blazes, Perry! she thought. She really didn't know what her connection was. Consciously and subconsciously, that very subject had racked her brain since her arrival in Acapulco. But, of course, the official cover, no matter how insignificant and immaterial she deemed it at this moment, was the issue at stake.

"Clark is my husband," she uttered blandly, feigning interest in a low-flying bird.

Perry would not play her game. He eyed her skeptically. "Let me tell you what I make of it. I see a guy who works with Intelnet, who certainly would suffer no lack of female companionship, who doesn't pay you the slightest attention, who couldn't care less when a former lover is caught with his naked wife. I can see the style of a flashy coast-to-coast marriage, but you, Cleo Sherlock, don't fit."

Cleo bristled. Why didn't she fit, her thoughts raged. Because her life was too dull, too boring? She was in no humor to be ridiculed for being conventional.

"Perry, Clark is my husband, whom I chose to marry," she stated definitively, as if losing her patience with a tiresome topic. The tension seemed to subside.

"I'm sorry, Cleo. It's none of my business. I just don't want to see you get hurt." There was a loaded pause. "I love you far too much," he confessed sadly, giving his horse a kick.

He galloped away and Cleo watched, her heart breaking. Tears began to stream down her cheeks. She saw Perry become smaller and smaller in the distance until he dropped from her sight.

She hated herself. Only a wicked spider would torture a genuine friend in a web of deception, but in one more week, she could make it up to him. Just one more week, and she'd have no tie to Clark. And then the tears became sobs as Cleo understood that she cried not for Perry, but for herself. The pain she had seen in his face during his confession of love, that vision of honest, frustrating pain, was the mirror of her own confused feelings for Clark. Just as Perry tried desperately to understand Cleo's curious situation in hope of salvaging a lost happiness, so Cleo struggled to read Clark. The only difference was that Perry did not suffer in vain. She was still in Perry's reach, whereas Clark was not in hers.

Cleo stroked Marina's mane in a conscious effort to put an end to the waterworks cascading down her cheeks. Beneath the life-giving sun, she was ready to accept that Clark had never loved her. He was simply doing a job—a job he did well. He had been at her beck and call only when she was a target. When she no longer needed protection, the attention stopped. And of course, that night in Reno when she was the center of his world, he was merely paying off a debt for her service, making sure she forgot being locked away in a crate. His reputation demanded that no harm or damage come to anyone entrusted in his care.

And Cleo could not fault him. He had advised her of his position as soon as she had declared her love and did not take advantage of her at night in the privacy of their room. As for the night in Tahoe when they had shared more than a bed, Cleo had asked, no, begged, for it. Clark would not have pressed her had she had the strength to refuse. *Clark Cannell, I submit that you will never belong to me,* she declared to herself, supremely in control. She would think of him no further.

Marina continued to plod the length of the beach, and Cleo grew concerned that Perry would not return. It struck Cleo that this was not the first time Perry had run away from her. In any event, she applied herself to the matter of returning to the stables, in spite of her total lack of riding skill. She had never been on horseback before, but she had certainly seen enough westerns, in more ways than one.

"Marina, will you turn back, please?" she addressed the mare hesitantly, and even more hesitantly pulled at one of the reins. Marina continued to plod along. Cleo was extremely uneasy. She evaluated her options. At last resort, she could dismount and lead Marina back to the stables, but like a supernovice, she feared ending up under Marina's hooves.

Marina ignored Cleo until she reached the rocky coast that no doubt marked the end of the Mayor estate. There the horse came to a full stop, and then obliged Cleo by reversing direction and retracing the route to the stables.

Cleo patted Marina's neck with a chuckle. "I'm really extraneous, huh, Marina? I guess some people are just meant to be towed along," she confided to her four-legged friend.

Perry must have known about Marina's round-trips, so Cleo excused him for leaving her on the beach with a horse she could not handle. The sun was now burning hot. The last time she had been on a beach, Clark had bought her a hat and had never left her side. But then he was only doing his job, she sniffed. But even when the job was over, had he not been considerate enough to leave her in a tropical paradise in the care of a former lover? Why must she always award Clark final credit?

It took the remainder of the morning to return. Marina took a few unscheduled rest stops along the way. When Cleo finally arrived at the stables, she asked about Perry and was told that he had gone to visit a friend in the city. She did not worry about him further.

She began to wander the grounds of the estate. It should have been just a leisurely stroll, but Cleo soon found herself busy, mentally calculating maintenance costs and estimating how much income Hal needed to support his lifestyle.

She passed the tennis courts, which were empty. The golf course appeared silent as well. It struck Cleo as odd that Clark's recreational activities included none of the amenities of Hal's resort. Then she promptly scolded herself for letting Clark encroach on her thoughts.

As Cleo crossed the lush lawn, she concluded that Hal, like Ian and Nareen, had the life he wanted. Did she have the life she wanted? The answer was a resounding no, but she was not dismayed. She knew, for the first time in her life, how to get it. It was up to her to make some changes, to say goodbye to California Investment, to take control of her life. Just as soon as the Intelnet game was over, she would make the proper changes. That was a solid promise she made to herself. There would be no more Clark, no more Intelnet, just Cleo Holmes, the way she was meant to be.

Renewed, she found her way back to the main house and walked into a whirlwind of activity. Hal's household was swarming with servants, many more than usual. Juan was standing in the foyer, giving directions and making mental notes.

"What's happening, Juan?" Cleo asked with friendly curiosity.

"Big party tonight, *señora*. Maybe one hundred people, maybe more."

Cleo pursed her lips. Clark hadn't bothered to tell her about the party. Would he tell her what to wear? Would he care?

"I get you lunch, *señora*?"

"No...no, thank you," Cleo replied quickly, aware that she had been preoccupied. "Please don't bother." She retreated down the hall, not wishing to add to Juan's burden.

She was heading for the guest suite when she caught sight of Perry's studio from the window at the base of the rear staircase. His Alfa Romeo was parked outside.

In an instant, Cleo shot through the passageways and out a back door to meet him, running across the lawn, dodging the spray of water sprinklers. She was eager to make a new beginning, not afraid of anything Perry might think or say.

The lawn took on the dimensions of a football field and Cleo imagined herself running for a touchdown with the sound of the crowd cheering in the stands. She knew this game, and she was winning.

She arrived at the studio, breathless and happy, ready for Perry, the always golden Perry. But the mood surrounding her student prince seemed so contrary to her own. He was leaning over the railing of the deck, staring soulfully at the ocean lashing the rocks below. Suddenly, Cleo felt selfish. For the past two days, she had been using him to fill her own needs, taking her happiness from him, while ignoring his needs in their unresolved relationship.

"Are the colors not mixing?" she asked cheerfully and was instantly sorry. Perry turned to her with a face full of trouble. She bit her lip, recognizing her mistake at trivializing his problem.

"That's right," he snapped. "Blue number twenty-eight isn't making it. I have a pretty frivolous life, don't I?"

"Perry, I'm sorry. I was just trying—"

"What is your impression of me?" he interrupted, then waved his arm over his head. "Look at this studio. Not many accomplished artists get a chance to live like this. I have a condo in L.A. and a flat in New York." He stared hard into the ocean to extract a truth. "I am successfully comfortable, not comfortably successful. You see, to do that, Cleo, takes more talent than my uncle's wealth can buy for me."

"Perry, everyone has moments of self-doubt. Why, you have more talent than..."

"I'm nothing, Cleo," he said, placing a finger to her lips to silence her. He smiled sardonically as if his next statement would make his assertion undeniable. "If I were something, Cleo, I would be with you."

He sank to the edge of a chaise longue, cradling his head in his hands. "I was content as a spineless stooge until you came to Acapulco and reminded me how I never face anything difficult, how I ran from you, ran from my family. I've backed myself into a corner, financed by my uncle, who includes me in his world because, for all his

underhanded dealings, he gets a kick out of being considered a patron of the arts. He enjoys being able to speak
of his nephew, the artist, but I know that deep down he
doesn't respect me.'' Perry wrung his hands. ''Every man
has his price, Cleo. Mine is just so damned low. How I
wish I could be free of him,'' he admitted, anguished.

Undaunted, Cleo sat beside him. She draped her arm
over his shoulders, ready to offer him all the comfort she
could give, but not knowing where to begin. There were
so many things she could say to ease his worries. But there
was one thing that she must not say before the end of next
week, no matter how badly he needed to hear that she was
not out of his life. She began with the obvious.

''What's stopping you from being free? You're not tied
to your uncle.''

''Cleo Sherlock,'' he said, laughing bitterly, ''my self-
reliant goddess. Don't you see? None of this is mine. I
don't even hold title to the Alfa parked outside. There's a
partnership deal I can get into, an art gallery in La Jolla
to be exact, but I can't even lay my hands on five grand
right away.''

Cleo smiled a calculating smile of checkmate. In one
morning, she had set her own life straight, and now she
would do the same for his. ''You have five grand,'' she
announced. Choosing her words carefully so as not to
wound Perry's pride, she offered him the money she had
won in Tahoe. He accepted, not needing as much coaxing as Cleo would have thought.

''Cleo Sherlock, you have always bailed me out!'' he
exclaimed, excited as a ticking Geiger counter.

In one tiny flash of realization, Cleo recognized his
statement to be accurate, although she had always thought
it was the other way around.

BEHIND THE WHEEL of the Alfa Romeo, Cleo drove Perry
to the airport. A three o'clock flight would take him to
Los Angeles, where he would sew up the deal and return
no later than tomorrow afternoon with a new life and a
new sense of self-worth. With the wind blowing in her
face, she listened enthusiastically to Perry's plans for the
business, which in Perry's inimitable style, grew more
fantastic by the minute. Destiny was theirs.

Cleo treated the drive back to the estate like the beginning of a Hollywood musical in which she, the star, was
singing the title song at the top of her lungs. Her hair was
flying in the wind and her smile was wide.

The movie was spiced up by limousines that passed her
at regular intervals. As the cruisers rolled effortlessly by
her, Cleo was tempted to wave to the mysterious passen-
gers hidden by the dark-tinted windows. When she arrived at the estate and saw limousines parked everywhere,
she was more than thankful that her hands had not left the
steering wheel. So this was where the action was, she
clucked. When Hallaran Mayor gave a party, his guests
didn't come by subway. Cleo felt she was definitely in the
swing.

She parked Perry's car at his studio, then walked down
the steps from his balcony to the beach. She took off her
sandals and shuffled in the sand at the water's edge, a
happy ending to her Hollywood musical, which would
turn into a box office smash when Perry returned. She
shared the beach with the sun and a few nameless sea
gulls, but now and then, she had the sensation that someone was watching her. Just nerves, she told herself. Nerves
of hope and promise.

When she returned to the house, it was alive with Hal's
guests. It was an international crowd, and Hal's servants

were flying. Cleo sneaked through the commotion to her room and took a lazy nap.

She woke to the sound of a mariachi band playing in the reception hall. The party was in swing. As Clark had not specifically invited her, Cleo considered skipping the entire affair. But she was hungry and going downstairs was the easiest route to dinner. Besides, it would be a treat to observe the international jet set in action.

After a quick shower, Cleo changed into the mint-green dress she had worn to Josh's wedding. She studied her reflection in the mirror critically. The color showed off her tan nicely, but the dress was too sedate. Experimentally, Cleo detached the overblouse, baring a spaghetti-strapped sundress. Then she dug in her suitcase for her jade beads. She fastened the choker around her neck. Better, she decided. Next she tied a magenta scarf around her waist. The color jazzed up the outfit. Satisfied, she went down to the party, a little miffed at herself for going to such pains just for the sake of eating.

Cleo hesitated on the brink of a grand-scale cocktail party that seemed amazingly successful. There was not a bored face in the crowd. No one looked familiar to Cleo.

Enjoying her anonymity, she headed straight to the buffet table and filled a plate. Establishing a chair against the wall as home base, Cleo hovered over the table and kept track of every new tray brought in from the kitchen. Everything was delicious, and Cleo made a business of eating. She was perfectly relaxed. She had only one purpose at this mixer—to eat.

After Cleo was sure she had tasted every dish at the buffet table, she lingered awhile to observe the crowd. Men far outnumbered women, most of whom were dressed in black and diamonds. Couples had begun to dance here and there to the salsa music interspersed between quiet beguines. And everywhere groups were gathered for intense conversation. Money talked, Cleo laughed to herself as she started to leave.

But Hal Mayor, the affable host, appeared at her side. "Hello, honey."

"Hello, Hal."

"I understand my nephew flew to L.A. It's a shame he had to miss the party when you two were getting along so well. I don't dance as well as Perry, but will you give me a try?"

With a smile pasted on her lips, Cleo took his arm to the tune of some slow, indistinguishable melody. She definitely did not like this man. The profile she had heard about him from Perry today confirmed her feelings. Oh, well, she thought, what was one dance with a deceitful Porky Pig. She owed it to him. She had been eating at his trough.

As soon as they reached a clear area, the band broke into a rousing salsa. Hal hesitated for an instant, leading Cleo to believe that he had changed his mind. Then he turned into a showman. "Let's do it, honey!"

He was Perry's uncle, Cleo thought, as he whirled her around the floor. They did the Charleston, the tango, the jitterbug, all rolled into one. Hal was enjoying himself, playing to the guests, who cheered him on. Although Cleo had not intended to become the life of the party, there she was, the center of attention, caught up in the excitement, proving, as always, that Cleo Holmes was no party pooper.

At the conclusion of the number, Hal was huffing and puffing. "That does it for me, honey," he said, just as a handsome Italian stepped up and asked Cleo for the next dance. Cleo declined demurely and withdrew, although it crossed her mind that she should dance with every man in the place just to spice up her memoirs. As she was making her exit, she saw a fresh tray of hors d'oeuvres being carried out of the kitchen, and not being able to resist, she trailed the waiter to the buffet table. She was studying the new puff pastry with interest when a pair of hands clasped her waist from behind. She knew instantly who it was. Her body tingled.

Clark whispered into her ear, "Another piranha attack? Don't be surprised if the chef takes you into the kitchen and begs you to fill up on peanut butter and jelly sandwiches."

Smiling, Cleo leaned over the table, picked up two pastry puffs and handed one to Clark as her answer. He popped it into his mouth. "Not bad," he said with a nod.

Cleo waited until he swallowed, then fed him the second pastry. As he bowed his head to take the morsel from her fingers, Cleo was struck by his willingness to be fed— a sure sign of friendship. She watched him chew like a little boy. This was the man she had firmly dismissed today. So how could she be so smitten, so moved by how good it felt to be near him, her friend of one week on this night of their anniversary?

"When are you and Hal opening on Broadway?" Clark said, his gaze moving aimlessly over the crowd. "Hal had to explain to so many people who the woman in green was that he sent me over here to claim you."

Cleo admired Clark's profile. He was a testimonial to a very successful party, she decided. For the first time since arriving in Acapulco, he looked happy, and the glow worked an intoxicating miracle in his handsome face, making it so, so easy for Cleo to fall in love. Then he turned to her.

"Dance with me?" he asked shyly, as if she might refuse.

She nodded, hiding the teary mist in her eyes. He swung
her into his arms and drifted away from the buffet to the
slow notes of a beguine. He held her comfortably close.
Cleo rested her head on his shoulder. He felt so good
against her. She wanted to melt into him. She wanted to
hold him forever. She kissed his shoulder like a devoted
puppy. This was the first time since their arrival in Acapulco that she had touched him. She sent telepathic messages in Spanish to the band, begging them not to stop.

Clark waltzed her onto the patio and into the fragrant
night breeze. The music was hard to hear, but it didn't
matter. Cleo floated on air. She felt his granite body relax and heave a small sigh when they were alone.

"Are you tired?" she asked.

"A little."

"You've had a busy week."

"Where's Perry?" he questioned softly, with no hint of
jealousy or sarcasm. Just friendly concern.

"He had business in L.A."

Clark nodded.

They were actually communicating, Cleo noted joyously. Not sparring, not bandying words in a contest of
wills. This was the man she had come to know outside of
Acapulco. It was Acapulco that had made such a difference in him. Why? And why had Clark not specified her
appearance at this gathering to maximize exposure of his
marriage to a flesh and blood Cleopatra? Question after
question came to sit on the sidelines of her bliss. Finally,
she yielded to her need to know.

"How long have you known Hal Mayor?" she began,
feeling Clark's muscles tighten.

"He's a long-standing acquaintance," Clark answered. The silence hung heavy.

"How much do you know about him?" Cleo persisted, knowing full well that in doing so, she was destroying the mood, perhaps irreparably.

"Your boyfriend must be telling you stories," Clark said, drawing away. Ice was forming quickly. "Have fun with your little schoolboy, Cleo, but keep him out of my business." The ice was solid.

Clark turned on his heel and left Cleo gaping after him. She barely had a moment to indulge in self-pity before a man in Western clothing but Bedouin headdress emerged from the shadows. He flashed a pearly white smile as a means of introduction. He looked young, conceited and dangerously sexy.

"Are you a spy, too?" he asked, a smile of intrigue lighting his face.

The question startled Cleo, but she covered her reaction with a blank stare.

"Come, come, Mrs. Cannell. No need to hedge. Permit me to introduce myself. I am Radul Jamar." He said his name as if he were giving her a gift. "I noticed you on the road today in that Italian excuse for an automobile. I must admit I watched you with my field glasses on the beach this afternoon. Why do they call you Cleo?"

"Because it is my name—short for Cleopatra."

"You are bold and courageous! I would not spy with such a name that draws attention. Or is that the idea?"

"I am not a spy."

He raised an exquisite dark eyebrow. "Perhaps I have offended you with the word 'spy.' It is a taboo in this country. In my country, spies are a way of life. Permit me. I am a graduate student at your Georgetown University, studying now and then, psychology. Motivation is my passion." His eyes were lively. "Why does a multitalented double agent like Clark Cannell take a wife unless she, too, is a spy? It is a very exotic mix, because she, too, must be a double agent, or else all is canceled. No matter which way the allegiances fall, the effect is negativity.''

''Your conversation is stimulating, Mr. Jamar, but I must go.'' Cleo marched off the patio. It was obvious he had had a lot to drink, and Cleo had her own problems. Matching wits with someone who fancied himself a logic philosopher was not on her agenda. She returned to the buffet table, ate three guacamole canapés and then left the party.

Cleo climbed the stairs, and walked down the dimly lit hallway, past the Aztec wall mountings, to her room. She was opening the door when someone came up behind her, clamping a hand over her mouth and swinging an arm about her waist, just below her breasts.

She shook her head trying to break free, and the hand covering her mouth fell away almost immediately. Cleo sensed in her struggle that the hold was playful, without malice, just firm enough to keep her pressed against the body of her captor.

''Let go! Stop it!'' She was hoarse, catching too little breath to be heard over the band downstairs.

''Your heart is thumping out of your very fine chest, Mrs. Cannell.'' It was a whispered tease sailing on the breath of alcohol. Having spoken, Radul Jamar released her, and Cleo spun around to face him defiantly. There was a devilish charm about him as he fluttered his palm at his chest to simulate her heartbeat. ''Fright? Or desire?'' he asked, unleashing a roguish smile.

''Anger!''

He was pleased with himself. ''I had to find out if you are a spy,'' he explained as if totally justified. ''You are not,'' he reported.

"What are you talking about?" Cleo put up her hand. "No. I don't want to know. Stay away from me," she warned, stepping inside the room.

"Do not be angry," Radul said innocently. "It was I who took all the risk. A highly trained spy reacting to my attack could have sent me to my grave. I am still a young man—" he flashed a devastating smile "—but death at the hands of a beauty such as you perhaps..."

Cleo started to close the door in his face. "Go downstairs and maybe someone will call you a camel."

He threw his head back to laugh and quickly placed his hand on the doorjamb. "You will hurt my hand if you close the door," he said to evoke sympathy.

Cleo obligatorily swung the door back. "You are drunk and disgusting and not necessarily in that order," Cleo rasped impatiently.

"I am drunk and resourceful," he corrected stepping into the doorway. "And not necessarily in that order." He leaned on the door frame.

Oh, what have I done? Cleo thought fearfully. *Clark, where are you?*

Radul adopted a professorial manner. "I have established that you are not a spy, therefore I conclude you must be very good in bed." He flashed his smile. "And I suppose I will find that out, too."

"Enough! Get out of my room or I'll—"

"Or you will what? Scream? You self-righteous American women." He laughed, turning to leave, then he stopped. "Seriously, Mrs. Cannell, you should learn to defend yourself. Strike out quickly against greater strength. Men, too, can be very vulnerable."

"Get out," Cleo demanded, pushing Radul across the threshold and slamming the door.

He was grinning at the click of the latch. The sound of the lock was next. "See," he crooned sweetly outside the door. "I have the greater strength, yet you win." He waited a moment, thinking that Cleo might respond. Then, chuckling, he left.

Cleo stared at the door until she was sure Radul was gone. Then she stomped across the rug and latched the balcony window. There, she thought, that would keep him out. But she wasn't really worried about his return. She suspected that he would pass out under a palm tree and sleep until morning with a drunken smile on his face. She ran the water for a shower, and by the time she was finished, she had forgotten the incident.

ALONE IN BED, Cleo kept thinking about Clark—how he had worked a magic spell on her at the party. She could not deny that he was still first and foremost the man of her dreams, her Superman. Sure, she knew how to banish him from her mind, and it worked . . . as long as he was away. Let him get near, and she was once again at his feet. Why? Was it his physical stature? If only. No, Cleo sighed, there was a quality about him as sterling as the silver candlesticks she had been drawn to in spite of her wish to avoid souvenirs. Well, it was obvious she knew what she liked—things solid in purpose, solid in worth. She chuckled inwardly, recalling Clark's assessment of himself on the shore of Lake Tahoe as a silver medalist in swimming. In swimming, she thought, and so much more. He was a noble being. A good guy in a western. Sure, he was moody. He could be surly and disagreeable. She knew that from the first night at the research lab. But could she blame him? He had been withdrawn, absorbed in a steady analysis of ways to stave off some earth-shattering event... and to save her life. How could she fault him for that?

He was behaving now as when she first met him. Was there something in Acapulco that was drastically wrong? Nonsense. Wild premise, Cleo decided. This was a vacation. And Clark had chosen to extend his stay. She sighed. It was more likely that she, herself, was the cause of Clark's biting aloofness, which really began in Reno, not Acapulco. She was the one who had gotten carried away on the Ferris wheel and set her sights on forever. It was Clark's intention to make crystal clear the absence of mutual feeling. He had decided to get off the Ferris wheel sooner rather than later.

But he had been so tender and so weary tonight. Something must have been wrong. *Turn over and go to sleep,* she told herself. *Your problem is simply that you love the man and will go to any extreme, hunting among the embers for signs of reciprocal feeling. It's over. Admit it. Consider it a fling.*

But last weekend was real, she heard herself imploring before the council of her rational mind. He had taken care of her, had given himself to her, and tonight... *Go to sleep,* she ordered.

CHAPTER THIRTEEN

CLEO WOKE LATE Saturday morning with a lazy, Saturday morning feeling. Warm and comfortable, she stretched out, enjoying the luxury. She must have slept well, she decided, secure in her being, happy.

Her eyes roved the sun-bright room. It was a cheerful habitat, light in design, lively in color—bringing forth the tropical beauty of Acapulco without trying to compete. She had not given it much credit before. There was a turquoise she liked in the weave of the rug. It led the eye to the palms at the window and picked up the pattern in the bedspreads. Clark's bed had not been slept in. And suddenly, Cleo rejoiced. No wonder she was at peace with herself! Clark had not been her first thought this morning. She was in control at last. It was good to be back.

Impulsively, she sprang from the bed to unlatch the balcony windows, filling the room with the sound of birds, the sweet smell of tropical flowers. She stood there for a while before going back to lounge in bed. She planned on seeing Perry when he returned later in the afternoon. Otherwise there was no reason to rush out of this pleasant setting filled with her own pleasant feelings.

IT TOOK HUNGER to pull Cleo out of bed around noon. In the name of lunch, she dressed, determined to avoid the crowd of guests that would also be sampling Hal's hospitality. Putting on her skirt and blouse gave her a fresh

surge of independence. She could not have felt more in
control had she been dressing to go to work. She studied
herself in the mirror and liked what she saw—Cleo
Holmes, still one of the best analysts around, but with a
great tan. Indeed, she had lost nothing in service to Intelnet. She had only gained.

When Cleo opened the door, her foot struck an object,
and she nearly tripped. Looking down, she discovered a
large gold gift box tied with purple ribbon. She glanced up
and down the hall. No one in sight. Enchanted, she sank
to her knees and began to undo the ribbon from the
package.

She lifted the top of the box. Inside was a bathing suit
in splashes of orchid and violet, a matching wrap and a
luxurious royal-purple beach towel. Dear Perry, she
thought. There was no need for a signed gift card. These
were his traditional colors for her. He had obviously called
someone in the city to deliver his gift. Cleo was delighted.

She quickly brought the box into the room and changed
into the suit, extremely pleased with its fit as she inspected her figure in the mirror. With the wrap, she was
respectably clothed, so she had no qualms about going
downstairs to find food.

A luncheon buffet had been set up both in the dining
room and on the patio. Cleo selected a banana and a small
cluster of green grapes from the patio buffet. She had intended on a larger breakfast, but the new bathing suit
made her conscious of her figure.

Fruit in hand she walked down to the beach just below
Perry's studio. She had the warm stretch of sand all to
herself. Hal's guests apparently preferred the pool and the
gardens to the surf. She spread out her prize towel, sat

down and ate the fruit. Then like a lazy cat, she stretched out and closed her eyes.

She soaked up the direct energy of the sun, and projected her resolve. After next week, she would return to California Investment with a great tan and a great story...and her two weeks' notice of resignation. She smiled. Porter would probably ask for more time. That would be fine. It would give her the opportunity to groom Josh for her position. And then? And then she would spend some time with Cassy in San Luis Obispo, get to know her niece. And then she would want to come back to Perry. Yesterday he had said he loved her. Maybe in another week she would be able to tell him the same. Maybe it was finally time for her to go to Athens with him. Oh, Nareen, Cleo thought, you were so right. People came into your life when you were ready for them.

Suddenly a call for help pierced the air. Cleo jerked herself to a sitting position.

"Help! Help!" It came again. A man's voice. Cleo jumped to her feet, scanning the beach. A man was drowning just beyond the wave break. Cleo ran toward the waterline, looking around for any other help in the area. She could swim, but she was not of rescue caliber. If the man was caught in the current, Cleo might not fare any better. But there was no time and no one around to help her consider the ifs.

"I'm coming," she called, splashing into the water, and plunging to a fast stroke. She clawed against the waves, knowing that she couldn't possibly be fast enough. If only she were Clark. The thought of him sustained her—helping her to try harder, to force herself to her limit, and then beyond. She pushed through the water, taking every breath with Clark, until she reached the dark head of hair bobbing in the water. Miraculously, she was not too late.

She reached out for the man. She touched him and took control. It was Radul Jamar, barely conscious, exhausted from his ordeal.

Cleo put her arm around his neck and began to swim awkwardly to shore, supremely thankful that the waves were with her. Later she would enjoy the irony of having Radul by the throat, but for now it was hard work. She was panting with the effort. She was forced to swallow a good deal of water, and the taste of drowning was a vivid warning of the power of the sea.

In shallow water, Cleo towed Radul toward the beach. His labored breathing was a relief to her. No longer able to float Radul at the water's edge, she coaxed him to stand, placing herself under his arm to support him. They stumbled onto dry sand. He was a crushing weight on her shoulders. At least he was alive, Cleo thought.

Suddenly, the burden lifted from her shoulders as Radul stood on his own. Then to Cleo's gasping surprise, he lifted her into his arms. He was no longer the man she had pulled from a watery demise.

"You are a good woman," he praised. "Rest, my friend." He flashed his pirate smile, his teeth gleaming in the sun. "You will forgive me. I wanted to talk to you again."

Cleo's eyes were wide in disbelief. He had staged the drowning. She offered no resistance. Now was not the time to fight. She needed to conserve her strength.

"I am most resourceful. I expected that there was no other way to get near you after last night," he explained, as he walked up the beach.

He laid her gently on the beach towel, placing a hand below her bosom as a trainer might to regulate the breathing of a tired athlete.

"Get your hand off me!" Cleo barked.

"As you wish." He smiled, lifting both hands in the air as terms of surrender.

"You want to talk, talk," Cleo snapped, realizing she was once again presenting a poor show of toughness.

"I want only to apologize for last night. You impress me. I like you even more today. You deserve a chance to know me."

"You pompous jerk!" Cleo said hotly, leaping to her feet. She yanked her towel off the sand, dislodging Radul in the process. He gallantly picked up her wrap and held it out to her. She snatched it from him. "I like you," he repeated as if she were auditioning for a show.

She stomped away.

"I must warn you," he called after her, "I always get what I want."

"How many times can you fake a drowning?" Cleo shot over her shoulder.

"I got you to come to the beach, did I not?"

His boast burst through her brain. The gift box had been from Radul! Filled with revulsion, Cleo threw the towel and wrap on the sand at his feet. He smirked, eyeing her bathing suit. "Do continue."

Mortified, Cleo stormed up the beach toward Perry's studio, glancing over her shoulder defiantly to make sure Radul did not follow. But he was running into the surf. She watched him plunge headlong into a wave and swim out to sea with strong powerful strokes. Cleo shook her head and climbed the steps to the studio. She admitted that he had a unique style. He was either treacherous or harmless; he couldn't be both. For sure, he had a large ego, a large libido and good taste in bathing suits.

Radul was instantly erased from Cleo's mind when a cab pulled up in the driveway. It was Perry. Cleo waved furiously and tried to contain her brimming excitement as Perry paid the driver.

"You look nice," he complimented her as his eyes shuttled between her slim figure and his wallet.

Perry said nothing as he carried a large painting wrapped in brown paper into the studio. Cleo was close behind. The suspense was unbearable. Cleo grabbed his arm. "Well, how did it go?"

"I've got to show you what I bought. It's a painting for you—an investment I want you to hold. It's guaranteed to appreciate in value a hundred times."

Perry tore off the wrapper and launched into an energetic exposition on the merit of the painting. At first Cleo indulged him. It was Perry's style to create fantasy out of the ordinary. Then she understood. Perry had not had the courage to make the break. He had converted her five thousand dollars into a painting instead. He had thrown away his future and hers, too.

"Oh, Perry," Cleo groaned, stopping him midsentence. "I'm so disappointed in you. But this is not the first time, is it?" She sounded like a scolding parent. Why not, she thought, he was still a child.

"Look, I can get your five grand back right now if that's what you're worried about," Perry sulked.

"I don't care about the money," Cleo said in exasperation. "Don't sidestep the issue. You were supposed to salvage your life. Instead you go on a...a shopping spree."

"Don't get condescending with me. We all get caught in some compromise in life. Look at you. What are you getting out of your marriage to Clark Cannell? A photo of a good-looking husband on your desk at the office you love so much. I overheard Clark tell my uncle that he married you to serve his purpose. So even you, Cleo, my exalted, hardworking queen of strength, even you are not above living a lie.''

Cleo was angry. She saw nothing but a shell of a man. He was irresponsible and immature. And like a spoiled boy, Perry was striking out, trying to hurt her feelings. A part of her saw every moment she had ever spent regretting the loss of Perry as a waste. And a part of her was weeping for every beautiful moment they had shared that would never be the same. She felt nothing for him but pity. Pity for an unforgettable old friend. And to that old friend, she spoke softly, ''I'll accept the painting if that is what you want. Sell it for me when you think it's at its peak.''

Her eyes circled the studio for the last time. The words came to her slowly. ''There will always be a place in my heart for you. I'm in the phone book—west coast. Call me if you ever need my help.''

With that, Cleo walked away. It was a final curtain. She was leaving Perry behind. Perhaps her respect for him would be restored if he called her back, if he ran after her. But he did not. With each step she put more distance between herself and Perry. She looked forward to tomorrow when the split would be complete. She could not wait to leave Acapulco.

Head held high, Cleo marched through the house in her bathing suit. She ascended the stairs like the supreme highness of the hemisphere. Once in her room, she crumbled.

She took a long shower, washing away the saltwater, both from the ocean and from her tears. She should have felt better when she came out. She did not. She felt like she looked—washed-out, deflated and lost. But she was in control. She refused to lose her control.

She packed her suitcase meticulously. She was more than ready to leave Acapulco, more than ready to reduce her presence in this room to one compact Samsonite suitcase. Then there was the matter of a slightly used bathing suit. She dropped it into its original gift box and disposed of it by asking one of the upstairs maids to place it in Señor Jamar's room. Most efficient.

Now all she had to do was wait until tomorrow. In her kimono, she curled up on the settee and watched television, spending the evening flitting mindlessly through the channels with the remote control while she concentrated on suppressing her feelings.

And just when the pain caused by Perry began to blur, a rather startling fact broke into her consciousness. According to Perry, Hal was aware of her paper marriage. If Hal knew the reason for her association with Clark, then Hal knew of CLEOPATRA. Ian knew about CLEOPATRA, and yet the marriage had been held up as legitimate in his eyes. She recalled what Radul Jamar had said when she first met him. Just what exactly was a double agent? Clark, himself, had used the term when he complimented her in Tahoe. "You have the mettle of a double agent," he had said.

The whole scenario was unsettling, but Cleo had no trouble dismissing it. Today she had discovered that Perry was hollow. She was not prepared to surrender Clark also. He was still her Superman. He was the one she had turned to when fighting the sea to save Radul. He was the one who had rocked her out of a humdrum existence and touched her life in so many ways. If she had not met Clark, she would never have seen Perry again. If she had not placed Clark's bet for a six-thousand-dollar win in Tahoe, she still might not know that Perry lacked substance. *Oh, Clark,* she thought. *You amaze me even in your absence.*

She dragged herself to the balcony window and searched for the moon. It was a weak thing—a mere sliver. It was hard to believe that this was the same splendid moon that had hung in a Tahoe sky, in a Reno sky. No wonder people wished upon the stars. No wishes could be made on this paltry Acapulco moon.

The door opened, and Cleo quickly brushed away a tear.

"Hi there," Clark said, pausing slightly at the sight of her.

"Hi," she answered meekly, her eyes following him as he went to the closet. He looked at her rather kindly as he grabbed his jacket off a hanger. Oh, Cleo thought, he was leaving her again, and she focused her eyes on the floor.

"Cleo, are you sick?" His voice was gentle, caring, and Cleo glanced up. She shook her head to his question, all the while wondering if she had correctly heard a morsel of concern.

"Didn't think so," he replied, slinging the jacket over his shoulder. "See you." His back was to her as he was leaving.

"Clark..." Cleo called softly, and he turned, somewhat alarmed.

"Where are you going?" she asked quietly. She didn't care about pride.

"Poker game," he said. He waited a moment, then headed for the door.

"Clark?"

Again he turned. He was patient.

"Will you do me a favor?" she inquired in a small voice.

He nodded. He waited.

He was a fine man, Cleo thought. He was leaving her, but at least he had stopped. *Hold me,* she wanted to say, but she spoke the words she had intended. "Tell me what time we're leaving tomorrow."

"Nine o'clock."

"Thank you." Her voice was tiny.

The door closed.

Fifteen minutes later there was a knock on the door. It was the same maid who had returned the boxed bathing suit to Radul Jamar. She was carrying a dinner tray.

"I didn't order this," Cleo said, immediately on guard. "Who ordered this?"

The maid smiled happily. "Your husband, *señora*."

When she was gone, Cleo cried.

CHAPTER FOURTEEN

CLEO PEERED through the porthole into the black night sky, then checked her wristwatch. In another hour, the plane would be landing in Washington, D.C. Due to missed connections and delayed flights, the trip had consumed all of Sunday. Cleo didn't mind. She was overjoyed to be leaving Acapulco behind, no matter what the cost. Clark, on the other hand, had spent the day in controlled fury.

The trouble had begun early that morning. Hal Mayor's attaché, not the regular chauffeur, had driven them to the airport and stopped in front of the Air Mexicana check-in. Cleo knew from the trip down to Acapulco that Intelnet agents always flew domestic airlines and were thus exempted from carryon restrictions on hardware and firearms.

"I'm booked on Southern Skyways," Clark said.

"Hal changed your reservation for a stopover in Houston," the attaché replied, handing Clark two tickets from his inside coat pocket.

Clark had taken his time reaching for the tickets. "Tell Mayor that no one alters my schedule," he stated coolly, and tore them in half.

Cleo had followed Clark like a puppy when he got out of the car, grabbed a suitcase in each hand and blazed a path to the other end of the terminal. She was so proud of her hero. He could not be manipulated by Hal Mayor. As a consequence, they had waited three hours in Acapulco and another three in New Orleans for flight connections. Clark had paced both airports while Cleo had skimmed a paperback novel.

That novel was now tucked into the seat pocket in front of her for some bored traveler to find. In the seat next to Cleo, Clark slept like a rock, the rugged picture of total exhaustion. Cleo adjusted his blanket and resisted stroking his brow. She knew now that Acapulco had been no picnic for him, and she was ashamed of herself for having missed the fact that he had been working hard these past few days. She did not even know where or if he had slept for the past two nights.

Earlier, on the flight out of Acapulco, Cleo had tricked Clark with surprising ease. In an earnest desire to understand his hostile departure, Cleo had asked him how he had liked deep-sea fishing. Caught off guard, he was blank until Cleo had reminded him about his fishing trip on Thursday. He had done slightly better on her later question concerning his poker game. No, Cleo thought. Acapulco had been no vacation.

And now he slept like a tired soldier. Her heart went out to him. They both needed to be away from Acapulco, away from Hal Mayor and everything Hal Mayor controlled.

Carefully, she slipped past Clark and groped her way down the darkened aisle to the lavatory. She blinked against its bright fluorescent lights as she locked the door and peered into the mirror. Even in poor, artificial light, she had an enviable tan—one that spoke of fun and adventure. As she washed her hands, she noted the contrasting milk-white skin beneath the wedding band. When exposed, it would highlight a loss more serious than the absence of a ring. But things might be different at Clark's

home, Cleo thought optimistically. There would be no
need for stifled pretense, and possibly she could relate to
him as a person. Maybe enough time remained for him to
love her not as a job, but as a person.

EXCITEMENT WELLED in Cleo during the cab ride from
Washington National Airport to Clark's home, and if she
allowed herself the fantasy, her home. He lived in a mul-
tilevel condominium complex on the Potomac in the
northwest section of the District of Columbia, not far
from Capitol Hill.

With a zeal that would warm a commission-minded real
estate agent, Cleo followed Clark through the common
interior and to Clark's corner unit on the third and top
level. The floor-to-ceiling door opened into darkness.
Clark entered, dropping his keys on a metal table in the
narrow foyer. He reached for the light switch and un-
veiled his home to Cleo's sight. He then secured the door
with three strong locks.

Cleo stood on the edge of a functional living center,
immaculate, efficient and almost futuristic in the number of electronic conveniences. A steel-framed shelving
system like a giant Erector set dominated one wall. It
housed two television sets, dual VCRs, a stereo system
with tape deck, several digital clocks and a personal computer with peripheral hardware. A large sectional sofa
arrangement, a well of navy-blue velour, was positioned
strategically in front of the wall unit. It was a virtual
command center for a man who demanded the maximum
in amenities at his fingertips.

His habitat was just like the bare metal table stationed
in the entryway to hold his keys. Functional. Nothing
frivolous—no lamps, only track lighting, no photos, no
art, no extraneous objects. Looking through to the

kitchen, over the counter that separated it from the main room, Cleo saw a microwave oven, a radio and another TV.

Cleo studied the scene with growing confidence that there was room in Clark's life for her. The tasteful but pervasive gray reminded her of her office. There was a clinical sterility about the place and not one item to suggest any personal attachment or affection, a condition that seemingly begged for Cleo to make it a home.

"There should be something to drink in the refrigerator," Clark said by way of welcome, followed by, "I'll sleep on the couch," which more than adequately squelched Cleo's optimism at establishing a permanent address here. Then he carried the luggage up the cantilevered stairs to the bedroom loft, leaving Cleo alone in the gray interior.

Cleo's shoulders drooped. Disappointment was no stranger in her relationship with Clark Cannell. It was Acapulco all over again. She brooded awhile, then plodded up the steps to the loft where she hung in the doorway watching Clark unpack. There was a king-size bed in the room, a stereo and another television. A telescope stood in front of a view that included the top of the Washington Monument.

Clark methodically hung up his clothes and put equipment in separate cases for storage. He was such a neat little bee, Cleo noted. Such a meticulous, ordered life he conducted.

Finally, Cleo peeled herself off the door frame and entered the room. She sat limply on the bed. She was so tired of being ignored. In frustration, she groped for words. "Clark—I know you've been under a strain this week. I sincerely wish I could have been of help. In fact—no that's presumptuous—I suppose what I'm trying to say is that I want to be your friend.''

She traced the stitching on the blue bedspread, preparing to be coldly rebuked by Clark. To her surprise, he sat easily on the edge of the bed, taking one of her hands, then the other. Cleo's heart soared. He had heard her. He had come back to her.

"We have four days, possibly less together. I can't say for certain. Tomorrow I'm going to work and resume the status quo.'' Cleo's elevated spirit lost altitude. The tone was too businesslike to lead to what she hoped. "I recommend the Smithsonian Institution and a tour of the Capitol. Keep yourself entertained.'' Cleo's spirit slipped into a nosedive. "Don't plan your time around me.'' Her spirit thudded into the ground. "I have a housekeeper, Mrs. Gunderson. She comes in on Monday and Thursday mornings. She'll be glad to help you.''

Cleo wanted to disengage her hands, but Clark held them firmly. Of course, she noted hotly, she was not yet dismissed.

"As for you wanting to be my friend—'' Clark appeared to grope for words ''—I would be grateful.'' With that he released her hands, leaving no doubt that she was now dismissed.

Later Cleo fell asleep in the cold, electronic bedroom after an exhaustive imaginary dialogue with Clark Cannell in which she berated him for his indifference, assailed his character, slammed his life-style and screamed that she did not care.

THE SMELL OF COFFEE woke her in the morning. Cleo quickly reached for her robe, refusing to be left sleeping as she had been in Acapulco. She dashed out of the room, but hesitated at the top of the stairs when she heard the front door open. She withdrew to eavesdrop.

"I smell coffee . . . Clark, are you home?"

"You caught me, Mrs. Gunderson."

"It's always nice to hug you. Even though you're late. I expected you last Monday. Baked you a cinnamon coffee ring."

"Cinnamon coffee ring? On Monday, you say? I knew I smelled hot cinnamon."

"Go ahead and tease me when I love you like a son."

Cleo continued to listen, in awe of their relationship. Was this the real Clark Cannell? Of course not. The real Clark Cannell was, as she had concluded last night, a cold stone who played with electronic components, incubating too much ego to ever see the error of his ways.

And while Cleo was making this assessment, Clark made the marriage announcement, which astonished Mrs. Gunderson and grated against Cleo.

"No teasing, Mrs. Gunderson. Cleo is asleep upstairs. We got in from Acapulco last night so she's going to be a little groggy. Will you take care of her?"

"For her anything and for you everything."

The door closed. Clark went to work, and Cleo was left in the middle of a pretense. She retreated to the bedroom to at least brush her hair before holding herself out to Clark's housekeeper. She was annoyed at having to play a part. If Clark had only shared with Mrs. Gunderson what he had supposedly told Hal Mayor, she would not be forced to go through this farce.

Cleo was only halfway down the stairs when Mrs. Gunderson met her with all the old-fashioned goodness of a Welcome Wagon. Cleo swallowed her first taste of guilt over lying to a kindhearted, elderly woman.

Mrs. Gunderson seated Cleo at the kitchen counter, made her breakfast and hung on her every word. It was agonizing. Cleo tried at every pause to steer the conversation away from herself, but it was useless.

Finally, she got Mrs. Gunderson started on a monologue, and Cleo was forced to eat four English muffins in the process. Mrs. Gunderson explained that she no longer needed to work but did so for Clark because he was like family. She launched into a detailed historical account of the many ways Clark had endeared himself to her, notably how Clark had counseled her wayward grandson.

Cleo tried to maintain a detachment from Clark's heroics. There was no reason to be swept away by his larger-than-life credits recounted by this fan club of one. To Cleo, the world was just one English muffin after another.

When the breakfast dishes were done, Mrs. Gunderson insisted on helping Cleo unpack. Consequently, Cleo was forced into more direct lies about how the rest of her things were to arrive by train from California next week.

Cleo hated lying to such a dear woman who was so thrilled to be in her company. She tried with all her ability to fashion truthful statements. She told Mrs. Gunderson more about the weather in Acapulco than the poor woman would ever choose to know. Mexican culture was another safe topic, and Cleo related it in encyclopedic detail.

When Cleo unwrapped the silver candlesticks, Mrs. Gunderson's eyes sparkled. "Oh, my dear, how perfect. Clark must have told you all about your new home." While Cleo hedged at the truth, she realized that the functional hunks of silver that Mrs. Gunderson was now examining did belong in Clark's home. It was uncanny that out of all the merchandise on the streets of Acapulco, the one item to which she had been attracted suited Clark so well. So be it, she decided. She would leave them as a memento for Clark. She would not, however, leave the photograph taken in the winter chapel that Mrs. Gunderson was now gushing over. Nope, Cleo thought. The photo—like her tan—would go home with her.

Mrs. Gunderson adored the picture and begged Cleo to explain the glass gazebo. So Cleo obliged. She described the winter chapel, recreating the crystal castle in detail. And in doing so, she fell hopelessly in love with Clark again.

Later Cleo walked to the bureau to stuff her clothing into a drawer for appearances' sake. Suddenly, Mrs. Gunderson uttered a cry of distress. Like a protective parent, she rushed past Cleo. "Oh, let me remove something, my dear. Clark should have called me," she said in a flurry.

From a corner of the second drawer, Mrs. Gunderson removed a black negligee. She was frazzled, considering it highly improper that Cleo should see evidence of another woman. "I tell you this means nothing," she said, waving a finger in the air and drawing upon the wisdom of her years.

Cleo tried to put her at ease, but basically her only effective move was to smile and accept attention from a woman very willing to love her to death.

"You know, Cleo," Mrs. Gunderson confided as she gathered up the laundry, "I see why he chose you."

Cleo sighed to herself. *Look me up if you ever get to San Francisco, Mrs. Gunderson. We can talk about it.*

CHAPTER FIFTEEN

CLARK WALKED through the door at seven o'clock to find the table set and the smell of a home-cooked meal in the air. He stood in the foyer watching Cleo light two long candles. *Cleo, Cleo, Cleo. Don't do this to me,* he begged.

Clumsy under his stare, Cleo had to strike two matches before the wicks took to flame. She knew that each moment that passed in silence made his approval less likely.

"I did this for Mrs. Gunderson's sake," Cleo explained uneasily. She lied. She had wanted to cook his meal, to put together a home in the middle of his steel-gray hideaway.

He approached the table and lifted a linen napkin from a place setting. He was frowning, disturbed perhaps by the frivolity of fine cloth on his table. The napkins and tablecloth had been a Christmas gift from his sister Claudia, according to Mrs. Gunderson.

"We better go out," Clark said. "You can eat this for lunch tomorrow."

Cleo could not believe her ears. She was dumbfounded, reality setting in only as she watched Clark lean over and blow out the candles.

"Sounds fine," she agreed, recovering swiftly, collecting the plates, clearing the table. She masked her disappointment, but it hurt to the point of humiliation that Clark had dismissed a whole afternoon of loving preparation. Like giggling teenagers planning a slumber party, she and Mrs. Gunderson had worked over a dinner of pot roast, popovers and fresh apple pie.

Then, predictably, Cleo's disappointment turned to anger. How rude of him, she thought as she replaced the dishes in the cupboard. Would it have killed him to eat her dinner? But he knew she had gone to a lot of effort. She wasn't the type of person who could readily whip up a meal. After all, he had seen, no analyzed, her kitchen, stocked with graham crackers and coffee. He was making it perfectly clear. No playing house.

IT WAS HARD to remain detached from the excitement of sight-seeing as Clark's silver Porsche sped by the White House and the Capitol Building. There was an energy here. A constructive energy. A patriotic pride. She felt it. She wondered if Clark felt it, too. But she didn't ask. He didn't want her in his life so she refused to push her nose to the glass while looking in.

The restaurant was French, the dinner delicious. Cleo admitted inwardly that Clark had made a better choice for himself by rejecting her dinner. She hardly spoke to him, deriving satisfaction through indifference to Clark and anything that concerned him. If Clark noticed her aloofness at all, he took it in stride.

They went to a movie afterward. Clark had asked Cleo to choose one. She refused. Undisturbed, Clark selected a foreign film, and Cleo paid the price for stubbornness by having to read subtitles. After a while, she just didn't bother. She turned to Clark to see if he enjoyed subtitles and then realized that he didn't have to read. He was tuned in to the original German. She hated him just to hate him.

After what seemed like forever, the movie ended and they drove home in silence. Traffic was sparse, the neighborhood was quiet. Though the hour was not late, Monday night imposed the curfew of a regular workweek.

On entering the condo, Clark paused, as was his habit, to park his keys on the metal table in the entryway. He should put a vase, a tray, anything, on that bare slab of metal, Cleo decided. Then she noticed something already there, another key, which Clark was fixed on.

"Oh, no," he muttered. Leaving her side, he bounded up the cantilevered stairs.

Cleo saw his towering frame sag in the doorway, silhouetted by the dim light from the bedroom. She scurried up the steps behind him, and took his place when he moved into the room.

A woman slept across his bed. She had a glorious mane of golden hair like that of a princess in a child's fairy tale. The woman stirred as Clark approached the bed.

"Candace," he said gently.

Cleo knew she should leave. But she was locked in a masochistic trance and couldn't stop staring at the flawlessly constructed beauty on Clark's bed. This was the kind of woman that rated a Clark Cannell. Candace, she said to herself, testing the quality of the name.

The woman eased her honey-rich hair from her face seductively. "Hello, Clark." Her voice was a pleasing murmur. "What did you do with my nightie?" she purred, sitting up on the bed. And then she spotted Cleo. "Who's this?"

The tone was accusatory, and Cleo reacted as though she had been caught in a crime. Dazed, she opened her mouth to make some sort of apology. And then she heard Clark say, "Candace, this is my wife."

Had she heard him say that? Yes, it was his voice. She was stunned. What about Candace? Her own presence legitimized, she looked sympathetically at Candace.

Candace was a woman of class. She spoke rapidly to the pace of embarrassment, but with dignity. "What a spectacle I've made of myself. I'm sorry, Clark. I didn't know. I should have called. I heard you were back in the office today." She swung her long, gorgeous legs over the side of the bed and tugged at her skirt. "Where are my shoes?" She looked frantically at the carpet along the edge of the bed.

Clark put a steady hand on her knee as he lowered himself in a deep knee bend and fished her navy-blue pumps from beneath the bed. "I'm sorry you had to find out this way, Candace," he murmured as he helped her into her shoes with care.

"I should have called," she repeated, dismissing Clark's attempts to ease her embarrassment. "Switchboard said you were back and I didn't stop to think. I had the emergency keys you gave me in Cairo and thought, why not."

Shrinking into the shadows just outside the door, Cleo watched Candace gracefully rise and stride regally to her trench coat draped over the back of the chair. "I'm due in Rome tomorrow. I wanted to see you before I left. I'm supposed to leave at 0600," she said as she rushed. From under her coat she resurrected a shoulder holster complete with regulation revolver that Clark helped her to fasten. *Oh, my God, she is an Intelnet agent, too. Don't rush, Candace,* Cleo pleaded inwardly. *You belong here. You are part of him in a way that I am not and could never be.*

Cleo retreated down the stairs to grant them the privacy they deserved. Without witness, Clark could tell his love the truth. To Cleo's surprise, they were almost directly behind her on the steps.

"Your sister called," Candace told Clark brightly. "She asked what was new with you. Would you believe I said, 'nothing'?"

"How long will you be on assignment?"

"Two weeks."

"Promise me you'll call. I want to talk to you."

"Sure, well, maybe... To tell you the truth, Clark, I'll need some time to adjust."

Cleo backed away into the darkness of the living room, but Candace sought her out. "I owe you a special apology for this scene," she said firmly.

By the single light in the entryway, Cleo could see that Candace's eyes were glistening, and Cleo could certainly identify with tears of loss. Clark had given Candace no secret sign, no clue as to the truth. Cleo understood every pain in Candace's perfect body and more. Much more.

But why should Candace go through hell needlessly? *Don't cry, Candace,* Cleo wanted to say, eager to help her, eager to set things straight. She had lied to Mrs. Gunderson all day. But those lies at least had made Mrs. Gunderson happy. The lies tonight only caused pain.

Cleo groped for a clue to give Candace. "Don't give it a thought," she assured her. Not good enough, she realized. "Ah...Mrs. Gunderson must have put some of your things away. I'm sure they'll be here when you get back." She was rambling. "Things are not always..." Clark had slipped beside her. He pinched her at the small of her back. "Uh...where you expect them to be," Cleo finished with the hasty substitution for "as they seem."

"Thank you," Candace said, thinking Cleo to be simpleminded. "Goodbye." She headed for the door.

Clark walked with her. He was careful to let her open the door. And he pulled up the collar of her trench coat around her neck as she paused in the doorway.

Candace drank in the moment and then tossed a light laugh. "Don't you dare walk me to my car."

Clark nodded and stood in the doorway obediently until Candace disappeared down the hall. Then he closed the door and leaned against it heavily, emotionally drained.

"I'm sorry, Clark," Cleo said, and then turned away. She felt miserable for them both. She felt wretched herself. What was she doing here? What was so important about this Intelnet game? But it must be important. Critical. Why else would Clark have bowed to duty and sent the woman of his life away without a word of the truth? *Oh, Clark,* she thought. *This is such a serious business, and you sacrifice so much.* Her hand moved absently to her back where Clark had burned his warning that the code of secrecy must not be broken at any price.

"Did I hurt you?" Clark said, beside her again.

She turned to him, shaking her head, her eyes filled with tears.

"No, Cleo, don't cry. It's not . . ."

He simply touched her shoulder, and in a burst of emotion, Cleo threw herself against him, clinging to him desperately and triggering his crushing embrace, which swept Cleo into the depths of her deepest dream. He lowered his lips upon hers and there was no return from this spontaneous passion.

Cleo pressed against him. It had been so long since she held him. She needed him, needed him as surely as she needed her next breath. Oh, God, she loved him. She raked her hands over his shoulders and chest with yearning, thrilling to the hardness of his body, his perfect form. She wanted him so much.

He kissed her throat, blazing a trail of searing pleasure and stirring her response from a bubbling caldron within. Cleo knew he was making up for being denied his golden blond love. She knew he ravaged her like a hungry bear deprived of his honey. She knew, she knew. But she wanted him on any terms.

This was wrong, Clark thought. He had to stop. He couldn't. He had held back for so long. He had died each time he had let her go to Perry. Yet he wanted her to have the happiness. Most of all, he wanted her safe. *Is this how you protect her?* he mocked himself. Still he could not stop. This won't hurt, he assured himself. This won't hurt the project and this won't hurt Cleo. Nobody would know. Above all, he wouldn't let Cleo know. He held her savagely, guarding against showing his love for her in his hands, his body, his face. *Don't talk to her,* he told himself. *Let her think it's animal passion.*

Clark worked his hand between their bodies to create the space to unbutton his shirt. Cleo's breath quickened in anticipation, and she spread her palms greedily across his chest, bared by his gaping shirt. Excited by her touch, he feverishly kissed her neck, her shoulders.

Cleo tore off her own blouse, baring her desire in unabashed invitation. Clark was stirred to passionate fury, obsession. He roved the curves and softness of her body, stripping the clothes that hindered his touch until Cleo stood at the edge of the sofa, stripped of everything but her desire.

The soft velour of the sofa felt heavenly as he eased her down upon it. But the sensation paled in comparison as Clark's magnificent body lowered upon her. She had waited so long to feel his powerful body above her. And now there was no past, no future, only the present, the sound of his heavy breathing, and his hot breath at her ear as torrid passion surged within. She matched his driving movements, moaning softly with pleasure, clutching his muscled flesh, until she cried out in final ecstasy.

Shuddering, he collapsed upon her, and together they caught their breath. Near in body and soul, Clark dared to look into Cleo's eyes. Such pretty eyes. Eyes that still said she loved him. *Stay with me, quick-thinking lady, and I'll make everything up to you.* There was a smile on her lips that intensified her eyes. He saw everything in her face. He made sure she saw nothing in his. He reached beneath the sofa for the sheet he had used last night. Unfurling it, he rolled over, allowing Cleo a cover if she wished.

Cleo was not upset that he had turned away. It was a fair bargain. She had asked for no more than he had given. She was no fool. She lay still beside him in the warmth of indescribable satisfaction. He had filled her physical need so expertly. Her emotional need she refused to let surface to mar this pleasure. Clark's emotional need, however, was another matter.

She turned to look at him, lying on his side, his face pressed into the sofa back. He had sacrificed his heart for Intelnet tonight. His commitment to duty extracted a heavy personal price, yet he did not complain. She wished with all her might that she could make things easier for him. In three days she would be gone and that would certainly make things easier for him. But right now, she wanted to ease his burden, to help him in any way she could.

She sat up, retrieved his long-sleeved shirt from the carpet and slipped it on, luxuriating in its cozy feel and faint scent. She rolled up the sleeves and then began to massage Clark's back. He muttered his appreciation, shifting his position to accommodate her as she straddled his hips.

Cleo started at his shoulders, squeezing his muscles as hard as she could. She knew it was impossible to hurt him and that a vigorous action was best. She worked lovingly down his strong back, varying the pressure as she kneaded his firm flesh, then beginning the process at the shoulders again, with the relentless effort of rowing a boat. It was not long before her fingers ached, but she continued to pinch and squeeze in a labor of love. In three days, she would never touch this man again.

When the strength had drained completely from her fingers, she continued to rub his back, hoping the love from her hands would be enough to soothe him. In a short while, Clark stirred.

He turned on his side groggily and reached up for Cleo's shoulders, pulling her to a position facedown beside him. His eyes closed, he sleepily caressed the back of her neck, then dropped his hand to massage her shoulders effortlessly.

Cleo rested her head comfortably on her folded arms, gazing at Clark, proud of herself for how relaxed he seemed and proud of him, her Superman. He would not take something from someone without giving in return. "You are a fair man," she whispered.

A joking smile came to his lips, and then he opened his eyes to study Cleo's unassuming face. "Fair?" he said, giving Cleo's shoulder a squeeze. He lazily closed his eyes again, continuing to grin. "I had thought excellent, good at very least, but fair?"

Cleo laughed, happy in the presence of a man so relaxed that he resembled the man she knew in Tahoe. The memory of their banter on the subject of his ego as they had floated on the dance floor, sizzled in the casinos and walked arm in arm on the beach, flooded her consciousness and laced her eyes with a mist that she banished by necessity with one blink.

For everything they had shared, Cleo quietly drew closer to Clark, and moved with deep regard and respect, she kissed him gently on the lips. It was an honest thank-you for eleven days in the life of Clark Cannell. Her boring, little life, as they had both termed it, would never be the same.

His eyes opened, then crinkled at the corners with a smile. Cleo looked into the dark gray eyes of her hero, the vista to the noblest, strongest soul she had ever known. With her heart full, she ran her fingers through his hair, and then unable to resist, melted into a lingering kiss, and then another. *Forgive me,* she said to Candace, in her last moment of rational thought. *I'm going to love you out of his mind.*

They made love again, in silence, more slowly this time, more controlled, with the sedate familiarity that comes to longtime lovers.

CHAPTER SIXTEEN

THE SPACE-AGE PHONE trilled at the center of the sofa well at 4:20 a.m. according to the pulsating digital time display. Cleo reached for the receiver. "Hello."

"Clark Cannell, please."

Clark's hand was already on the receiver as Cleo passed it to him.

"Cannell," he said routinely, then forcefully, "I told you never to call me here." Aware that Cleo was watching him, he turned his back on her. "Give me twenty minutes."

He replaced the receiver roughly and bounded up the stairs. Cleo never let on that she knew the voice to be Hal Mayor's. She sat against the cushions, her legs drawn up to her chest, listening to water running in the shower upstairs.

A few moments later, Clark dashed down the steps flinging a jacket over his shoulder. "I have to go," was the abrupt explanation. The door clicked behind him, then clicked twice again as he threw the dead bolts with his key.

Alone in his electronic hideaway, Cleo wrestled with why a call from Hal Mayor would drag Clark out at this early hour. It would be understandable if he had been willing, but he had been less than charmed by the telephone call and gruff in his response.

She went to the kitchen and started a pot of coffee. Thoughts rolled over and over in her mind like clothes tumbling in a dryer, churning the names Hal, Perry, Candace—especially Candace.

Last night Cleo had seen Clark toss his personal life to the wind to guarantee the success of project CLEOPATRA. He had sent the woman who shared his world, including friendship with his sister, into the night—to Europe, without so much as a hint of the truth. Yet Clark had told Hal Mayor something less than the sworn story and carelessly enough for Perry to overhear. If Clark had discretion over the truth, he would certainly have told Candace. Cleo bit her lip in speculation. She was too ignorant of the facts to make a judgment, but something seemed wrong, very wrong.

How could she be sure? Whom could she talk to? Her instincts told her to find Alex. She liked him. She trusted him. She recalled the night she had agreed to the whole, crazy Intelnet plan, when she had sat at the table with Edmondsen, Alex and Clark. It had been a stuffy affair. Only Alex had treated her like a person. Yes, she could talk to Alex.

But how could she get in touch with him? She could search for him at work, but to do so would broadcast her need all through Intelnet, wherever it was located, and however large it was. She rummaged through drawers until she found the phone book. Her finger ran down listings for Matlow, finding a Matlow, A. She frowned and looked up Cannell, Clark. He was unlisted. Alex would be, also. She shut the phone book. There had to be another way.

She systematically searched the shelves, compartments and fold-out desk of the living room wall unit. She searched for a personal address book. Last month's phone bill caught her attention, but on inspection, no number was repeated, and naturally calls within the local area were not separately listed.

Then Cleo went through the computer diskettes, lingering over a disk labelled ROSTR. Switching on the personal computer, she inserted it and loaded the data. She watched the cursor flash until a roster of names in random order was displayed on the screen. Bingo. Cleo advanced the cursor until she found Alex Matlow, complete with address and phone number. She seized upon the number, memorized it, then shut down the computer and replaced everything.

She was poised over the phone when she stopped abruptly. What if the phone was tapped? She could not broadcast what she was about to say. It was 5:55 a.m. by the digital clock.

Hardly five minutes had elapsed before Cleo was dressed and walking briskly down the block to a group of shops arranged around a common parking lot. There she found a public phone and dialed Alex's number fitfully.

"Hello?" A voice groggy, but definitely Alex's answered on the second ring.

"Alex. This is Cleo," she said, slightly out of breath.

"Cleo, what's wrong?" he asked, instantly alert. Cleo could imagine him swinging his legs over the side of the bed, hunching over the phone.

"Nothing is wrong, Alex. Sorry to call so early, but I wanted to catch you before you went to work." She stopped unsure of how to proceed. "Alex, I'm calling from a public phone." She paused again. "How many people know that I'm not really married to Clark?"

"Four. You, me, Clark and Edmondsen." Suddenly it was all clear to Cleo. Clark was a double agent, at home in the dirty nest of Hal Mayor's politics. The only honest person in the whole Acapulco fiasco was Radul Jamar.

Alex judged the stillness. "Cleo, are you telling me you've told someone else? We're too close for any upsets."

"No!" Cleo shook her head violently for emphasis, aware that Alex could not possibly see her, but too nervous to control the frantic response.

"I—I'm just upset, Alex." Cleo fashioned an answer quickly. "Candace was here last night and it broke her heart. I was wondering why you couldn't bend the rules a bit."

Alex drew a long breath, the kind reserved for the final piece of a jigsaw puzzle as it is inserted into place. "Don't worry about it, Cleo. Clark can work it out later. And, Cleo...Candace can handle it. She and Clark have an on-and-off, meaningless physical relationship. Trust me on it.... Quote me on it." There was a buzz in the background. "That's my alarm. It was much nicer waking up to you."

"Thank you, Alex. I owe you fifteen minutes," Cleo replied blankly, replacing the receiver like a robot. She was mindless, mechanical. She moved to a bench outside the storefront of a dry cleaner. There she sat motionless, staring straight ahead, overcome by a numbing realization. Hal Mayor had the same ugly hold over Clark that he had over Perry. Clark and Perry, though men of different substance, were equal prey before some insidious evil.

In a daze, Cleo watched cars traveling through the parking lot, driven by people who scurried in and out of a doughnut shop like ants. How nice it would be to run into a sweet shop and then drive away, never to know or care that Clark Cannell was a double agent. That much she was aware of.

When the dry cleaning store behind her opened for business, Cleo left the bench without so much as a blink to acknowledge the proprietor's morning greeting. She began to walk stiffly toward the Washington Monument according to the view from Clark's bedroom window. She was oblivious to the pedestrian traffic springing up around her. The phone call to Alex became a mental tape recording to play, rewind and play again.

She should have told Alex the real reason for her call, and in doing so, bought herself relief from the whole affair. But how could she expose Clark so easily, ruin his reputation, his career and certainly his life, with allegations she, herself, could not accept as true? She loved him too much, she believed in him too much, and fearfully wondered whether she was making a mistake of faith over fact. Was she incapable of objectivity?

But even when she stripped Clark of every shred of her love, a task that required a concentrated effort, he stood before her too much a hero to be a traitor to his country. Had he exposed CLEOPATRA to Hal Mayor? She struggled with conflicting pieces of a puzzle, sifting through data and the absence of data. Analysis was her craft, but she was a long way from California Investment and her proven set of rules.

She recalled the night in her own bedroom back in Oakland at the outset of this Intelnet scheme, when Clark, directed only by his sense of decency and fair play, confided his ignorance, explained the danger and swore to keep her alive. In Tahoe, Clark had pronounced CLEO-PATRA the single largest contribution to world peace in the last two decades, and had stated that CLEOPATRA meant more to him every day. Cleo believed him, but wasn't pretense the core of his profession?

The Washington Monument stood like a candle to freedom, reassuring Cleo that, geographically at least, she was not lost. She had come onto the campus of the national grounds at the Lincoln Memorial. She looked at the tranquil reflecting pool stretching across the lawn and recalled the night in Reno when she had shared Clark's life as a member of Ian's troupe. Hadn't Clark run into Hal Mayor by chance at the Cordoba estate? Wasn't the visit to Acapulco intended as a short social visit, a visit on Cleo's behalf at Ian's urging, a visit that had been extended only after Clark had spent a day with Hal?

Some change had occurred in Acapulco, and Hal Mayor was pivotal in that change. Cleo strained her imagination for some reason why Clark would sell out CLEOPATRA. He was not weak like Perry. He could not be bought for easy, material comfort.

Cleo had never been to Washington, D.C., before, but she felt at home in the nation's capital. The monuments, the symbols of the nation, were like old friends, helping her focus her mental turmoil. The heart of the nation belonged to every American. This was Clark's home, and every day he breathed a sense of American history, American honor. He couldn't be a traitor.

She walked along the Potomac River and around the tidal basin to the Jefferson Memorial, thinking and rethinking. The sky was overcast—providing a canopy conducive to thought. It was a long walk and by the time she had come full circle, returning to the grid of city streets and federal office buildings, she was sure of only one thing. She was hungry—both for food and for information.

Cleo was standing across from the Bureau of Printing and Engraving. The campus of the Smithsonian Institution was just ahead. There would be food for visitors, tourists. That was one problem solved. The other was more difficult. What source of information could she tap without official consequences? What source was available off the record? Perry? She couldn't depend on him. Radul Jamar? The man who had blatantly declared Clark a double agent as a matter of social chitchat? Of course. Radul Jamar, the resident rogue, would be glad to share his logic with her.

Crossing the street, she hurried to a phone. She dialed directory assistance and spelled Radul Jamar phonetically, hoping that he did not use an exotic spelling, replete with silent *h*'s. Would he even be listed? Please, please, she thought, and was rewarded. She dialed his number in a rush. It was past noon. Please be home. She counted rings. One. Two. Three.

"Radul here."

"Radul Jamar. How are you?"

"Who is this?" he purred.

"Cleo Cannell."

"Ahh, Mrs. Cannell. A delightful surprise. Why do you call?"

"I lost a bracelet on the beach. I wondered if you might have found it in the towel?"

"An expensive bracelet?"

"No, it's very cheap. It has sentimental value."

"Let's talk about it. Where are you? At home?"

"No. I'm at the Smithsonian at an information kiosk."

"Which one?"

Which one? Oh, he was aggravating. "I'm on 15th Street looking up at the Capitol."

There was a long pause. Too long. "Hello?" Cleo prompted.

"I will pick you up for lunch," Radul said. "I owe you. Now describe this bracelet to me."

Cleo gulped. "It was just a chain."

"What kind of chain?"

Did he know she was lying? "Gold. Gold plated."

"Was it—what do you call it—a charm bracelet?"

"No, it was just a chain—a simple chain."

"What kind of clasp?"

"Just ordinary." What was Radul doing, Cleo thought.

"No engraving?"

"No." Cleo was getting impatient.

"Where did you get this bracelet?"

"Radul, can we talk about this when you get here?"

"I am here!"

"What?" Cleo turned around at the sound of a horn. There sat Radul Jamar in a red Mercedes convertible, a cellular phone at his ear, looking very pleased. The man was full of surprises, Cleo thought, hastening toward him.

"I have call forwarding from my home phone," Radul explained when she was close. "Get in," he said cordially, flipping the door handle.

Cleo hesitated.

"We go to lunch over there—in the open." He tossed his head in the direction of an outdoor café with tables under an awning. He lifted both hands off the steering wheel and smiled. "I assure you I am quite harmless."

"I AM SORRY about your bracelet. I will buy you any bracelet you want," Radul said over lunch.

"I only asked if you had seen it, not to replace it."

"But I caused you to go to the beach. I want to be a friend. I live here. You live here...."

"I probably just misplaced it somewhere."

"Permit me at least to say I am sorry. You say it had sentimental value. Perhaps this bracelet was given to you by your husband?"

"No."

Radul raised an eyebrow. "A boyfriend, perhaps?"

"No."

"You don't have a boyfriend?"

"No."

"That is too bad. You need a boyfriend. Marriage to an intelligence agent can be lonely." He smiled sympathetically. "I can take care of that." His eyes were dancing.

Cleo was rejoicing. He was so predictable. She could handle him easily. "I couldn't possibly take a number and wait in line for you," she said coyly.

"You underestimate yourself, probably me also. I like you. We have more in common than you realize. Espionage is a very close family." He knitted his fingers together and treated Cleo to his piratic smile. Cleo gave him an equally naughty smile, hoping he would continue. "You and I, you see, are on the outskirts. I, from a family dealing with spies in the business of power, you, the chattel of an American spy. The difference between us is that you are naive, a delightful quality in you, which I shall enjoy molding."

"And how do you come to know so much?" Cleo asked.

"The privilege of a royal purse. As you Americans say, the spoiled-brat second-born son. My birthright entitles me to a kingdom's inheritance with no traditional responsibility of the firstborn son. And that is why you can trust me. I have everything—which assures my future. I care only about the present."

"Why did you call my husband a double agent?" Cleo inquired nonchalantly.

"Because he is smart. And smart men can take advantage of money while testing themselves in a very dangerous trade."

"So it's just the guess of a psychology student. You have no proof," Cleo scoffed, disguising her gleeful relief.

"It is self-evident," Radul said.

Self-evident? Cleo laughed inwardly. Radul was just a pompous windbag who loved to hear himself talk. How wonderful. The strongest accusation against Clark had been cleared away.

Radul removed a cigarette from a gold case and began thumping the cigarette upon it. "You might care to warn your husband that he is playing with fire. Hal Mayor is not used to dealing with men of strong will. It is an explosive combination," he stated, flicking his lighter for effect before holding it to his cigarette.

"Who is Hal Mayor?" Cleo asked.

"Who is Hal Mayor?" Radul was amused. "Look at that row of street lamps." He cocked his head. "Hal Mayor donated them. He is a public benefactor, an influence-monger in Washington and, most successfully, a monger of military weapons in secret. For detail, or proof, as you say, you had best ask my father's council. I do not make it my business." Radul eyed her curiously. "You ask many questions, my friend. What do you trade for answers?" he inquired provocatively.

"Lunch." Cleo smiled, placing her credit card on the tray and flagging the waiter.

Radul did not press to drive her home. Bowing to her preference, he simply helped her into a cab. "This is my card. I have taken a suite at the Columbia Regency while my apartment is being painted."

Cleo took the card out of courtesy. "You made up cards for a temporary suite?" she asked, glancing at the address before dropping it into her purse.

"Why not?" he said playfully, his smile charming as his hands rose to his chest. "I am popular."

"It must be self-evident," Cleo said, joining him in tongue-in-cheek humor.

She relaxed on the ride to Clark's home. Lunch with Radul had been a joy. Many things were still unclear, but it was self-evident—to use Radul's word—that there would never be an alliance between Clark and Hal Mayor. Cleo had already seen the friction between them, and Clark had no motive in money. Had he not magically made six thousand dollars out of a quarter in Tahoe and then given it away? Perry must have been mistaken. He had overheard something, put two and two together and come up with five. Perry was not a careful, detail-oriented person.

When the cab pulled up in front of the complex, the driver raised the flag on the meter before Cleo opened her purse. "It's okay, ma'am. Your friend gave me fifty to take you wherever you wanted."

"So he did," Cleo remarked, sliding out of the cab and thinking that Radul was not such a bad rogue.

Standing on the sidewalk, Cleo noticed a pretzel wagon down the block in front of the shopping center where she had sat so miserably this morning. So that was the root of Clark's pretzel habit, she noted, giving thought to buying him a few for dinner as a secret peace offering for thinking the worst of him this morning. No, she thought, smiling, as she entered the complex. She would let him warm up the pot roast. The day had certainly taken a turn for the better. Even the sun was winning its battle against gray clouds.

As Cleo sailed into the condo and closed the door behind her, she sensed a strange presence in the air, a shad-

owy feeling that she was not alone. She turned quickly.
She was right. She screamed. But it was only Hal Mayor.

"Gee whiz, honey," he said.

"Hal! Excuse me. How are you?" said Cleo, looking
past him. "Is Clark here?"

"No, he's not, honey."

The answer stunned Cleo. Hal *was* an intruder, and she
felt justified in rage. "What are you doing here?" she
demanded crisply, acutely aware that this was not her
home, either.

"Easy, honey. The door was open."

Cleo felt a stab of compunction. She had not locked
Clark's door when she flew out this morning.

Hal continued, "While I was in this neck of the woods,
I dropped off Clark's briefcase." He pointed to an aluminum case in front of the hall closet. "I knew he
wouldn't want me to leave it in the lobby so I let myself
in."

Cleo looked Hal straight in the eye. "He doesn't own a
case like that, Hal."

Hal winked. "Relax, honey. This is not a wife test."

Confirmation. Hal knew all about the phony marriage. Cleo wanted with every fiber in her body to throw
Hal out of Clark's home and out of his life. Instead, she
said, "Could I get you a cup of coffee?" Right now she
needed information more than revenge.

"Thank you but I've got to get along. Here are two
tickets to the dinner show tonight at the Waterfront Yacht
Club. Clark knows where that is."

Cleo had lost her gambit. "Clark can't possibly use
these tickets," she said defiantly.

"No?"

"He made other plans," she snapped.

"How so, honey?"

"Don't call me honey!"

"What plans, Ms Holmes?"

"Oh, how should I know, but what gives you the right to barge into his life, order him around and sneak into his home? I should have you arrested like a common criminal." Cleo was nearly screaming, her voice trembling with anger.

"You love him very much, don't you?"

The question disarmed Cleo. "That is none of your business. But yes, I do, very much." She spoke defensively. She was more than visibly upset.

"And does he love you?"

Cleo was completely wrung out. In total frustration, bearing the entire weight of the morning, she answered wearily, her eyes to the floor, "No, Hal . . . he doesn't."

"It's a shame."

Cleo glanced up and saw Hal smiling rather kindly. He did not look like a fiend. He looked more like someone's uncle. "Just be sure Clark gets the tickets," he stressed, and then he was gone.

Cleo raced to the window and checked his departure through the vertical blinds. After his chauffeured Rolls-Royce had cruised out of sight, she descended upon the case like a vulture. It was moderately heavy and sealed all the way around with a continuous strip of aluminum tape, three inches wide. If she opened it, there would be no way to disguise the entry, but she had to know what was inside, whatever the consequences.

She hauled the case to the kitchen counter and pried at the tape with a knife. She panted as she pulled at the industrial-strength adhesive. Her fingers were raw when she finally ripped it from the case.

She released the latches, her heart pounding on the verge of discovering the connection between Clark and

Hal. She opened the case to the extent of its hinges. Inside lay guilt. Measurable guilt. Bundles of crisp thousand-dollar bills packed solidly. Cleo fanned a bundle and counted the stacks in horrified disgust. They amounted to a cool million. Cleo recalled what Perry had said—every man had his price. Including Clark.

CHAPTER SEVENTEEN

CLARK CAME HOME, as usual, at seven o'clock. Cleo was simmering on the sofa as she had been for an hour, her legs crossed, her arms folded.

"Hal Mayor was here," she called to him coolly as soon as he shut the door. "He delivered your case."

"I see it," Clark answered.

"I left it on that awful entry table of yours. You really need something on it. You should get an expensive knick-knack, or two."

"Really? Why don't I just leave the case there?" He smiled agreeably.

"What a good idea. It's a shame I didn't leave the aluminum tape on it."

"I noticed," Clark replied, not bothered by her hostility. "Did Hal leave these tickets?"

"What is the million for, Clark?" Cleo demanded, her voice quivering with rage.

Clark calmly took a seat on the sofa and sorted through the mail in his hands. He spoke without looking up. "First, I'll point out that you had no right to open the case, and second, it is none of your concern."

"It *is* my concern. You once sat in my bedroom and told me I had the right to know. Since then I have spent almost two weeks devoted to the preservation of something called CLEOPATRA. I have been pretty damn useful to you. I may owe you two days in Tahoe when you were prepared to guard me with your life, but I've paid my way since then, and I *demand* to know with whom I've been associated. Are you a double agent?''

Clark waited until she was finished. Then he proceeded to open an envelope. Her demand had been wasted.

"Clark!" Cleo pleaded. "I'm your friend! If you're a double agent, stop. Refuse. I know how treacherous Hal is.''

"The dinner reservation is for eight o'clock,'' he informed her, reading the outside of another envelope with interest before tearing into it.

"Clark, I want to help you!'' Cleo cried, gripping his sleeve.

"Then get ready.''

"I'm not going with you.'' She sat back in the sofa, folding her arms. "I refuse to eat at Hal Mayor's trough. I told him you had made other plans,'' she said, sniffing.

Clark dropped the mail and grabbed her by the shoulders, fire in his eyes. "Cleo! Tell me exactly what you said to Hal.''

She was rebellious, defiant. She said nothing. He shook her shoulder. "Cleo, don't play games with me.''

She let him wait, glaring at him, before telling him what had actually happened. He inhaled deeply and sat back on the sofa. "I am going to dinner and you are coming with me,'' he said firmly, his eyes hard, "because you have forty-eight hours on your official agreement with Edmondsen. You are in no position to second-guess that, no matter what you think of me. You may, however, exercise your right to glower at me like that during dinner. In fact, I should like nothing better.''

And all through dinner Cleo did just that. She never said a word unless she had the opportunity for sarcasm or to throw an insult. Clark nodded to many people at the club, all of whom seemed to offer him a sympathetic nod regarding his seething dinner companion. Cleo knew she was the picture of ugliness, glaring at Clark while he sat with perfect features, perfect manners, the perfect gentleman.

The floor show at the yacht club tried to pass as a program of exotic dance. It was mostly an exhibit of female bodies for the enjoyment of male club members. Cleo found it disgusting, typical of Hal Mayor, but she used the time wisely.

Disguised in the appearance of watching the show, Cleo reassessed her situation and planned her strategy with Clark. It was pointless just to be angry at him. She had to talk to him, she had to reason with him. She was determined to pull the truth out of him once they got home.

It was that resolve that allowed her to behave civilly on the ride back to the condo and to sit on the sofa like a docile pet, watching Clark remove his tie. He appeared to enjoy her submission.

"From here on in, Cleo, don't answer the phone," he instructed.

"Okay," she replied sweetly, building a rapport. It was ironic, she thought, that manipulative skill, the very thing she had found unsettling in Clark, was what she had practiced twice today—once on Radul and now on Clark.

She focused on the flashing light from the electronic box attachment to Clark's phone. It signaled a message pending, but Clark was pointedly ignoring it. Cleo regarded it calmly as just one of the mysteries she would unravel this night.

Suddenly, the rude sound of the buzzer at the building security entrance pierced the room. It was an ugly, forbidding sound.

"Ignore it," Clark told her. He was watching the door, tensed for action, and reading his behavior, Cleo was afraid.

He drew his revolver and sat down on the sofa beside her. Now she was thoroughly frightened. She knew that Clark was waiting, expecting trouble. She kept silent, her heart beating like a jackhammer.

Then there was the chime of the doorbell. Cleo started. Whoever had been outside the complex was now inside, just beyond the door. The door would not stop a bullet. Or two. Cleo panicked.

"Ask who it is—calmly," Clark whispered urgently, putting his arm around her shoulders.

"Who is it?" Cleo called out, making a concentrated effort at keeping the petrified squeak out of her voice.

"Edmondsen. Open up."

Cleo exhaled in relief, but Clark did not release his grip. "Tell him to wait a minute," Clark instructed between clenched teeth.

"Just a minute," Cleo parroted.

Clark again whispered urgently, rapidly. "Go to the door. Let him in. You have not seen me since dinner. You drove home alone."

"Clark, it's Edmondsen," Cleo stressed, turning to him and discovering she was looking into the barrel of his gun. Aghast, she was quick to understand that he had not been protecting her but holding her hostage.

"No argument, Cleo." He pulled her, gasping, from the sofa and led her to the door, the gun held close to her neck. He slipped into the hall closet after threatening in gesture his ability to observe her and aim his gun through the slats of the louvered sliding doors.

Cleo's hands shook as she unlatched the door. Her stunned mind raced. Clark, with all his superior skill, was an unbeatable foe. If she ran outside once the door was opened, Clark could easily shoot her, and Edmondsen as well...unless Edmondsen was also armed, and he shot Clark first. Anguished and horrified to be plotting harm to Clark, she opened the door cautiously, then stepped back in surprise against its force.

"Clark in?" Edmondsen said, swinging the door wide, looking past Cleo into the room.

Cleo shook her head, her mouth agape.

"I was afraid of this," he said, pushing into the foyer and closing the door behind him as if poison gases filled the hall. Cleo, barely breathing, was fixated by the click of the door. She had wanted to keep the door open. Now they were both trapped in the narrow entryway in point-blank range of Clark's precise marksmanship.

"My, God! You're white as a sheet," remarked Edmondsen, finally taking notice of Cleo. "Sorry to scare you when you're alone like this. Here, I have your plane ticket to San Francisco. You're leaving tomorrow," he said, digging inside his coat for the ticket and handing it to her as an apology for his forcible entry. Cleo could see he was not wearing a shoulder holster.

"I've been trying to get hold of Clark all night. Damn, I see he hasn't picked up our signal," he said, catching sight of the flashing light on the phone. "Do you know where he is?"

Cleo evaluated her chance. This was the moment to shift her eyes to the closet. Instead, she made a pitch for information. "Is he in trouble?"

"He is about to get himself killed." Edmondsen wiped sweat from his brow.

Cleo saw that the stodgy dull man she had met almost two weeks ago was shaken to wit's end. "What's wrong?" she asked.

"The core of CLEOPATRA was drained from our computer banks. We have aborted CLEOPATRA. I repeat, aborted CLEOPATRA. If you should see Clark before I do, tell him we have withdrawn all backup support. If Clark takes any action on his own, he's a sitting duck."

"And this is all you want me to tell him?"

Edmondsen nodded, suddenly aware and embarrassed that Cleo had led him into revealing more than necessary to a civilian.

"Where did you last see him?" he questioned, regaining his formal manner.

Cleo looked at Edmondsen and spoke clearly. Her decision was implicit. "We had dinner at the Waterfront Yacht Club. He took a cab, and I drove back here."

Edmondsen nervously absorbed the information, then turned to leave. "Thank you for all your assistance, Ms Holmes. I'll be in touch about the stipend. Have a good trip home."

Cleo closed the door, keeping one hand on the knob. In a moment she would know if she had been a fool. She turned and watched Clark ease out of the closet.

"Thank you, Cleo." He threw her a second glance, slow to realize that she was cowering in the corner. "Get away from the door. I'm not going to hurt you," he said wearily, moving into the living room.

"Clark, did you hear him? The mission is over," Cleo implored, taking a few steps after him.

"Yeah, I heard."

"Clark, why are you hiding?"

"What flight are you on tomorrow?" he asked, turning to her with a contemplative frown.

Cleo fumbled with the ticket envelope. "Ten o'clock, TWA."

"That's good. Your official duty is over."

"Clark, I'm worried about you."

"Save it, kid." He set his revolver on the coffee table and began to unbutton his cuffs.

"Clark, I know you drained the computer banks for Hal Mayor. I know CLEOPATRA is still active to you. What makes you think I'm going to fly home tomorrow and let you sell us out?"

"Go ahead, Cleo. If you're so sure I'm a double agent, run out and tell the world and see how far you get. Your word doesn't mean much against mine. I remind you that all you really know about CLEOPATRA is what Edmondsen told you at the outset, and now he told you it's over and to go home. You are out of it."

"I came close to being out of it tonight," she snipped, indicating the revolver. "Would you have used it on me?"

Clark's nostrils flared with anger. He picked up the gun and stormed toward her, his face contorted in an ugly scowl. Courage drained from Cleo's body. She had gone too far. She had been too flip. He was in a rage. She stepped back, shrinking in fear, seconds from whimpering.

Clark reached out and roughly grabbed her hand. He slapped the gun into her palm. "What do *you* think?" he snarled in disgust. And then he walked away.

Plastered against the wall, speechless, Cleo watched him return to the sofa. He proceeded to make up his bed for the night, and Cleo retreated to the loft, carrying the gun.

She was assailed by many fears, all of which seemed to converge in the pit of her stomach. With no idea of what she should do, she sat on the bed, facing the bedroom door with the airline ticket and gun in her lap. She didn't know what was going on, and she didn't know Clark anymore.

The lights downstairs soon disappeared into darkness. Cleo knew Clark had settled on the sofa for the night. Instinctively, she dialed the lights in the bedroom to the dimmest setting and sat quietly, maintaining her vigil at the door while her insides continued to churn in panic. She had Clark's gun and he was asleep, so logic told her not to fear him. But she could not forget how easy it had been for him to thrust a gun into her neck. What had possessed him? What madness had driven him into conspiracy with Hal Mayor and into hiding from Edmondsen, who was sweating to save him?

The airline ticket was her way out of this tangled torment, so foreign, so incomprehensible. Only the night stood between this insane game and her freedom to walk away. But she was now a full-fledged player, the stakes were sky-high, and to walk away would be unconscionable.

Action from her was imperative but impossible. Analysis of the incoherent facts at her disposal served no purpose but to tighten the knot in her stomach.

Cleo let an hour pass to ensure that Clark was sound asleep before starting to pack. It was her only solid move. The front door was unlocked. If she could just sneak away from Clark, she would be in a better position to think of a way to keep him from killing himself and whoever stood in his way. From the closets and drawers, she quietly gathered her belongings, scolding herself for packing. How could she possibly save the world toting a suitcase? But her chances of saving the world even without a suitcase were nil. The only real thing that was expected of her by Edmondsen, a ranking official of Intelnet, was to be on the plane to San Francisco at 10:00 a.m., and that, at least, she could do. But before heading for the airport she would take a cab to Alex's home and correct her error of not telling him about Hal Mayor in the first place.

Cleo packed in fear, looking over her shoulder constantly. What would happen if Clark found out what she was trying to do? Her only hope was in silence. If she was quiet, she could escape. More than once, she clutched at an upset stomach, refusing to admit to growing nausea.

At last, everything was packed. Cleo stuffed a blouse into her purse to make sure nothing rattled, and made her move. At the top of the steps, she set her suitcase on the carpet, doubling over as she clutched her stomach. Nausea drove her to the bathroom and she was panicking. This was no time to be sick.

She leaned over the basin hoping against hope to avoid turning inside out. But it was as inevitable as it was graceless. Her body convulsed, forcing tears into her eyes. Instantly, she felt better. Perhaps she was still on track. Perhaps she had not awakened Clark. She let the water run into the basin at a slow stream while she sank to the edge of the bathtub and rested her head against the cool basin.

Everything was fine. In a few minutes, she would resume her escape. She would just get her breath and then—the click of a switch flooded the bathroom with light. Clark loomed in the doorway. A scream caught in Cleo's throat. Clark lunged at her. In a flash, he had lifted her pitifully limp form into his arms, "I told you not to order the crab crepe," he said.

He placed her on the bed and then pulled a wastebasket and a box of tissue within her reach, exaggerating his movements to call attention to the security items. "I'm going to make you some tea."

"I don't want any tea." Cleo was defiant, never taking her eyes off his face. Lying helpless before him, she accepted her fate, ready to suffer the full brunt of his rage without accepting any token courtesy.

"Okay," he said easily, as he sat on the edge of the bed. He placed his hand with confidence on her forehead. Cleo was tense with confusion. After a moment, he explained, "I have no idea what this is supposed to tell me. My specialty is making tea. So if you need a doctor, you'd better tell me."

Cleo shook her head nervously, struggling with the contradiction. There was no way Clark would have shot her if he refused to let her suffer with food poisoning. She kept staring at him, looking into his eyes. They were kind eyes, caring and considerate—consistent with his easy bedside manner. He sat quietly, patiently, soaking up her apprehension like a sponge. Cleo waited for him to mention the suitcase at the top of the stairs. He did not. She waited for him to threaten her, to punish her. He did not.

Then he took her hand from her stomach and replaced it with his own. Very gently, he began a soothing circular motion, relaxing her tightened muscles and taking away the ache. He watched her carefully to make sure he wasn't hurting her.

Cleo kept her eyes on his face. He was an enemy. He was a traitor. And...and he was such a damned good friend, she decided, precipitating a sob that drew an instant reaction from Clark. Mistaking tears for illness, he bent over her with increased concern. Cleo pretended a cramp, reaching out for him. "Hold me," she begged.

With speed Cleo judged too fast for ordinary compassion, he took her in his arms, lying down beside her in bed. Cleo buried her face against his chest while his hand pushed firmly against the small of her back, pressing her soft abdomen against his strong body. "Take it easy, quick-thinking lady," he whispered. "Give your pain to me."

Cleo held him as close as life itself, and there was peace in the world. "I love you, good guy," she told his warm, furry chest.

He gave her a polite little laugh, a modest response to what he must have considered gratitude. *I love you,* she told him again, this time silently. He continued to hold her tenderly, working magic into her body to make her whole again.

Cleo drifted with memories as she rolled in and out of waves of nausea, heeding Clark's whispered messages to relax. She remembered walking with a man on the shore of Lake Tahoe, and how beautiful the world looked when she held his hand. She remembered sitting next to a man on a Ferris wheel rising toward an orchid moon, where she held him in her arms and touched the stars, where he kissed her in the moonlight and locked her in a dream. The same man now held her, comforted her, wrapped her in warmth on the relaxed brink of slumber. She knew she loved this man. She was certain of her heart, and more. *You love me too, Clark Cannell, and I will save you from the devil himself, if I must.*

CHAPTER EIGHTEEN

WHEN CLEO AWOKE, it was morning. Rain was beating against the window, and she was alone. She jerked herself upright. How could she have let Clark slip away? She had not intended to let him out of her sight. Horrified, she called his name. He was gone.

What time was it? There was a note covering the face of the digital clock. She reached across the nightstand to remove it, saw the time at 7:26 a.m., and anxiously read the penciled message. "Take it easy. If you feel lousy, stay here. We'll book you another flight."

Cleo sat back against a pillow, relieved. There was no urgency in the message; the writing was carefully printed, not hastily scrawled. Clark's gun lay on the bed where Cleo had left it. Perhaps all was well.

Then the phone rang.

"Hello."

"May I speak to Clark, please." The voice was feminine.

"I'm sorry. He isn't here. He's probably at the office."

"No. I just called there. Switchboard won't connect me anywhere else without a code."

"May I take a message?" Cleo offered, sensing frustration in the caller's voice.

"Well, this is his sister. I'm at the airport. He is expecting me, I think. Someone called early this morning saying that he needed to see me as soon as possible, so I took the first plane I could get from New York."

Cleo's pulse raced as huge pieces of the puzzle, which had eluded her for so long, flew at her like a meteor shower. "Claudia, who called you?" Cleo asked urgently.

"I don't know.... Who is this?"

There it was. The reason Clark needed Intelnet backup withdrawn from CLEOPATRA. The reason he needed to act alone. Clark was being coerced into counterintelligence with Claudia as leverage.

"Claudia, listen to me," Cleo urged rapidly with military command. "You are walking into a trap. Go to a waiting lounge past the metal security detectors. Which one is closest to you?"

There was a pause. "Eastern."

"Wait for me there. Please. My name is Cleo Holmes... Cannell. I'll show you ID. Don't let anyone near you. I'll explain when I see you. This phone may be tapped. Claudia, be careful. Do you understand?"

Across an excruciating silence Cleo waited for Claudia's response, praying she would cooperate with a stranger. Then it came. "I'll be waiting," Claudia agreed skeptically.

The alarm bells were clanging in her head as Cleo slammed the phone receiver into its cradle. Speed was critical. The ball was in her court. Professional thugs were about to pounce on Claudia, and Cleo had broadcast the complete rendezvous plan over public wires.

Cleo dashed to her suitcase at the top of the stairs. She tore through its contents, strewing clothes on the carpet to get her gray trench coat, a veteran of San Francisco fog, which was about to do battle with Washington rain.

Like a whirlwind, Cleo threw herself into the coat while rushing to the bed, where she pocketed Clark's revolver. On the way downstairs, she stooped to pull her fuchsia scarf from the clothes heap, and draping it around her neck for use as a rain bonnet, she flew down the steps.

Downstairs Cleo dialed information, then a cab company, with her eye on Clark's car keys on the entry table. If her hunch was correct, there would be a Porsche waiting for her in the garage, and the cab waiting outside would serve as a smoke screen. She gave the address to the cab dispatcher with conviction. Today she knew no limitation. The resolve was set as surely as blood coursed through her body and her nerves stood on end. She was prepared to do anything and everything to keep Claudia out of malevolent hands and to deliver Clark from the same.

As Cleo marched squarely to the door, she swung the million-dollar briefcase off the entry table without missing a step. For whatever lay ahead, she would have bargaining power to boot.

She took the elevator to the basement garage. As expected, the silver Porsche lay waiting. Wherever Clark had the misfortune to be, he was without his car, without his revolver. *Don't worry, my darling,* Cleo spoke to him, as she stabbed the key into the ignition and started the engine.

She drove to the airport. She didn't need the map she had found in the glove compartment and spread open on the passenger seat. The route came back to her in reverse of the cab ride from the airport Sunday night. Interpreting the ease of navigation to some cosmic force that affirmed her quest, she drove the car like a silver bullet through the pouring rain.

Rain pelted her unmercifully as she ran to the terminal entrance. Cars formed an endless convoy in search of convenient parking, but Cleo had found a space near the terminal. Another cosmic nod, she thought with confidence.

Once inside the terminal, she fought the impulse to continue running. Her better instincts held her to a brisk, motorized walk. Unerringly alert, Cleo observed everyone and everything as she headed toward the baggage lockers and deposited her million-dollar cache in return for a locker key.

Then she cut a trail into the interior of the terminal, taking her bearings from the directional signs that led to the waiting area for Eastern Airlines. She was well into the concourse before realizing that the security checkpoint, which she was using as Claudia's first line of defense against armed kidnap, would not discriminate in favor of Clark's revolver. Without breaking stride, she shifted the gun from her pocket to her purse. At that moment her appreciation for airline security shot sky-high along with her pulse rate.

A man, wreathed in sinister vibration to Cleo's sensitive sonar, was tucked away along the corridor near the metal detection barrier. He nursed his aggravation on a cigarette. It was Hal Mayor's attaché, the man who had driven Cleo and Clark to the Acapulco airport.

Recognition was not mutual. Her plan on track, Cleo withdrew her wallet from her purse.

She curtsied before the security attendants, batted her eyelashes into a vivacious and vacant stare and spoke in a cute whine. "Oh, oh, I forgot about you boys. My gun is in my purse and I'm meeting my momma. Be lambs and just hang on to it for me here, okay?" Leaving her purse innocently on the conveyor belt, Cleo trundled through the detection archway before the attendants could refuse.

The next hurdle would be recognizing Claudia. On last encounter, Claudia had been three inches tall on a sixteen-inch television screen and had worn ballet slippers. Cleo's apprehension vanished on sight of a woman, regal in stance, exquisitely packaged in a designer black raincape and expensive high-heeled boots. Claudia Cannell stood apart, her back to the observation window, so aristocratic with her hair pulled severely off her face, so obviously a prima ballerina, so obviously Clark's sister.

Cleo approached Claudia, holding her driver's license in her hand like an official badge. "Claudia, I'm Cleo Holmes Cannell, Cleo Holmes for real, Cannell for the sake of the tapped phone."

Claudia's lips moved to a tight smile of tentative cordiality, and Cleo felt Clark's presence. She steered Claudia to a row of seats in a secluded section of the waiting room and explained her story as rapidly as possible. Claudia listened like an impartial judge until Cleo told of Hal's attaché.

"What does he look like?" Claudia asked.

Cleo answered without a pause. "He's big. He's mean-looking. He has a mustache, dark hair, dark complexion. He's wearing a trench coat, chain-smoking—"

"I saw him. He was watching me when I spoke to you on the phone," Claudia said, becoming more aware. "Now tell me again—how did you meet my brother?"

Oh, Claudia, please, Cleo thought. They were wasting time. She answered frantically. "Alexander Matlow gave me a pretzel in a BART station to take to him. It was part of a joke, I suppose. I had orchids in my hair, I was in a good mood, I..."

"I believe you, Cleo Holmes. What is your plan?"

CLAUDIA RAISED THE HOOD of her cape over her head as they rose from the chairs. Together they traveled to the security checkpoint like sisters of the same convent. "This is my momma," Cleo offered, while retrieving her purse. Twenty brisk steps later both women slipped through the door of the rest room, which opened into the corridor.

Exactly seven minutes later, Cleo stood in the corridor at a pay phone, talking to an automatic time recording, while monitoring the progress of a woman in a gray trench coat with long damp hair beneath a fuchsia scarf. The woman walked down the concourse, handed her ticket to an airline attendant and boarded flight 902 to San Francisco, departing as scheduled at ten o'clock. Only when the plane rolled away from the gate did Cleo replace the receiver. She readjusted the hood of the black cape over her ponytailed hair, fixed the position of the attaché by a glance of her heavily made-up eyes and began to click the high-heeled boots down the concourse. So far she was in control. Claudia was safely tucked away in the sky for the next five hours while Cleo, in place of Claudia, located and liberated Clark. If she ever needed to do a job well, it was now. *Don't fail,* she begged of herself. *Don't even think of failing.*

Artfully inspecting the heel of her boot, she confirmed that the attaché was following her. Her lips were set in determination against the constant pounding of her heart. For Clark's sake, she would not fail. *Clark needs you, quick-thinking lady.*

The boots clicked a determined rhythm, one click for every three heartbeats as she approached the terminal exit, then one click for every four beats as the automatic doors swung open into the morning air, crisp and clean from the earlier rain. She slowed her pace on the wet pavement and headed for Clark's car. She could feel the attaché following her. Her hand tightened over the revolver, which she held against her thigh beneath the cape. She controlled her breathing. At the very least, she could control her breathing. *Don't fail,* she warned.

She could feel the attaché closing in behind her, closer, closer. From the corner of her eye, she saw a black BMW sedan crawling through the parking lot. Was it also stalking her? Suddenly, it accelerated past her, screeching to a halt behind Clark's Porsche.

A man climbed out of the car, poised for abduction. There would be two of them in on the assault. Wait for the moment, Cleo told herself. Wait. Then it happened. The attaché grabbed her from behind and the accomplice swooped upon her. Cleo put up a token struggle. They were pushing her into the BMW. It was working, Cleo thought. Then the hood fell to her shoulders.

"Damn, this is the wrong one," the attaché growled, pulling Cleo back from the car by her collar.

Discovered too soon, Cleo seized the moment and started to swing the revolver into the attaché. But before she could assert herself, she heard, "Stop! Police!" and the attaché flung her to the pavement.

A policeman was on foot, about a half a block away.

"Stay away!" Cleo cried. There was no time for law and order. She was scrambling on her knees as the attaché and his accomplice climbed into the BMW. No! She couldn't let them get away. What could she do? What would Clark do?

She aimed the revolver with both hands as the car started. She fired at the rear tire, using the gun to avert disaster as Clark had done in Ian's yard. But all she managed to do was draw screams from witnesses and jar her bones as the charge exploded.

The policeman was now behind her. She could feel the nuisance of his presence. He was trying to restrain her. "Hold it. You're okay now," he said.

Cleo twisted violently, shaking him off like a cobweb. "Go away!" she screamed authoritatively. "Special detail, narcotics!" she yelled without shame and hurled herself into Clark's Porsche, never losing sight of the BMW.

The Porsche engine roared and belched exhaust smoke, ready to race. Cleo let the clutch fly out and the car jerked forward as she stomped on the accelerator. In wild pursuit, Cleo drove recklessly. Then she slammed on the brakes. A Grayline bus crossed her path like a lumbering giant, obstructing her way—and her view. Cleo leaned on the horn. But nothing changed. She was hysterical. She threw the gearshift into reverse, and changed course.

But when she was clear of the bus, the BMW was gone. She was no longer hysterical. She was devastated. She considered returning to the policeman, but that would be a waste of time. Like Cleo, he had had no chance to get the license plate of the car. He was of no use. She drove on in desperation. She had lost her only link to Clark. Where was he? She had not a clue in the world.

She sifted through her minimal resources, trying to build a desert from a few grains of sand. But one of those grains was Radul Jamar. She drove to the grand trickster himself, the address on his business card looming in her mind like a giant billboard.

The sick feeling in her stomach returned. What if Radul was not in his hotel suite, waiting for her like a dependable cuckoo in a clock? What then? One thing at a time, she told herself, pacing herself, calming herself. Clark's life was at stake. She had to be in control.

And her control could not have been more smooth, more perfect, as she took the elevator of the Columbia Regency to the thirtieth floor and glided on the plush carpeting to the door of Radul's suite. She knocked. She waited. She panicked. She knocked again. There were footsteps. She regained control. Total control.

CHAPTER NINETEEN

A DELIGHTED RADUL JAMAR in a burgundy silk robe greeted her at the door, his teeth gleaming white against his dark, devilishly handsome features.

"Do come in, Mrs. Cannell."

"Thank you," she said coolly, as she stepped into his deluxe suite, a museum of gilded French provincial furniture with heavy draperies tied away from narrow windows with gold braid.

"May I take your coat?" he offered with saccharine chivalry, his hands already on her shoulders.

Cleo wanted to jerk away, to scream, "no, there is no time." But that was no way to maintain an adversarial advantage. Instead, she unfastened the clasp at her neck and allowed him to gallantly take her cape and drape it over a chair.

She seated herself on the sofa with what she hoped was aristocratic carriage and crossed her legs elegantly. Radul, eyeing her with charming appraisal, did not miss a glimpse of Cleo's skinned knees before she smoothed her skirt.

"You look like a piece of Egyptian art, Cleopatra," he said, studying her heavy eyeliner. "Let us see," he continued theatrically, gesturing toward the antique clock on the mantel. "You arrive at my door less than twenty-four hours since our lunch together. An Australian boomerang could not be more reliable. Do not mistake me. I am most happy to see you. But since you have not had sufficient time to miss me, I cannot credit this visit to my personal charm. That makes me unhappy."

"Oh, you shall be happy, Mr. Jamar," Cleo cooed.

He raised his eyebrows quizzically, and a smile spread slowly across his face in wicked fascination as he took a seat at the other end of the sofa.

Cleo put her hand into Claudia's handbag, and drew out a key. "This key is yours," she said, holding it in front of her, "if you can tell me where my husband is." She held the key at its tip and displayed it on the emerald-green cushion, which lay between them.

"This key, Mrs. Cannell?" Radul inquired, edging closer to inspect it, like a mad wizard contemplating some rare ingredient for a potion.

"This key opens a locker containing—" Cleo paused for impact "—one million dollars."

Radul waited a moment to be sure Cleo had nothing further to say, then threw back his head and laughed into the vaulted ceiling. Cleo was dumbfounded, ignorant of where she had gone wrong, where she had lost control. She could have counted every one of Radul's gleaming teeth before he composed himself and gave a roguish smile.

Cleo sat behind a mask of calm as he spoke slyly with tantalizing slowness. "If this key of yours is so valuable, what is to prevent me from—" he paused, and Cleo's fingers inched instinctively over to the key "—taking it by force?" He dropped his hand over hers, pinning it to the pillow and impounding the key. His eyes danced devilishly.

Cleo didn't flinch. She raised her chin for a haughty bearing and stated with cool certainty, "Your personal honor makes such robbery impossible."

His hand relaxed as he nodded and appraised her approvingly. Holding her gaze, he lifted her hand from the pillow, then bowed his head and planted a kiss into her palm. Cleo heaved a quiet sigh of relief.

He regarded her affectionately, caressing her hand. "You, too, Mrs. Cannell, are a most astute student of psychology, but I'm afraid you have made a grave error. I am a rich man. Why should I lift a finger for one million dollars—" he let her hand slip from his "—when that sum, in which you place so much faith, is but a fraction of the amount of interest my holdings accrue overnight while I am asleep?" He waved his hand into the air to emphasize the insignificance of the amount to him.

Inwardly, Cleo crumpled. The force of his epicurean life-style, the luxury of his surroundings, the habitat of no graduate student she had ever known, closed around her, mocking her. She had relied on ordinary greed, only to find that his immeasurable wealth negated it.

Still, Cleo remained resolute. Playing to greed had failed, playing to his ego must not. She spoke steadily, eyeing Radul skeptically. "So I have made an error in thinking you could be persuaded by a plebeian sum. Did I also make an error in thinking that you can ascertain the whereabouts of my husband?"

Baited by the challenge, Radul was quick to boast, "I can find out in one, maybe two, phone calls."

"Ha! I thought you would know such matters first-hand," she scoffed, sitting up on the sofa to leave.

"You doubt me?" Radul trumpeted with indignation, his temper at a boil.

Poised on the edge of the sofa, Cleo twisted toward him and ran her eyes over him as if he were a useless piece of baggage, not worth the effort of review. Slowly, she let an indulgent smile creep across her face as if granting him one more chance to prove his virility.

She cocked her head, dragging the ornate, gold-encrusted phone across the coffee table to Radul's knees. "Prove it," she breathed provocatively.

Soberly, he picked up the receiver, intent on the ultimate challenge. Cleo settled back onto the sofa to maintain her flawlessly cool exterior, elated that she was just seconds away from Clark's location through the power of eavesdropping. Her ecstatic victory was short-lived. Radul conducted his conversation in his native tongue, and Cleo knew she was once again at his mercy. Still, she inspected her nails leisurely.

After Radul replaced the receiver, he, too, settled back on the sofa. He pursed his lips into a wry smile. "Only one phone call," he told her smugly. He paused for her reaction. Finding none, he resorted to theatrical speech. "So it appears *I* have the information *you* want. *You* have one million dollars, which I have refused. Perhaps you have another commodity you wish to trade...."

Cleo stiffened. The implication was clear. The thought of making love to Radul repulsed her. But Clark needed her. His life, his future, depended on her action. It was such a small price to pay for Clark. She minimized the horror of it. Perhaps all she had to do was play to Radul's ego. Perhaps he would be content with her flattery, her willingness.

With one graceful movement of her hand, Cleo removed the barrette that secured her ponytail. She tossed her head so that her hair fell over her shoulders. "I would hardly call what interested you in Acapulco a commodity," she purred and edged closer to him on the sofa. She flirted with her eyes, but Radul was largely unresponsive.

Hiding her quiet desperation, she rested her hand on his knee.

"Are you trying to seduce me?" he remarked at last, highly bored.

Cleo retracted her hand, humiliated.

Radul gave a snobbish sniff. "I make love only to women of my own choosing. Women of consummate appeal. I am not prey to random seduction on the whim of even the most meticulously groomed woman, much less a woman who has obviously slept in her wrinkled clothes. And forgive me, Mrs. Cannell, but that eyeliner you should best avoid."

Cleo bowed her head, unable to hold his penetrating gaze, feeling ashamed in defeat. But she would never concede. Where was the shame in saving Clark? How could she even consider defeat?

Undaunted, she stood suddenly and turned her back on Radul, who thought she was leaving in a huff. Cleo heard him say her name in a conciliatory fashion, but before he could say more, she turned sharply to face him, her fingers at the top button of her blouse.

"I ask you please to favor me with your choosing," Cleo spoke softly. "Wrinkled clothes can be removed. Just tell me what you want."

Radul regarded her soberly and said nothing. She swiftly undid the top button on her blouse, proving her sincerity. Still Radul said nothing.

Cleo didn't know what to do. She felt she might cry. She reached for the second button.

"Cleopatra," Radul said. "Come here."

She approached him hesitantly.

"Give me your hand."

She held out her hand, and he took it delicately, as offered. And then he gripped it as a friend, one friend to another. "You are a courageous woman," he said with respect, the edge of ridicule absent from his voice. "I am a rich man so I do not take your money. And I am an honorable man. So I do not take pleasure from your body when it is obviously your concern for your husband that forces you to do this. I will tell you where he is."

Cleo looked amazed.

"You see." Radul smiled. "I am not such a bad character. I only make a bad first impression. Your husband is on Hal Mayor's pleasure ship. You know where it is. I believe you had dinner at the Waterfront Club last night. The ship is moored on the east side with the large yachts in berth 7E. The plan is to set sail at 2:00 p.m. for something of a dinner cruise.

Cleo looked at the clock on the mantel and panicked.

"You have plenty of time," said Radul, giving her hand a firm squeeze before letting go. "The catering manager at the Waterfront was born in my country. I will call him and arrange for a delay to 3:00 p.m."

Overwhelmed, Cleo rushed to her cape. Radul helped her with it. "You have a car?" he asked.

She nodded. "You will call?"

"Right now." He picked up the phone. "Also, I would have called you a camel."

Cleo pressed her eyes shut for a moment. "Thank you, Radul. Thank you so much."

His smile was slow, and shaded with sadness. "You shame me, my friend. In Acapulco, I called for help and you chose to save my life. You call for help now, but I do not know if I am saving your life. You choose a dangerous game. Take warning and good luck, my friend."

She rushed out and Radul made the call. He arranged for the delay easily. Life was easy for him. But when he put down the phone, he picked up the key Cleo had left on the sofa and worried that he had done the wrong thing.

CHAPTER TWENTY

CLEO HURRIED through the lobby, stopping briefly at the entrance to check the street for anything suspicious, then ran out into the misty rain to the silver Porsche. There were storm clouds above.

She revved the engine while she threw the Porsche into gear and raced toward the marina. She scanned the rearview mirror constantly, prepared to detour if pursued by a black BMW. Only once did she spot a black car, which made her heart leap into her throat. Otherwise, everything appeared to be going smoothly.

She piloted the car through the gate of the marina, her heart flying as fiercely as the wind-slapped flags of the yacht club, and proceeded to the east pier where the large seagoing yachts were moored. She came upon berth 1E and looked down the row of commercial charter boats. Through the rain, she saw a white, luxury vessel with two decks and a pilot's bridge, *Hallaran II* painted on the stern. The club's catering van was parked by the ramp to berth 7E.

Suddenly, Cleo jammed on the brakes, reducing her speed to a crawl. The black BMW sedan that she had so far avoided was parked in front of the catering van. Straining to see through the windshield, she saw Hal Mayor's attaché standing sentry at the ramp, supervising the catering load.

Cleo had not expected difficulty in getting aboard the yacht. Immediately, she tore off her black cape to avoid recognition. She hoped the Porsche would go unnoticed, a blend of gray in the rain, as she rolled it into an unobtrusive parking position in front of berth 5E. The rain was heavier now, beating forcefully on the roof of the car.

Cleo clenched the steering wheel for a moment, her lips moving in silent prayer to lift the limits of her conventional mind, which told her that boarding the yacht was impossible. Then she slung Claudia's handbag over her shoulder, feeling a fiendish satisfaction at the weight of Clark's revolver within, cracked open the door and slipped out of the car. She plotted a swift path to berth 7E, walking behind posts and moorings. The rain was in her favor.

Another man joined the attaché on deck. They appeared to be in relaxed conversation. Judging her opportunity, Cleo then ran the final distance to hide behind the rear wheel of the catering van. Her position was strategic, but her mind was not one step closer to boarding. What could she do? She waited and watched the gatekeepers.

Then one of the caterers surfaced from the depths of the yacht and presented a clipboard to the attaché. In a matter of minutes, the caterers would run down the ramp, hop back into the van and, much worse, the yacht would depart. Cleo crouched low and moved to hide behind the BMW. Her chin brushed the rain beads off the chrome bumper as she desperately tried to think of a way to get on board. She needed to distract the guards.

As she crawled around the BMW for a better view of the yacht, she saw her opportunity. The driver's door was unlocked. She opened the door wide enough to shimmy inside, and sprawling across the seat, she threw the gear-shift into neutral and released the parking brake.

Her heart beating in her ears, she slunk headlong to the rear of the car. She braced her arms against the bumper and gave a hearty shove. The car rolled easily, and Cleo advanced her position as the front wheels hit a section of downward-sloping concrete, gaining momentum, at which point Cleo gave another shove and scampered to hide behind the van.

It's working! It's working! she reveled in retreat. Elation pounded into her brain, numb from panic but keyed for survival.

The BMW was rolling toward the dock's edge to crash into the rubber bulwark and create the distraction Cleo needed to board the yacht. She poised for her moment like a runner in the starting blocks and became bolder in observation. It was now or never. The men had noticed the rolling car. The attaché began to sprint toward it but was too late. The car collided with the bulwark, which unexpectedly gave way, causing the car to slip over the edge of the dock and nosedive into the water. It was an impressive spectacle, which brought the second man and the caterers to the attaché's side to commiserate as the BMW filled with water and started to sink.

Cleo scurried along the pier and charged up the ramp unnoticed. She boarded the yacht and faded into the canopied shadows.

Drawing the revolver, she began to sneak from porthole to porthole. The interior was dark and empty. Obviously, the entire party was on the deck above. Stealthily, she made her way to the base of a ladder at the rear of the yacht. She glanced around furtively, then ascended. Stepping quickly out of the main walkway, she flattened herself against the exterior cabin wall and proceeded to search.

She was holding her breath, edging to a porthole for a glimpse inside, when someone struck her between the shoulder blades and pinned her to the wall. Once the revolver was wrested from her hand, the pressure to her back ceased, and she was allowed to turn around.

"My goodness, Mrs. Cannell."

It was Hal Mayor, a hospitable smile spreading across his lips as he looked down at a shivering, rain-soaked woman with eyeliner streaking down her cheeks. Her wet clothes clung to her body, making her appear smaller than she was.

"Where is Clark?" she demanded fiercely.

"Well, I don't recall sending you an invitation, honey, but come join us anyway." Smirking, Hal took her arm firmly. Just then the yacht's engines started up.

Cleo allowed Hal to lead her down the passageway. She had been caught but was still on target. She was going to Clark, and together they could escape anything. She was suddenly aware of being cold and slightly nauseated. She had not eaten since the day before and felt terribly weak. But soon everything would be all right. Soon she would see Clark, and Clark would take care of everything.

Hal showed Cleo into a large wood-paneled cabin furnished like a cozy den in the English countryside. Two men in dark suits were nursing drinks. The glowering attaché was talking in low tones into a portable phone. His airport accomplice was looking out the porthole. The yacht was leaving the dock.

"Guess who I found on the prowl, packing firepower?" Hal said, laying the confiscated revolver on a shelf. "You know anything about this?" He was addressing the back of a large leather chair, which was swiveling in his direction.

The man in the chair was Clark, healthy, unharmed. At the sight of him, Cleo breathed a sigh of relief, but faltered on the eerie expression of nonrecognition on Clark's face. He eyed her with detached curiosity, swirling his drink around the ice cubes in his glass. He did not seem like a man coerced. He seemed like a willing participant and more. The status of his chair, his commanding position at the table covered with maps, made him a leader.

Clark threw Hal a look of boredom and shook his head. Hal was amused.

"Bed this girl for one night and she can't let you out of her sight," Hal joked, drawing laughter from around the room, except for the attaché and his accomplice, who appeared uneasy.

The scene was not as she had imagined, but Cleo forged ahead. "Clark," she said under the belittling stares of the men in the room. "Claudia is safe. Hal tried to kidnap her, but we switched places. She is safe."

The attaché stepped toward her, but Hal motioned him back. "The little girl is delirious, Clark. The rain must have soaked her brain," Hal remarked casually.

Clark glanced at Hal in agreement, shaking his head again as if bored by these feeble accusations from a wet nuisance. But Cleo saw it. The flicker in his eyes. She knew him too well. He was not fooled. She wore black high-heeled boots, boots that Clark knew were not her own, but of Claudia's sophisticated taste. He was undoubtedly her partner in principle, but what could he do? There were five men in the room. His gun was on a shelf behind Hal.

Cleo reached clumsily into her handbag for a tissue, then another, like a pathetic waif. Then she was ready.

"Freeze," she shouted, pointing the miniature gun Clark had given her at the outset. She took the room by surprise, drawing quizzical stares at her toylike weapon.

She was trembling as she stood alone against the roomful of suited muscle. A loaded stillness descended upon the cabin. Now what, she thought.

Her lips quivered in a smile of nervous happiness when Clark slowly rose from his chair. "Good girl," he soothed, coming toward her, walking into the barrel of the gun. Cleo started to warn him not to block her sight of the men in the room, but he was already reaching for her wrist, taking hold of the gun, which she gladly relinquished to his experienced, capable hands. It was over. They had won.

Then he clamped down on her wrist in a vise grip. Her eyes went wide, seeking Clark's reason. In answer, he jerked her forward, throwing her off balance, and then pushed her backward, letting her fall to the bench built into the cabin wall behind her. Her eyes were as wide as her mouth.

Clark tossed Cleo's gun to Hal, who examined it with interest. Clark returned to his chair. "You shouldn't take me for a fool, Hal. The kid is wearing my sister's boots— so I believe her. Fortunately, for you, the kid also claims my sister is safe."

Hal shifted uneasily. "You have my word, my men would not have harmed her. You realize with stakes this large I needed the insurance." He leaned forward in his chair, presenting Clark with a submissive posture.

Clark gave Hal a long, hard look. He began to nod knowingly. "I suppose I would have done the same in your shoes." He grinned. "I suppose it's hard trying to strike a deal with the best agent Intelnet ever produced."

Cleo's face stung with humiliation. She had been such a fool. A simple fool. How could she have fallen in love? How could she have been duped by a man in a game he played for ego and personal gain? Impaled on a stake of reality, she listened to the idle words of the man she once worshiped.

"What are we going to do with her?" Clark asked. "She obviously knows too much about me."

"We'll leave her to the sharks," Hal said.

"No good," Clark mumbled. "She is officially in my custody. I'm responsible for her till she's out of D.C. Let's not forget my reputation."

"Okay, I'll ship her to Acapulco with Johnny," Hal replied, indicating the attaché as he sipped his drink. "Stick her in a car with my spineless nephew and run them over a cliff. I knew he'd come in handy someday."

"No!" Cleo screamed in rage, springing to her feet. She could not let her own stupidity claim Perry's life, too.

"Tie her up. Take her to the lower cabin," Hal ordered, no longer willing to waste time.

The attaché approached Cleo zealously, enjoying the prospect of settling a debt with her. The accomplice moved in to assist him, but Cleo refused to be taken. If she could just break free, she could jump ship and swim back to the dock. It could not be far. The yacht was still in the channel.

She went wild and struck the accomplice in the throat, sending him sputtering backward. The attaché moved in to subdue her, but she scratched and thrashed in a fury. She kicked his shins unmercifully, scoring solid hits to the bone. But her struggle amounted to nothing as he arrested her forearms. Set on survival, she remembered Radul, the only honest man in this whole band of thieves, and his lecture on self-defense. With a swift jerk, she

raised her knee in the attaché's groin. He let out a tremendous groan of pain and doubled over pathetically. But
Cleo could not win. The accomplice caught her, pinning
her arms behind her.

Trapped, Cleo saw the attaché rise to his full height, his
grimace of pain turning to fury. Cleo saw it coming, but
there was nothing she could do. He hit her in the stomach
and she gasped for breath. She couldn't fight anymore.
They were too strong.

She crumpled slightly but the attaché had her pinned in
place. Helpless, she let her eyes rove about the cabin while
her rational brain lectured her. *You fool,* she heard repeatedly. Already nauseated, she felt weak, terribly weak.
The figures in the room began to blur—except for Clark,
whom she saw as clearly as if under a spotlight from
heaven. He reflected a cool white light, unmoved, apath-
etic. It was crystal clear that Cleo meant nothing to him.
When the attaché forced Cleo to move, she fainted.

CHAPTER TWENTY-ONE

LYING ON A HARD BUNK in a lower-level cabin, Cleo regained consciousness. She stared blankly at the low ceiling, sure only that she was alive. Her hands were tied with rope behind her back, her legs were bound at the ankles. Her arms felt as if they had been twisted from their sockets and replaced badly. Her stomach ached. Her clothes were dry, but they felt like stiff parchment against her skin.

The cabin was empty except for the bunk and a heavy wooden chair. It was dark but for the gray light of a rainy day, visible from the partially curtained porthole. She did not know how long the yacht had been under sail. They could be well out of the Potomac River and into the Chesapeake Bay by now. What had Hal said? Leave her to the sharks? No. She was obviously freight—assigned below deck, waiting for a contrived death with Perry.

At the recollection, Cleo's blood boiled. How dare these thugs and thieves rob her of her life? How dare Clark Cannell talk of her disposal as easily as swatting a fly? She would show that beguiling, blasted double agent that she could not be sold out as easily as he had sold out the free world.

Swearing they would never get her to Acapulco, Cleo twisted her wrists against the ropes. But it was useless.

The ropes were too tight. Frustrated, she sat up to look at her ankles, wincing at the stab of pain the effort brought to her stomach.

Her ankles were not bound as tightly as her hands, an apparent oversight and certainly a blessing of the leather boots. Twisting and rotating her foot at the ankle, Cleo began to pull her right leg out of the boot. She held her left leg rigid as a counterresistance, and strained against it until her breathing was rapid. Panting, and gritting her teeth, she thought of Houdini, strained and pulled, then strained and pulled again. Soon she was grunting, and then with a final tug, the struggle ended. Her right leg was free.

She extricated the boot from the ropes with her foot, and shifted in the bunk so that the boot lay beneath her wrists. Her fingers tested the edges of the silver buckle that adorned it. The underside was unfinished and sharp. The tingle of victory coursed through her body.

Sitting on top of the boot, Cleo began to rub the ropes against the buckle. It would be no instant success, but if perseverance had its reward, Cleo had perseverance to give. She sawed on the ropes relentlessly, tired and fatigued in the awkward position, but undaunted.

She knew that Claudia had arrived in San Francisco by now and had called Alex at home. Cleo was confident that Alex was searching for her at this minute and that rescue was at hand. After all, Clark's Porsche was parked at the marina, and certainly after her airport scene the police would be looking for the car.

Even so, Cleo was devising her own plan. Once free, she would sneak out. She suspected that the door was not locked since she was tied up. Alternatively, she was prepared to break the porthole with the chair. Then what? She didn't know, but she had come this far to save Clark.

Now she could certainly save herself. She, alone, was responsible for her predicament, and she was angry—angry at herself and angry at Clark as she sat sawing the ropes against the buckle.

Hours passed in the dark. Hours in which she felt faint, hungry, physically exhausted. She couldn't guess the time. She only knew it was night. She could feel the frayed outer layers of the rope. More than half the bulk remained. The rope would be off before the sun came up, she told herself, switching to the buckle of the other boot. Just as long as the ropes were off before the yacht docked, she would be fine.

Then the yacht's engines sneezed to a halt and Cleo's blood turned to ice. In pitch-darkness, she speculated in the depth of fear. She knew they were not in port. They were in the ocean somewhere and at a dead stop. Why?

Furiously, she sawed at the ropes. What reason would there be to stop in the middle of nowhere unless to throw her to the sharks? She panicked. *Don't be so self-centered,* she scolded. Why would they stop the boat just to throw her off? But she sensed danger. She was in the precarious position of being unwanted cargo no matter what lay ahead.

Perhaps a half an hour passed while Cleo breathed in absolute fear, listening to every creak as the yacht rolled in the waves. Then her worst suspicion was confirmed. She heard approaching footsteps.

She was terrified. Her arms were still bound. She was quite helpless. Only a miracle would save her now. She curled on her side, lying on the boots and tucking her legs behind her. She shut her eyes, pretending to be asleep as the door opened. If the visitor was making a routine check, he would see her, as expected, and leave.

But the visitor didn't leave. He entered the cabin. He shut the door behind him. Then Cleo heard the most chilling sound of her life. He locked the door. Trapped with the unknown in the dark, Cleo's heart beat like a jackhammer. She clung to the flimsiness of her pretense. Certainly, murder on this ship would not have to take place behind a locked door.

The visitor crouched beside the bunk. Cleo could do nothing but pretend. She felt an exploring touch to her lower abdomen, right where the attaché had thrown his punch. Rape sprang into Cleo's mind, and rage dispelled fear.

Determined to sink the ship with hands tied behind her back before she would submit, she shot up to a sitting position, but was caught in a smothering embrace, her swearing muffled in the chest of a man she knew.

"Shh." His voice was a soothing whisper. "Remember me?" he said, his hands dropping to apply a pocketknife to the ropes at her wrists. "I'm the guy who promised to keep you alive. You certainly are making it tough, quick-thinking lady."

It was Clark. Clark had come back to her. Her special hero. Tears welled in her eyes. At the snap of the ropes, Cleo's arms flew around him.

"Oh, Clark, I'm so afraid," she sobbed, clinging to him like a child.

He wrapped her in his arms, trying to give strength to her wilted, fragile form, imagining the untold hurdles she had gone through, hating himself for what he was about to do. "You're a real pro, ma'am. Got your legs untied without me."

Cleo shook her head. "I'm no pro...I'm sick, Clark. My stomach hurts," she whimpered feebly, no longer needing or wanting to be brave and strong.

"I know, baby, I know." He held his hand briefly to her stomach before reaching into his pocket. "We're going to get out of here," he said, unfolding a tightly compressed plastic tube into a wide ring, which he fastened as a collar around her neck. "Listen to me."

Cleo listened like an obedient child, resting against Clark's powerful chest, safe at last. He introduced her hand to a cord hanging from the plastic collar. "When I lower you into the water, swim away quietly and as fast as you can. Don't stop for any reason. Pull down to inflate this only when you're so far away, you can't see the ship lights. We don't have much time. Can you stand?" he asked, raising Cleo to her feet, then bracing her as she swayed. "Hold on to my neck. I'll carry you."

"No. I'm fine," she insisted, determined to do her part in the escape.

She grasped his arm, and he unlocked the cabin door and looked down the passageway. Cleo blinked against the light as Clark quickly pulled her out and closed the door behind him.

With the stealth of a commando, he led her down the passageway and parked her at the base of a ladder. Cleo waited while Clark climbed ahead. When he signaled, she followed him, willing herself from rung to rung, until Clark hoisted her onto the deck.

Stooped over, they ran to the stern of the yacht. Cleo welcomed the cold, the fog. She and Clark were escaping. They crouched at the railing behind plastic storage drums.

"Hurry," Clark urged, directing her to a sitting position at the edge of the deck and getting a grip on her arm as she dangled her legs over the side. "I'll stay here till you're out of pistol range."

"You aren't coming?" Cleo gasped in disbelief.

"Later," he said, keeping a lookout around them.

"Clark!" she protested.

"The water is going to be cold. Don't be afraid." He tightened his grip on her arm, preparing to lower her over the side.

"No! Clark, I won't leave you!" she cried, grabbing the railing to resist him.

"Cleo, don't make me hurt you."

"Oh, Clark, come with me," she pleaded. "Please come with me. Now!"

"Soon," he said, his watchful eyes darting around the deck.

"Promise me," she implored, her hand to his chest. He turned to her and Cleo desperately searched his face. She didn't want to leave him.

Clark had broken his vigil to look at her. He allowed himself this moment, for there might not be another. And when his moment was spent, he drew her close and kissed her, hoping she would know how much he loved her and praying that the part of him she chose to remember would always make her happy. "I love you, Cleo," he said with all his heart. Then he swung her over the side, and dropped her into the water without a splash.

Cleo felt the shock of the ice water on her feet first. Then the searing cold rose evenly up her legs until it engulfed her and she became part of a vast inhospitable sea. She might have panicked, but her love for Clark was stronger than fear. Hearing his voice as if he were beside her, she followed his instructions explicitly. She swam away from the yacht quietly, as fast as she could, pushing through the freezing black water into darkness. The faster she swam away, the sooner Clark could leave his watch. The sooner he could leave his watch, the sooner he would follow. The current of the sea was with her, and she lost sight of the yacht almost immediately in the fog.

She swam farther and farther into the darkness, rising on the crest of waves and falling. She was losing directional reference and she was scared, but Clark was with her. He loved her. He had said so.

She kept swimming until she was sure that she was a considerable distance away from the yacht. Then she reached for the cord at her neck and pulled down sharply while treading water. The collar inflated around her neck. It became a tight-fitting buoyancy device and she floated easily. Now she would not drown even if she fell unconscious. She had done what Clark had told her. Now there were no instructions in her head. Now what?

She drew her legs up to her chest and clasped her arms around them to conserve heat in the fetal position. She was shivering badly. Cleo knew the danger of hypothermia, but she was not worried. Clark, himself, had put her in the water. He would join her soon. But when? How? No matter, Cleo thought. *He loves me.*

Ironically, she had feared being thrown overboard to the sharks most, and now wasn't that her exact situation? *But Clark loves me,* she repeated.

Her confidence in Clark was unshakable, but she realized she was rapidly succumbing to the cold. It was getting harder and harder to form coherent thoughts. She was getting drowsy. Soon her arms and legs dangled in the water listlessly. But Cleo hung on to her mind. Clark had said soon, and soon meant any moment.

And then the sound of an explosion ripped through the night, and a fire temporarily lit up the sky. *Oh, my God!* Cleo thought. It was the yacht! The yacht had blown apart.

She screamed Clark's name and tried to swim toward the diminishing blaze, glowing through the darkness like a red-eyed devil, slowly closing its eyes. She tore at the buoyancy collar, believing that it hindered her swimming, but she couldn't tear it from her neck. Her fingers, like her cold strangled body, would not function.

And then reality ripped through her, extinguishing any feeling not yet frozen by the sea. The yacht was gone. So was Clark. His death would have been instantaneous—as certain as her own as she waited to die, lost and forgotten in the middle of the sea. Clark had not come with her, but soon she would go to him.

She surrendered to the sea, the dark and the drowsiness overtaking her. There was no reason to resist. Nothing mattered now—except perhaps saying goodbye to someone. No one would know what happened to her if she didn't say goodbye . . . no one would ever know . . . no one knows now. . . .

Now. It couldn't be more than nine o'clock in California, this Wednesday night. From behind a glass wall, Cleo saw her sister, Cassy, putting her daughter to bed in a crib by the glow of the clown lamp that Cleo had sent as a gift at birth instead of visiting. Cassy was smiling at the baby who would wake into Thursday—a Thursday that Cleo would never see. She tapped on the glass, but Cassy didn't hear. Then Cassy turned out the light, and Cleo saw no more.

It came out of nowhere. A whirring sound. It got stronger and the water around Cleo rippled in concentric circles. With effort, Cleo looked to the sky. It was a helicopter hovering above her, descending like a giant bird on a nest, dangling a rescue hoist. Joy pulsed through Cleo's body like the thrill of a new dawn. She was not dead. Clark was not dead. The nightmare had been reversed.

With pinpoint accuracy, the hoist dropped directly in front of her. Cleo managed to wedge her shoulders through a triangular sling that held her securely as the hoist was reeled out of the water. For a while she hung in the air suspended beneath a great flying beast. Then two sets of arms guided her waterlogged body through the cargo door into the belly of the craft. She could hear shouts above the roar of the rotor. Hands worked quickly to disengage the hoist, the collar. Hands slapped a coarse blanket about her shoulders. Hands were lowering her shoulders to the floor of the helicopter. These hands were attached to a face she recognized. Alex. It was Alex of the old team, Cleo and Alex, and anybody got a pretzel? And . . .

"Cleo, where's Clark?" Alex asked urgently.

The words tore through Cleo's delirium, destroying her euphoria. Alex didn't know where Clark was! Frantically, Cleo tried to create a voice. "On the boat," she murmured with effort. Her lips wouldn't respond, but Alex understood.

He shouted orders to the pilot. "Keep circling! And get copter three in the air with the searchlights. Notify the Coast Guard and any ship in the area."

The second man continued to swaddle Cleo in blankets, tucking them around her legs.

"Cleo," Alex asked again, inches away from her face. "Did you see Clark jump before the yacht blew up?"

Cleo relived the horror that the joy of rescue had eclipsed. That ugly ball of fire had been real. The nightmare had not been erased. She shook her head in agony.

"Keep circling," Alex barked, leaving Cleo's side to climb back into the cockpit. "If he jumped, we'll pick him up."

The man kneeling beside Cleo pressed a hot liquid to her lips. Cleo moved her mouth in a combination of a plea and a demand. "Find him. You found me."

Miraculously, the man understood her slurred speech. "We picked you up by the transmitter in your collar," he explained. "It's a Model UX 344 that will float you even when you're unconscious. We wondered why we got a signal so soon before detonation. Cannell only had one. He gave it to you."

Cleo withdrew into her failing body so that the truth would not hurt so much. The yacht, the explosion, the buoyancy device, the helicopter had all been planned, with Clark in control. It was Cleo's resolve to save him that had cost him his life.

Cleo heard Alex cursing in the cockpit. He was dropping flares, which confirmed ship wreckage only. The darkness was oppressive. She heard the man, the shadow above, shout to the cockpit. "Her body temperature is too low. We gotta get her back now."

Alex cursed again. The helicopter was turning back, aborting the search.

No! No! Cleo strained to say. But it was just an echo in her head. And then there was no echo at all.

CHAPTER TWENTY-TWO

CLEO WAS SEMI-CONSCIOUS. The world passed in shadows as she groped along a floor on hands and knees for scattered pearls from a broken necklace. Whenever she found a pearl and clasped it in her hands, there was a burst of light, and she could see around her. Then there was darkness and she groped again for the next pearl and the next moment of consciousness.

She was packed onto a stretcher by two bodies in white uniforms—crisp, starched uniforms. There was a swishing noise and wind. The helicopter was taking off behind them.

She was in an ambulance, the interior bright and white like a sterile cocoon against the night sky. A paramedic was intent upon her forearm, and a bottle of clear intravenous solution hung on a pole above her.

She was alone on the floor again. It was important to Cleo to find each pearl. She wanted the necklace to be complete. She knew it was just a matter of perseverance in the dark. She could do it. She would restring the necklace, no matter how long it took.

She was inside a hospital emergency room. It looked like a television program. Lab coats moved like windup toys, wielding stethoscopes, giving injections. She was linked to machines. There were more needles. There was a bath, a warm water immersion. *You're flooding my floor,* Cleo protested. *I can't find my pearls.* And then, lily pads emerged over the water of a warm, fragrant, tropical pool. Cleo breathed the warm, balmy air, relaxed, blissful.

Her eyes opened clearly upon a team of nurses above her. The pearl hunt was over. A physician was reassuring. He asked her a few questions, which she answered hazily. He told her to rest. Everyone was so obliging.

There was another injection before Cleo was transferred to a single room where she floated warm and happy in a comfortable bed. There was a window in the room, and a crescent moon was showing through the clouds. All was right in the world, as told by the contented smile on Cleo's lips.

Nurses entered the room throughout the night, announced by the muffled squeak of the door. They would hover over her like guardian angels, then leave. They became part of the dream parade and pleasant sensations that ebbed and flowed around Cleo as she rested comfortably.

Someone was standing at her bed, holding her hand. The hand holding hers was a warm hand, a loving hand that played with her fingers, massaging them...leaving a weight on one of them. Cleo murmured and a kiss fell lightly on her lips—a goodbye kiss. *Wait,* Cleo called. This person was a friend. A good friend. *Don't go.*

She awoke suddenly. A nurse was beside her bed taking her pulse. "Hello. How do you feel?"

"Where am I? What time is it?" Cleo asked.

The nurse was cheerful. She had apple cheeks and wore a smile pin near her name tag. Ginny. "You're at the U.S. Naval Hospital. You've slept for almost fifteen hours. It's 5:00 p.m. Thursday."

Cleo sank back into the pillow. She had awakened safe and sound, on the other side of a nightmare, on a Thursday.

"A Mr. Matlow has been calling about you all day. He left his number—" Ginny pointed to a notepad by the phone "—if you need to speak to him tonight. A Mrs. Gunderson brought you some clothes. She was crying so hard even though I assured her you were fine. Maybe you should give her a call, too."

"Was Clark Cannell admitted to this hospital?"

Ginny was puzzled. "There's no one by that name on this ward. We get all emergency room admits."

Cleo turned her head away to hide her grief. Ginny took Cleo's pulse again and made a note in the chart. "We've been feeding you on an IV, but dinner will be here at six." She smiled. "Take a look at your flowers," she said before leaving the room.

When the door swung shut, Cleo cried miserably, her shoulders heaving with sobs. Mrs. Gunderson knew Clark was dead, but did she know that Cleo had killed him? If only tears could bring him back. Cleo cried in vain, knowing that the great sobs racking her body would not make Clark whole. How would she be able to bear her grief? Nothing, nothing, nothing could ease her pain, her sorrow, her guilt.

Cleo cried openly until Ginny returned. Guarding her privacy, she dried her eyes and held back the tears as Ginny set a dinner tray in front of her and encouraged her to eat. Of course, Ginny could be perky and effervescent. She had never known Clark. But Ginny could not be easily fooled. "You'd better eat," she advised kindly. "You can cry much better after eating."

And Cleo did eat, a ravenous appetite rising to the surface and compelling her to finish the meal, but not without guilt. A physician entered her room just as she finished the Jell-O, red cubes with strawberry or cherry flavor, but basically just red and sweet. Cleo wiped the tears from her cheeks quickly.

Dr. Scott introduced himself as the staff physician assigned to Cleo's case. He joked about her healthy appetite, removed the IV insert, listened to her chest, palpated her abdomen and generally pronounced her fit. "I'll discharge you tomorrow," he decided before exchanging a few more pleasantries for the sake of bedside manner.

Cleo counted the seconds until he left to continue his rounds. It was excruciating to hide her loss from cheerful strangers. She yearned to talk to someone. She did not want to call her sister. Not yet. Too much explanation would be in order. She needed someone to understand her now. Someone who also missed Clark.

She couldn't call Alex. He had been checking up on her only out of duty. The last thing in the world he would want to do was comfort the fool for whom his best friend was sacrificed. She had to suffer alone.

She considered for the first time the tiny flower basket on the bedside table. It was a jaunty collection of yellow daisies, blue bachelor buttons and red carnations, cheerful enough to make a hat for Ginny. Who had sent them?

Mechanically, she reached for the envelope and removed a note. It was written in a fine hand:

Dear Cleo,

Whenever I pestered Clark about getting married, he'd say, "in a blue moon to a girl with orchids in her hair." I have the ones you were wearing the day you met Clark—pressed on paper, of course. I wondered why Alex mailed them to me last week. Take care.

                              Claudia Cannell

Fresh tears streamed down Cleo's cheeks. She would never forgive herself, but apparently Claudia had forgiven her. Perhaps Claudia realized that she, and not Cleo, could be lying in this bed, and Clark would still be lost.

That thought gave Cleo the courage she needed to call Alex. Quickly, she dialed his number, which she knew by heart. She let the phone ring forever. There was no answer.

In between bouts of tears, she redialed his number constantly over the next hour. At nine o'clock, Ginny brought in a sleeping pill, which Cleo promptly refused. Ginny left it on the nightstand according to Cleo's wishes.

Just when Cleo was about to give up on Alex, his "hello" broke the repetition of rings.

"Alex, this is Cleo," she began timidly.

"How do you feel, Cleo?" he replied kindly, bringing new tears to Cleo's eyes. She didn't deserve such kindness.

"I'm fine," she choked.

"Hey, Cleo. Don't cry. It's over. We all did our best."

"I loved Clark, Alex. I didn't mean to hurt him," Cleo sobbed, the dam breaking loose.

"I know, Cleo. Claudia told me all about it. Have you been trying to call me, Cleo?"

"Yes," she whispered.

His voice was soft. "I'm sorry I wasn't here for you. I had a debriefing. How long have you been awake?" He checked his wristwatch.

"Four hours, five, I don't know." She choked.

Alex cringed. She wasn't supposed to suffer. "Cleo, aren't you taking any sedatives?"

"I'm looking at a sleeping pill. I don't want it."

"Cleo, I want you to take it. There's no use in crying all night like this. Please, Cleo . . . for me?"

Cleo had never been able to resist when he said please. He made sense. And right now she needed someone to tell her what to do. "Okay," she agreed, reaching for the pill and swallowing the smooth capsule without water. "Okay."

"Good! I'll ransom you out of that hospital tomorrow morning. Early! Now let me tell you what went on. I'm very proud of myself. Listen closely."

Ego, Cleo thought morbidly. Alex had it, too. An ego that thrived on Intelnet, an ego that could buoy him through the loss of his best friend.

"As it turns out, I have no apology to make to Intelnet for recruiting you. Do you remember the mural in Hal Mayor's study? Something like nymphs?"

"Yes."

"One of them was you, right?"

"Yes."

"Well, that was the connection that Clark discovered by accident in Acapulco. It had nothing to do with CLEOPATRA, with your name or your briefcase."

"I don't understand."

"The man who contacted us in the BART station was Miguel Diaz, an ex-policeman with a history of mental disorder. He worked for Hal as a stable manager for a year. He may have wanted informant status concerning an operation in Brazil. We don't know. What we do know is that he never intended to expose Hal's racket of selling military secrets to the highest bid. That would have been courting death. But apparently, Miguel Diaz thought he stood accused when he saw you as a custom message from Hal, straight out of the mural. It drove him to suicide."

Cleo was stunned. She had missed the connection completely. "Why didn't Clark tell me?" she asked sadly.

"You know the answer to that one, Cleo. Hal would have pulled you apart if he thought you were more than a pretty little girl."

"If only Clark had told me."

"You can't say that, Cleo. You don't know this business. You don't know Intelnet. Clark knew he was on lethal turf. For Hal to have kept his reputation so spotless over the years, his crime network had to include some of the most influential people in Washington and Intelnet. Including Edmondsen. Clark didn't even tell *me* that one till Monday."

"Edmondsen?"

"Yes, he's in jail tonight. I'm afraid you'll have to kiss the stipend he promised you goodbye."

Stipend? *Oh, Alex how can you be so trivial?* Cleo wanted to scold, but she was getting drowsy. She just listened. It had been a mistake to take that pill.

"The only way to smoke out the entire Mayor network was to promise Hal the details of CLEOPATRA, because Hal knew that no one other than Clark would have the guts to leak something so big. Hal was the broker in the deal, bringing together all players who came to the CLEOPATRA bait for profit and power. The attraction was so strong that even Hal didn't know some of the players—those using fronts and go-betweens. And Clark had to make sure he identified them all. He was walking on eggs trying to keep the balance. You know, trying to build on the greed and mistrust without coming to the attention of our command personnel and without jeopardizing actual deployment of CLEOPATRA.

"Clark devised a plan whereby he gave CLEOPATRA away in pieces but withheld the final code, which would tie it together and make it operational. That way—with each party in on the deal holding a separate piece of CLEOPATRA—he built a mutual dependence into the network.

"According to the agreement, Clark was to transmit the final code by coordinating a radio relay on board the *Hallaran II* at midnight on Wednesday. Of course, the code he transmitted made no sense, but that wouldn't be apparent until all the pieces had been matched up.

"We were monitoring the transmission from the surveillance chopper. Worked like a charm. We got a fix on every player. We got them right where they live."

Alex's words were blurring in Cleo's mind. The mission. The successful mission. A veritable coup for Intelnet. She didn't care.

Alex was in his element. "And as soon as the final code was dropped into place, they figured out they had been double-crossed, and one of them beamed a signal that detonated the yacht. With all the mistrust going around, Clark suspected there might have been an explosive charge planted on the hull. But there was no time for us to look for the explosive and remove it. And if Clark had shared his suspicion with Hal, then Hal would have known Clark had no intention of cooperating. The rest you know."

Cleo was drifting but she saw the ugly ball of fire again. She closed her eyes. She could still see the flames on the back of her eyelids. She squeezed her eyes shut, squeezing out the flames. "Is Hal alive?" she murmured.

"No one on the yacht survived. Interesting point, Cleo. By default, your friend, Perry, inherits the bulk of the estate. He has control of the whole empire. What do you think of that? Cleo? Cleo?" He paused. "Good night, Cleo," he whispered, happy she had fallen asleep with him.

He had not expected her to be so coherent. He had been careful to call the nursing station about her every three hours to make sure she did not wake up into a hell all alone. He had been designated Cleo's keeper, and he did not take the assignment lightly. He deemed himself her guardian, her buffer, her best friend. But Intelnet matters had boiled over into critical and had kept him from adhering to schedule just when Cleo must have needed him most.

He did not hang up the phone, leaving it instead on the armrest of his sofa and covering it with a pillow. Cleo had fallen asleep with the phone at her ear, and if he got off the line, the telephone disconnect signal might wake her. It was important that Cleo sleep until tomorrow.

CHAPTER TWENTY-THREE

WHEN CLEO WOKE the next morning, she was angry. Angry at the world for its stupid ways and angry at everyone she knew. She ate breakfast, got dressed and refused to shed a tear. Her feelings frozen, she looked as stiff and fierce as a totem pole in winter.

She was standing at the window waiting for Alex to arrive, when a nurse on the day shift brought in a tiny package wrapped in brown paper. "Someone left this for you at the nursing station," she said.

Cleo was curt. "Leave it on the bed."

The sun was shining. After two days of rain, the sun should have looked good. It didn't.

The phone rang. It was Alex. "You're a free woman! I've had you discharged from the hospital. Meet me in the lobby."

"Okay," was all Cleo said. She glanced around the room. She was wearing everything she needed to take with her. She was leaving Claudia's flowers behind. Claudia's note, she had torn up into little pieces earlier. Oh, the box, she thought, staring at the bed in disgust.

She approached it with a sense of obligation. She took it in her hands and tore off the brown wrapping carelessly, exposing a velvet box. A ring box, she noted, curiously.

She looked at her own hand where the silver wedding band was still in place. She could not find it in her heart yet to take it off. If only the hospital staff had removed it along with her clothes in the emergency room. In fact, she recalled that they had. She would almost swear to it. Impossible. It was still on her finger.

And now the ring box. She opened it slowly, and sat down on the bed, entranced. Inside was a key—a key to an airport locker, returned by Radul Jamar, a very noble pirate. As he said, he was not so bad—he only made a bad first impression. A smile cracked Cleo's lips slightly as she thought of him as a friend, and she lost some of her icy crust.

When she met Alex downstairs, she was still frozen, but without as much hate. Alex gave her a long hug when he saw her, and she thawed out a little more. "I'm late," he apologized sheepishly. "I couldn't get away."

He seated her in his serviceable old Volvo, and they drove in silence to Clark's home so that Cleo could collect her things. Mrs. Gunderson had thoughtfully put the key to the condo in the pocket of Cleo's jacket.

There were no parking places when they arrived. Alex made several passes of the street, which amounted to slow torture for Cleo. Then he parked a block away at the shopping center. By the time he stopped the car, Cleo was breaking up inside, but she refused to cry. She got out of the car before Alex came around to meet her.

"You look terrible," he said. "You can't go up and pack this way. Let me buy you some lunch."

To Cleo's horror, he steered her to the pretzel wagon. How could he be so insensitive? She resisted. "Alex, no. I can't bear it."

"Please, Cleo...I'm starving." He purchased two pretzels, handing one to Cleo, while he paid the vendor.

"Okay. Let's go," Cleo said impatiently. She turned on her heel.

"Hey, wait!" Alex pulled her back. "You didn't get any mustard." He picked up a yellow plastic bottle and began to squeeze it over the pretzel.

"Alex, I don't . . . like . . . mustard." Her speech was an emphatic, pained staccato.

Alex's eyes were twinkling. "But someone you know does. Tell him that dinner is catered by me, and you—"

"Alex!" Cleo screamed, her eyes exploding in joy.

"And you—" he paused, letting a knowing smile spread over his lips "—are the very best I can do." He was grinning now from ear to ear, and nodding into Cleo's overwhelmed face, his eyebrows high in merriment.

"Oh, Alex!" Cleo cried, starting to run, hesitating, returning. "Oh, Alex! Do you know what you are?" She was breathless, unbridled. "You're a . . . a . . ." She couldn't think. She couldn't wait. She wanted to run. She did. She turned. "You're a hopelessly sensitive sentimentalist!"

"Jolly good!" he called out to her.

Cleo barely heard. She was running down the block, running to Clark. He was alive. He was real. And he loved her. He said so.

She stabbed her key into the main door and ran through the common interior. Hang the elevator! She galloped up the stairs, panting, breathing in great gulps of joy. She raced to Clark's front door. It was unlocked, open. She reached the foyer and tossed the pretzel on that empty entry table, but it was no longer empty. The wedding picture, the Tahoe wedding picture, had been framed.

Clark came out of the kitchen. He must have been cooking. He looked natural, comfortable, as if nothing had happened. The smell of home cooking was in the room. The table was set. "Howdy, ma'am," he said.

Cleo flew to him, and he opened his arms wide.

"Clark, you're alive!"

He raised her off the ground when she hugged him. "More than you know, my precious, precious darling."

"Oh Clark, you're alive," Cleo repeated, still in shock, clinging to him. "How did you do it?"

"Silver medal in swimming, remember?" he teased, letting her feet touch the floor again. He laughed, caressing her back. "Didn't have to go far, though. I was picked up by a Coast Guard cutter. They were swarming the harbor because of some foiled drug bust that went on at the airport by someone in a Porsche. But you wouldn't know anything about that, would you?"

Cleo shook her head, laughing and crying against his shoulder. He took her hand and led her to the sofa. They sat down on the edge. Clark studied her face.

"How do you feel?" he asked, holding her hand firmly.

"Fine," Cleo answered faintly, still overwhelmed.

Clark gently wiped a tear from her cheek. "When I saw you at the hospital, you had a smile just like that on your lips," he said, touching them lightly.

"You came?" Cleo remembered. The good friend at her bedside, holding her hand. Her left hand.

"Of course. But I couldn't stay...." He wound a strand of her hair behind her ear. "There were so many loose ends to tie up. But I never left you really. You were in everything I did." He looked at her hand, held tightly in his, then returned to her face. "I resigned from Intelnet yesterday. Sound okay to you?"

Cleo spoke in a tiny voice, nodding lightly to her hero. "Okay."

"I booked a cruise out of San Francisco to Hawaii. Sound okay to you?"

She was still nodding. "Okay."

He showed her his free hand, shyly. "I didn't take my ring off. Is that okay, too?"

Nodding vigorously, Cleo threw her arms around him and held him tight. She was looking over his shoulder at the entry table. She saw the pretzel with its mustard halo, sitting smugly beside a bride and groom in a crystal castle, and somewhere, way up above, Cleo knew there was an orchid moon.

FOLLOW THE RAINBOW...

Sally Garrett
RAINBOW HILLS SERIES

If you enjoyed *Weaver of Dreams*, Book One of Sally Garrett's trilogy celebrating the inspiring lives of three strong-willed American farm women, you're sure to enjoy Book Two, *Visions*, even more. Abbie's cousin, Eileen, discovers strength and courage she didn't know she had when she becomes a single parent struggling to save the family farm. And in time she makes the greatest discovery of all—broken hearts do mend when healed by the transforming power of love!

Coming from Harlequin Superromance next month, is *Visions*, Book Two of Sally Garrett's Rainbow Hill Series.

Harlequin Superromance

COMING NEXT MONTH

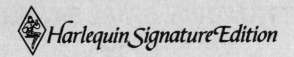
Harlequin Signature Edition

Carole Mortimer

Merlyn's Magic

She came to him from out of the storm and was drawn into his yearning arms—the tempestuous night held a magic all its own.

You've enjoyed Carole Mortimer's Harlequin Presents stories, and her previous bestseller, *Gypsy*.

Now, don't miss her latest, most exciting bestseller, *Merlyn's Magic*!

IN JULY

MERMG

ATTRACTIVE, SPACE SAVING BOOK RACK

Display your most prized novels on this handsome and sturdy book rack. The hand-rubbed walnut finish will blend into your library decor with quiet elegance, providing a practical organizer for your favorite hard-or soft-covered books.

Only $9.95

Approximately 16" x 8" when assembled

Assembles in seconds!

To order, rush your name, address and zip code, along with a check or money order for $10.70* ($9.95 plus 75¢ postage and handling) payable to *Harlequin Reader Service*:

Harlequin Reader Service
Book Rack Offer
901 Fuhrmann Blvd.
P.O. Box 1396
Buffalo, NY 14269-1396

Offer not available in Canada.

BKR-1A

*New York and Iowa residents add appropriate sales tax.